Banned Book
Banned Author

By J.R. Slade

Hilltop Publishing
Brown Summit North Carolina U.S. A

Banned Book Banned Author
Published through Hilltop Publishing

ISBN: 979-8-218-68329-0 (Paperback Edition)
ISBN: 979-8-218-70156-7 (Ebook Edition)

Dedication

For Thekla, my wife who has been my greatest supporter, and who endured the countless hours I spent in solitude while working on this book.

I also dedicate this work to my son Jamie and his wife Tracey, to my daughter Annika, and to my granddaughters, Zoey and Leah.

May Zoey and Leah grow up to learn the true history of the world — and of the people who suffered to make it better.

Author's Note

This novel was born out of a deep yearning to give voice to those who've been silenced.

Banned Book, Banned Author is a work of fiction, but its roots are real. It was shaped by the echoes of censorship. The ache for those in exile, and the quiet resistance of writers who continue to speak truth in lands were doing so can cost them everything. As a retired global citizen and a storyteller, I've carried the weight of stories that rarely make the headlines—stories of journalists imprisoned, books pulled from shelves, and families forced to flee their homelands in the dead of night.

This book is also personal. In 2014, I published a memoir about my deployment to Iraq. That experience taught me that bearing witness is not a passive act—it is a responsibility. And now, through fiction, I continue to honor that responsibility by preserving voices and truths that authoritarian forces often try to erase.

Pelin, the protagonist of this novel, is not just a writer. She is a survivor, and a woman who refused to let fear silence her convictions. Her journey mirrors the path of many—past and present—who risked everything to stand up to power and protect the dignity of her people.

To readers who find themselves in these pages, who recognize the quiet cost of resistance or the loneliness of exile: this story is for you. And to those who've never known that silence can be a weapon—may this book be an invitation to listen deeper, to question louder, and to protect the freedom to tell our truths.

Thank you for reading and thank you for bearing witness.

— J. R. Slade

— 1 —

Kemal returned home after evening prayer and immediately sensed that something was wrong. The flames in the fireplace cast flickering light on Pelin, his wife, standing motionless in the middle of the room, looking as if she might collapse at any moment. It wasn't just her stillness that caught his attention; her face was gray, her posture curled. In her right hand, she clutched her phone to her ear, desperately trying to maintain contact with the caller. To Pelin's surprise, he had introduced himself as someone she knew but hadn't spoken to in years.

As Kemal approached Pelin, she spoke in a quivering voice. "Kemal, do you remember when I told you about the dream I had, that they were coming? This time it's no dream. They are coming to arrest me."

Kemal stood emotionally numb, trying to make sense of what she was saying. She was being targeted because of her latest historical fiction novel. There was blunt criticism of the regime throughout the book. Despite knowing the risks, Pelin refused to be silent. She published the book denouncing the regime, fully aware of the danger it would likely put her in—one she had hoped to avoid.

"Who's coming, and what are we supposed to do?" Kemal asked.

"The caller suggested we leave now. He even advised that I go into exile, or I could face years in prison."

Though the air was thick with tension, Pelin paused just long enough to tuck a few loose strands of her black hair beneath her navy hijab. She felt more decent now. Her scarf outlined her cheek-bones and dark brown eyes.

Kemal stepped into the room across the hall. His well-trimmed beard identified him as a Muslim man, a middle-class professional. He searched the walnut cabinet for his silk prayer rug and leather-bound Quran. These had been given to him by his grandfather and to him they were priceless necessities.

The decision to flee had been made, and now Pelin and Kemal discussed the escape plans they'd already thought about. Now they were real. Pelin had previously been warned by government agents that she could face serious consequences unless she ceased her criticism of the regime. Now, with the threats becoming a reality, she was preparing to leave her beloved country and start anew elsewhere.

They hurried to pack. Kemal yanked open drawers and tossed a few garments onto the bed. He packed only one extra pair of jeans, jogging pants, T-shirts and underwear. Pelin was in her office, snatching up photographs from the bookshelf, including the one from their wedding day. She didn't have time to cry, she was too busy gathering what she thought was necessary.

Her plight mirrored that of her father, who had also stood up to government injustices . . . and likely paid for it with his life. Pelin inherited his stubbornness. She refused to abandon her work.

Pelin's troubles began when the public prosecutor saw her latest novel displayed in a bookstore window, on a narrow cobblestone street in Istanbul's Beyogu district. Her name was familiar—someone they had been quietly monitoring for stirring unrest. He entered the store, picked up a copy, and after reading only a few paragraphs, he pushed for the book to be banned, claiming her writings misrepresented the truth about the government. He accused Pelin of spreading disinformation and propaganda.

The release of her latest book, *A Dishonest Government*, would earn her worldwide fame but also drew the ire of the ruling political party. Disappointed but not surprised, Pelin learned that her most successful novel on the international market was being banned in her own country.

The very issues she had written about were becoming reality. Every day, Pelin could see more clearly the dangerous world she'd gotten herself into. She stood on the brink of experiencing what many before her had faced: the hardships of being a refugee, an outcast. Now she was preparing to leave her home, her mother, her friends, and her culture—all because of a novel. Pelin's words were written as fiction that tells truth.

Adding to her troubles, Pelin had published two scathing opinion pieces in a national newspaper earlier that day. After the book and the articles, the Minister of the Interior had had enough; he decided he would no longer tolerate criticism of the government and chose to make an example out of Pelin. The prosecutor quickly ordered a loyal staff member to draft warrants for her arrest.

Not long after the first visit she got from a secret task force member, Pelin was told her name was on the government's blacklist. She knew the government would pursue her as a direct threat. She had always thought she would be prepared for whatever punishment awaited her if they returned with more serious allegations. However, the prospect of being locked in a prison cell was something she could never prepare for.

Kemal stood near the fireplace, frantically rubbing his sweaty palms together and feeling the heat rising in his cheeks. He admired everything about Pelin—her bravery, intelligence, and dedication to her beliefs. He knew he couldn't stand by and watch her be persecuted.

Taking a deep breath, Kemal told Pelin, "I believe they are trying to silence you because of who you are." His voice cracked as he spoke. "They know you are the daughter of a man who also stood up to their injustices, and inspired others to do the same." Hearing Kemal speak about her father stirred a surge of emotion in Pelin. He understood what was happening to her and why she was being silenced.

Pelin had embarrassed the regime on an international stage. She represented hope for others who also disagreed with their style of governance. The Minister of the Interior understood the significant impact her words and work had on her followers.

She was the daughter of a well-known political activist, which made her a target that the Minister wanted to silence. Her father had faced harsh punishment for defending democracy. When she was a teenager, he often told her, "To deal with your dark times, you must exercise your imagination." His words inspired her to become a writer, to use her craft to express her critical views on fascism and heavy-handed governance.

Being fluent in five languages is a rare gift for anyone. Pelin spoke Turkish, Arabic, German, Russian, and English. That helped her build a diverse global following and deepened her insight into the cultures she often wrote about.

She frequently contributed to the *Guardian* in the UK and *Die Zeit* in Hamburg. Before her last novel gained attention, it had been difficult to find her books in some Western countries. But the banning of her book sparked an increase in recognition of her writing, shining a spotlight on Turkey and on the conservative factions in America, where the banning of books has notably risen in recent years.

Pelin had no time to ponder politics or anything else that might have contributed to her situation. She was caught in a difficult struggle against the regime. Her choice to go into exile wasn't just for her own protection; it was a bold step for the benefit of all. She was fighting for human dignity—a fight for the right to live without fear, and for everyone to be able express their opinions without retribution.

Both Pelin and Kemal understood the challenges. They grew up as Afro-Turks in a country where many were unaware of their community's existence. Their ancestors had been brought to Turkey centuries ago as slaves during the Ottoman Empire, and even after slavery was officially abolished, they continued to face discrimination and marginalization.

From their perspectives, Pelin and Kemal had fought for democracy all their lives. They refused to let their race hold them back, working harder than their peers to achieve their goals. Determination and perseverance were their greatest allies, using their voices to advocate for free speech and democratic values, leading them to become highly respected journalists in Turkey.

Kemal found himself at a crossroads when he left his job as a journalist to join Pelin's fight for democracy, demonstrating his commitment to her cause, albeit with reservations. He wrestled with his dedication to Pelin while grappling with the harsh reality they faced. The thought of leaving a career he genuinely loved weighed heavily on his mind.

Pelin's concern shifted to Kemal. His worried look was hard to ignore. He was struggling with the only two choices they had: stay and face the threat of a lengthy prison sentence for Pelin, or seek exile, which meant leaving their homeland—and his career—behind.

— 2 —

Keeping his head down, Kemal urged her to gather her belongings, hoping she wouldn't see the pain etched on his face. They were leaving behind nearly everything familiar, with no chance to say goodbye to family or friends. The looming threat of Pelin's arrest overshadowed their heartache.

Kemal held back tears as he packed the few items he deemed important. He didn't want the woman he had vowed to love and protect to witness his unraveling. Additionally, as the head of the household, tradition dictated that men should not appear weak during crises. "As soon as we're settled, I'll write to inform my boss and closest colleague about my sudden departure," he said, fearing this could be the end of his long journalism career—a lifelong dream, along with the hope of living and working in a peaceful city with Pelin.

Stepping into the kitchen, Kemal called his brother in London. This was a conversation he had dreaded. "Tarek, I only have a minute or two. Things are heating up; it's no longer safe for us here," he said. Tarek had moved to London five years earlier for similar reasons. Since a faction of the Turkish Armed Forces attempted a military coup in July 2016, the country's democracy had been precarious. Kemal used to joke at the end of each call, "Keep in mind that one day, Pelin and I just might knock on your door."

Now that joke had become reality, and Tarek understood the gravity of the situation. Though the conversation was brief, it was enough for Kemal to inform Tarek that the regime was coming to arrest Pelin; they would catch the next flight to London before it was too late. "I'll be on the lookout for your arrival," Tarek replied, bewildered by how something written could incite such fear in a well-established government. In the eyes of the regime, Pelin's book had transformed from a literary work into a symbol of resistance, threatening to ignite a larger uprising.

Kemal finished packing what they could carry, shredding documents and destroying items he didn't want anyone else to see. As he stepped outside to dispose of the remnants, he stayed alert. Before moving, he scanned the area. The nearby lamppost was dim, but he could see the bright lights on the barge by the river. His heart raced when he noticed two men—one rummaging through the dumpster with a flashlight and the other standing nearby with a large bag half-filled with aluminum cans. They startled each other.

Retracing his steps, Kemal saw another man stumbling off the wall of the building, having just left the corner bar. He appeared to have drunk more than he could handle. As Kemal fumbled with the stiff lock, he heard voices and spotted two bright orange embers glowing nearby. He realized two men were sitting on a bench across the street, smoking and chatting. He cringed inwardly and froze, unsure if they were watching him.

When the two men stood up, Kemal straightened his posture, torn between fleeing or standing his ground. The men began walking toward him. After struggling with the lock, he finally managed to open the door and hurried inside, closing and locking the glass-plated door just as they passed by.

Kemal gasped with relief, but anxiety at the thought of flying to London gripped him. There they could lay low until tensions in Istanbul cooled. Tarek's townhome wasn't large, but he was willing to accommodate them.

"I would feel much better if we didn't have to go there," he thought. London had its own issues with immigrants and people of color, especially those who looked like them. Although Pelin was uneasy too about traveling to London, there were no alternatives.

"We don't have much time or choice. We'll have to adapt to the situation as it unfolds. Thank God we have somewhere to go," Kemal replied. He knew the hardest part lay ahead.

After ensuring that they had their most important things, in the middle of the night they left their home. They slipped through the narrow back alleys of Istanbul, walking as fast and quietly as they could. They ducked under laundry lines and hurried by noisy bars and coffeeshops. At each sound she heard, Pelin felt her heart beating faster.

They were grateful to have escaped in time. Creating some distance from the police let them breathe again. As they hurried through narrow streets, the sounds of distant sirens faded behind them. "It's not the safest route in ordinary times, but I think it's better to travel through the back alleys until we're farther from the neighborhood," Kemal told Pelin.

She stopped and glanced over her shoulder at the sound of voices behind them. "Those are just late-night scavengers, searching for leftovers from the restaurants and bars," Kemal reassured her. "Don't worry; they'll help us blend in and keep us concealed from the police."

Kemal's phone buzzed in his pocket. He hesitated, then pulled it out. "It's our neighbor," he muttered, answering before Pelin could stop him. "Hello?" Pelin spun around, eyes wide. "Kemal, are you serious right now?" He turned his back slightly, shielding the call. "Yes… yes, I saw them too. No, I don't know why they came. I'll call you back." Pelin grabbed his sleeve, she spoke with a sharp but low voice. "We don't have time for this! We have to go. Now." Kemal ended the call, slipping the phone back into his pocket. "He said the police swarmed the building. Four cars."

"We knew they'd come," she snapped, continuing to walk. "Next time, don't answer. We're not safe until we're across the bridge."

After a few more blocks Pelin's anxiety eased a bit. "Kemal, we live in a country that doesn't fully accept us," she said quietly. "I believe that if our appearance were different, we wouldn't be facing this situation. As Afro-Turks, we've spent most of our lives trying to be recognized in our own country."

Kemal acknowledged that Afro-Turks continued to fight for legal recognition and the same rights as other citizens in their homeland.

"Books like mine have been written before," murmured Pelin, "but the moment I shine a light on corruption, I become an enemy of the government."

It wasn't just her latest novel; Pelin consistently highlighted these disparities in her work. Her recently banned book delved deeply into these issues, featuring characters that illustrated the many inequalities between Afro-Turks and other Turkish citizens—particularly how the government constructed invisible walls. Writing about these realities illuminated the darkness. She believed that by sharing these inequalities with her readers, she could change perceptions of their government. She also held onto the belief that confronting their past could better equip governments to thrive in the future.

Kemal wrapped an arm around Pelin, pulling her closer. "We have to get moving. We have just a few hours to get to the airport," he said, preparing to call a taxi.

"Kemal, are you okay? Did you forget that taking a taxi is too dangerous? We talked about this just moments ago."

Pelin had contacted a family friend who owned a fishing boat. He agreed to take them across the Bosporus to the Asian side, under the cover of darkness. Small fishing boats were rarely stopped by authorities, making it their best —maybe their only —chance to escape. He would meet them at the docks around midnight.

The cool night air was thick and foggy, with the scent of salt lingering as they cautiously approached the water. Every step was taken in silence, their eyes darting around, suspicious of their surroundings. A distant horn from a passing ferry broke the stillness.

Kemal flinched. In that tense moment, Pelin tightened her grip on his hand.

She scanned the dock for her friend's boat and spotted a clock on the boathouse; the second hand moved slowly, an agonizing reminder that time was slipping away.

Then she heard footsteps nearby. A patrol officer strolled along the dock, shining his flashlight over each person he passed. As he approached Pelin and Kemal, he hesitated, adjusting his radio.

Pelin held her breath, hoping he would move on. But he didn't. Instead, he turned and aimed the flashlight directly at them before stepping closer.

Kemal clenched his jaw. Pelin turned her back to the light, searching for her friend's boat among the others. She scanned the rows of boats, trying to identify which one was his.

Where is the boat?

Finally, Pelin spotted her friend's fishing boat and the far end of the pier. He was waving his hand, gesturing for them to hurry. She breathed a sigh of relief. She and Kemal didn't waste time, they hurried down the dock, where he almost slipped up and fell into the water. No one spoke a word, as they were pulled aboard. The friend loosening the ropes as Pelin and Kemal made their way down the steps into the lower level cabin. They all understood that time was a factor.

— 3 —

Once across the river, Kemal and Pelin stepped onto solid ground, they were relieved that the dizzy swaying of the fisherman's boat was behind them. They would take a taxi to Sabiha Gökçen International Airport for a direct flight to Heathrow International in London. Each second felt like a ticking time bomb.

Less than an hour after they left home, one of Mr. Hasan's most reliable reporters informed him that Pelin and Kemal had left the country. Like many others watching the breaking news, the reporter saw the broadcast on a state-run TV channel.

The *Daily Times*, known for breaking news, experienced a quieter newsroom hours after hearing about Kemal and Pelin's home being raided. To support Kemal, Mr. Hasan called his top reporters to a conference. Worry creased his face. "Hold the story," he told the reporters. "We won't be reporting on Pelin and Kemal fleeing the country." His reasoning was that he didn't believe all the details had emerged when the news first broke on state-run television. He also thought the news about Pelin might jeopardize the couple's escape.

The reporters in the room exchanged confused glances. The television continued running the story about the couple's disappearance. Mr. Hasan shook his head, disgusted, as he watched images of Pelin flash across the screen. "There is not enough substance to their report. It's all propaganda." The editor and other senior members of the *Daily Times* viewed the state-run television news report as another tactic used by the prosecutor's office to intimidate those who opposed the government.

"I should have warned him," Mr. Hasan muttered while running his hand through his thin gray hair. He imagined Kemal and Pelin running in the middle of the night, seeking safety, their lives forever changed. "I let him down. I let them both down." This was something he would grapple with for a long time, he thought.

Upset about everything that had happened so far, Hasan sent the reporters to their usual duties. He went to his computer and clicked on the email. He hoped that against all odds, Kemal would read it. He sent a late email offering help, and an apology for remaining silent when it mattered most.

As he typed, Mr. Hasan vowed to himself that he would make this right. The *Daily Times* may not have broken the story, but they would uncover the truth behind it—no matter the cost. As the owner of the paper, he had allowed his thoughts of saving his newspaper to override his thoughts of humanity. Looking back, he recognized the danger and uncertainty that Kemal and Pelin faced. Disappointed that he hadn't done more, Hasan felt he had let one of his longtime employees down. Now all he could do was contact Kemal through email.

Mr. Hasan continued the email, informing Kemal that two men who claimed to be from the chief prosecutor's office had come to visit him. They said they had a warrant for Pelin's arrest. Surprised to receive the email from the paper's owner, Kemal took a seat on a nearby bench to continue reading. "I'll catch up," he yelled. Pelin kept going, not wanting to stop until they reached the terminal. Kemal uncrossed his legs and planted both feet on the walkway. He was shocked to receive an email from the newspaper's owner. The contents astonished him as well. He didn't know that two men had come to Mr. Hasan's office seeking information on Pelin.

Kemal now had a clearer idea of how serious this matter had become. He had always praised Ismael Hasan, one of the few newspaper CEOs in the country to promote a person of color to the position of lead columnist. Not only that, but Kemal was practically free to publish what he wanted if it sold papers. His worries gave rise to another irrational thought.

"It's a trap," Kemal thought. Perhaps Hasan was being coerced into working with the security agents to save his paper.

Kemal finished reading the email, which left him confused. He hoped he was mistaken. But because of the complexity of the situation and his lack of sleep, irrational thoughts were continuing to take over his mindset. When he stood up from the bench, two uniformed police officers approached him. Kemal wanted to flee, but the officers surprised him, and he felt weak in the knees and couldn't. Pelin waited up ahead, unwilling to leave Kemal alone with the officers.

"Sir, show us your passport," commanded one officer. Pelin's heart sank when she looked back and saw Kemal being questioned by the police. She stood still, not wanting to draw attention to herself. For the moment, she worried the police would arrest Kemal and carry him away. She had no idea what she would do without him by her side.

After a few minutes of questioning, Kemal was free to travel. He felt more anxious than before as he ran to catch up with Pelin and never looked back. Never mind the look of doubt on the policeman's face; Kemal's passport was in order, proving he was a citizen. Luckily, the police neglected to check for any posted bulletins showing arrest warrants for him and Pelin.

"Now what, Kemal?" Pelin asked. Kemal grabbed her bag and pointed toward a line of taxis. After some distance from the police, Kemal shook his head. "That was close. We need to get out of here before they come back," he told Pelin. They rushed to the front of the line and hired a taxi.

Before loading the bags into the taxi, Kemal stopped to answer Pelin's original question. "Yes, everything is fine, at least for now." He told her that the police claimed to be looking for a family of immigrants and that his name didn't match the name they were searching for. With that scare behind him, all he wanted to do was get to the airport and leave.

"What about the email you were reading?" Not wanting to upset her again, he wasn't entirely truthful. The boss's email was a simple check-in to ensure they were okay, he claimed. He had seen a news flash about police activity in their neighborhood on television.

Kemal made a sour expression after misleading Pelin about the email. He promised himself to tell her the truth once they were settled. Still, he couldn't stop thinking about the email. Although Mr. Hasan sent it with good intentions, he worried that by sending it, might attract unwanted attention to himself.

He had known and worked for Mr. Hasan for over twenty years. Their relationship began back in university, long before Hasan purchased the *Times*. Reflecting on their long relationship, Kemal calmed down and gave Mr. Hasan the benefit of the doubt. He swore to himself that he would respond to the email as soon as he was out of harm's way and time permitted.

Considering the email's contents, Kemal realized how serious the matter was, had he and Pelin not fled. Relieved that they had made it to the boat and gotten across the Bosporus, Kemal put his arms around Pelin and took a deep breath.

She tried to be optimistic: they'd gotten out before the agents arrived. They'd eluded capture when Kemal was questioned at the dock. Pelin feared the police would return after discovering the arrest warrants against her, but so far, their luck was holding.

Tension rose as Pelin thought about leaving without knowing how long they would be gone, and the uncertainty ahead. The decision to leave Turkey was the better choice, compared to the alternative of staying and facing the potential consequences: imprisonment or death. Still, neither had any idea what awaited them.

— 4 —

With her boarding pass pressed close to her heart, Pelin let out a deep breath but still felt far from total relief. A long journey lay ahead. She sat in an uncomfortable bright orange chair near the terminal gate, her legs stretched out on her luggage and her head nodding with sleep. Kemal eased his phone out of his jacket to answer a call. This time the call really was from a neighbor.

"I've seen the police going in and out of your home several times already; are you okay?" The neighbor grew concerned when he heard loud knocks and saw a small crowd gather across the street from Kemal's home.

Pelin sat up in the chair, worried now. She was afraid that it was someone with more bad news: "Who's calling now?"

After he ended the call, Kemal scooted his chair closer to her. "Don't worry, it wasn't bad news; it was the neighbor across the hall. He saw the police going in and out of our apartment and wanted to know if we were okay. He also said that the entire building was surrounded by police."

"The police mentioned that they were looking into complaints about Pelin being involved in activism. They also said its possibility that she was inciting an uprising." The neighbor told Kemal. Kemal was just thankful that he and Pelin made it out in time and were able to get some distance from their pursuers.

Pelin overheard his response. Her voice carried the weight of her anger. "No, Kemal," she said, firm but not unkind. "And I know

I've said this before, but I need you to hear it—really hear it. It's not just about the book I published

She paused, searching his face, her tone softening.

"It's more than that. It's about who we are as a people. We were always just shadows to them—allowed to exist, but never truly seen. And now that some dared to notice us, to say we mattered… they'd rather erase everything than admit we ever belonged."

Pelin went on to explain to Kemal what she meant. "It's a shame that the very same individuals who helped build the country are the ones left to suffer. That's another part of our history that the majority are trying to erase. Afro Turks have spent most of their lives trying to be recognized as citizens of a country where they were born. It's unfortunate that in that very same country, they are still fighting for legal recognition and the same rights as all citizens living here."

This issue wasn't just laid bare in her latest novel; Pelin had consistently included these disparities in her work. In her recently banned book, this was one topic that one of her fictional characters addressed. The character highlighted the many disparities between Afro Turks and other Turkish citizens.

Writing about these issues gave her hope, and by sharing these inequalities with her readers, she hoped they would change the way her people were perceived. Pelin also hoped that one day the world would confront its past. Her belief was that this would better equip her culture to flourish in the future.

Kemal listened intently as he put his arm around her, drawing her closer to him. However, his concerns were in the present moment. They still had almost two hours to wait until they would start boarding their flight. These were tense moments. Pelin jumped at every announcement that came across the PA system, fearing an order to report to security. Kemal was in his own state of despair. He did what he could to calm them both down.

"Okay, Kemal, the emails," Pelin demanded.

He had hoped she would forget. He was reluctant to bring up the emails he'd gotten from his boss. Sharing that information would not be comforting. He would rather they talk about something more positive. But Pelin's strong eye contact and raised eyebrows said it all. She wanted to know.

Kemal shrugged and gave her a weary smile. He told her about the email and the two men who had gone to his boss's office, seeking information on her.

"How could they?" Pelin was disturbed that the Minister of the Interior would involve Kemal's boss.

"That's the reason; now it all makes sense," she hissed. There were things she hadn't told Kemal, as well; things that she didn't want to worry him with.

Pelin filled Kemal in on what had taken place at her office, days before she received the phone call. She informed him about the two men who claimed to be from the prosecutor's office who had come to her office. Fortunately for her, she was out when they arrived. They also left a threatening message with her secretary. The message from the men stated that they had solid evidence that she was working to overthrow the government. Pelin had wondered whether this was a threat meant to shut her up. She couldn't help wondering why they would warn her ahead of time if they intended to arrest her? She had discounted the event and was bent on not staying silent.

"It was obvious that the secretary was shaken," Pelin recounted. "Before they left, they told her that she was working for an illegal terrorist."

Kemal and Pelin no longer trusted anyone outside their close circle of associates. They agreed that leaving their homeland was no mistake. It had become necessary. The visit from the agents had not been "only an empty threat." It was a precursor to arrest.

The couple tried to rest in the uncomfortable airport seating; Kemal tucked his coat over her legs, sensing her chill from the air condition.

Pelin noticed Kemal kept staring out of the window and occasionally looking down at his phone. "Are you not able to sleep?" she asked. She reached for his hand under the warm coat that he had spread over her legs. Pelin looked directly at Kemal, trying to get his full attention. She was ready to be completely honest and explain everything that had happened up to this point: how she'd been dismissive of the agents' threats, and about the caller from the evening before. But since he never revealed his identity, she could only share what the caller had told her during their short conversation. However, the caller did mention that they had once been acquaintances.

Pelin apologized to Kemal for the disruption she had caused in their lives. Her words were brief, they weren't alone, and it wasn't the time to go into full detail about all her feelings of sorrow. She took time to reinforce her love for Kemal, reminded of his care for her by his warm coat on her lap.

"I love you even more Kemal, and without you saying a word, by coming along with me, you have shown how much you truly love me." She was asking for his forgiveness for the harm she had caused him. "If I could do anything to change the situation, I would." This was the reality they were now living. Kemal listened but held his tongue. Never mind that his wife struggled with her emotions; he saw that she was doing the best she could.

Their conversation was interrupted by an announcement. "All passengers bound for London England, may now begin boarding the plane in the following order." The announcer called passengers according to their physical abilities and seat numbers.

It had been a long night. Being able to board the plane brought each of them a little relief. Kemal and Pelin flopped down in their seats. Kemal fell asleep as soon as the plane burst through the clouds. Not Pelin; too many thoughts were jumbling in her head. Constant reminders of recent events that had caused her to flee her home filled her mind. She had done what she had to do.

The only serious grief she felt was having to leave her mother. Everything else, she could start from square one. Two promises she made to herself: to be there for Kemal, and to stay the course and fight for the things she believed in. While some considered her voice to be the loudest, Pelin did not want the campaign to be all about her. She reminded herself that the struggle was for every citizen of her country and their right to free speech.

— 5 —

The plane landed at the west of Heathrow; the roar of its engines faded as it taxied to the gate. Tarek stood at gate 16, surrounded by the noise of the busy airport. He looked towards the doorway, hoping Kemal and Pelin would soon appear. After taking a second look in that direction, he finally saw them being escorted by a customs officer. When the officer spotted a red flag on the screen indicating that Pelin was wanted by the Turkish authorities, he gestured for them to step aside. Moments later, they were led away from the counter through a door that clicked shut behind them. Tarek sensed that something was wrong but had no idea what.

Tarek stood frozen, as he heard the customs officer barked orders. Maybe this was the end. The escape plan had failed, and now they were being arrested. He wondered why his brother and Pelin were the only noncitizens pulled from the line. The customs officer seemed intent on examining them more thoroughly. His eyes sharp and unblinking, as if the red flag in the system had confirmed that Pelin and Kemal were wanted for arrest.

It took almost two hours of investigation before they were finally released.

It soon became clear that Pelin and Kemal were seeking asylum, and they were free to go. "My brother is waiting on the other side," Kemal reassured the official, emphasizing that they would be staying with Tarek while they awaited asylum approval.

"You will be contacted at a later date for more details," an officer informed them, referring to a date for a hearing.

Pelin felt relieved that she and Kemal had weathered the first storm. The two of them took the escalator down to the lower level to claim their luggage, where they finally reunited with Tarek. He rushed to Kemal, embracing him, and kissing him on each of his whiskery cheek.

"I am so happy to see you both," Tarek said. "It's unfortunate that you had to come under these circumstances."

Pelin felt ashamed, worrying that Tarek blamed her for putting his brother in this situation. She hoped he understood that the harsh measures taken by their government had forced them both to leave their homeland.

It didn't matter that they were in the UK; Pelin realized they needed to be better prepared for the challenges ahead. It was comforting to walk through the airport without the fear of being followed. As they made their way toward the exit, Pelin struggled with her luggage. She'd packed more than she realized. Tarek turned to help her, but she refused his offer, insisting she was okay with her mammoth bag. "It's got wheels," she smiled.

They exchanged smiles as they navigated through the crowded terminal to the luxury limousine waiting outside. Tarek had hired one of the best transport services in the city. Once they were seated and the doors were closed, they were on their way. The shiny black limo made a right turn onto East Lane. "This is the Brent neighborhood, a few blocks from Wembley," Tarek narrated, an impromptu tour guide.

Though the two of them had visited the UK before, they had not been to this area. Pelin moved closer to the tinted window for a better view and was surprised by the number of tennis courts she saw. With tennis being her favorite sport, she hoped time would allow her and Kemal to play on one of those courts soon.

"So, this is where you live?" she asked Tarek as the limo eased up in front of the building. "Impressive," Kemal added, already liking what he had seen of the neighborhood.

"It's not cheap, but when I moved in five years ago, I got a break. I was also younger. In the summer months, there's always some type of tournament being played," Tarek explained. From his balcony, he could hear the loud cheers from the fans, especially during the night matches. "I should warn you that during tournament season, there are crowds all over the neighborhood. Those who can afford it rent out their homes and leave town."

Occasionally, Tarek looked away, trying to hide his joyful tears. It had been years since he had seen any family members, and he couldn't express how he felt about having Kemal and his wife staying with him for a while. He was determined to do whatever was necessary to make them feel welcome, wanting them to know that his home was their home. He lived in a medium-sized three-bedroom townhome. "It's not the largest place, but we will make it work."

Tarek was single and had moved to London immediately after graduating from Oxford with a PhD in tech. He landed a job as an engineering technologist at the London Stock Exchange. The office was over on 10 Paternoster Row, right in the city. Despite being the chief engineer in his department, some felt he was out of place, with a few even accusing him of being appointed merely to comply with federal policies on diversity. The most amusing part was that some workers thought he was the custodian. Tarek didn't let their assumptions interfere with his duties; he knew who he was and what he was there to do.

"I'll let you guys get some rest and make any adjustments you need to feel at home. I'll give you a tour of the city tomorrow."

Six weeks passed, and Tarek's hospitality remained unwavering. He ensured Kemal and Pelin were comfortable, providing them with a place when they had nowhere else to go. The atmosphere in Tarek's home was warm and welcoming, but Pelin felt a need for independence. For her, the honeymoon was over. She worried about how to voice her need to leave while acknowledging Tarek's kindness. She wasn't sure why she needed to leave, but Pelin had always trusted her perceptions of what she needed. So she decided to speak as kindly and as frankly as she could.

"Thanks, Tarek. You've been the best, but it's time for Kemal and me to get down to business and figure out where we go from here," she told him.

Tarek was sad to hear her say that it is time for her and Kemal to move on. But he nodded. "I understand, Pelin. Just know you are always welcome here."

"I never wished to leave our home, and I assure you we will return to it someday, though I cannot say when." She looked away, trying not to reveal her emotions. She was still committed to her purpose, to create a nation that was just and fair to all its citizens, and her desire to find a place of her own, a home ground to craft her strategy, felt important.

Kemal was also wrestling with his thoughts. He shared Pelin's desire for a new beginning, a place where they could return to normalcy. He looked toward the future.

Tarek supported whatever decision Kemal and Pelin made. He helped Kemal find a townhome in Emerald Gardens, a place not far from his home, near the Wembley Park neighborhood.

Pelin was happy that the two of them would be on their own again. Her next step was to get back to work. Kemal was also eager to resume his career; it had been eight weeks since he wrote an article for the paper—he'd never gone so long without filing a story. Yet, they both understood that moving out on their own offered no guarantee of safety. The regime had connections beyond the seas, and Pelin remained a target.

On their first morning in their new home, Pelin awoke to the smell of brewing coffee. She drifted into the kitchen of their little flat and observed Kemal quietly; his expression shone with contentment, yet she sensed his mind drifting back to early mornings in their Istanbul kitchen. This London flat was theirs, and it was safe, but they were a long way from their homeland, and their journey was not yet complete. They had secured a new place to call home, but the real challenge was just beginning.

— **6** —

Kamal and Pelin took a few days to adjust to their new place, gradually settling in while figuring out their temporary life in London. As they wandered around the new neighborhood, the unfamiliar streets and faces reminded them of how much had changed for them. The hum and bustle of London was not so different from Istanbul, but the people were very different . . . it was a colder place.

"This neighborhood feels like any other big city," Kemal told Pelin. He noticed they were one of few minority couples on the streets. "Like all other cities in the world, people seem to group themselves by income and race," he added.

Pelin nodded, watching people hurry by on the sidewalk. "It looks like no one really knows their neighbors here. Everyone's just rushing to wherever they need to be," she said. She watched the young adults walking with earbuds in their ears, and a phone in one hand, coffee in the other.

A group of teens on skateboards zoomed past, glanced at Pelin, and made comments about her hijab, pointing and laughing. They exchanged remarks and skated off. Neither Pelin nor Kemal understood what they said, but it reminded them that young people are pretty much the same everywhere, no matter the language. They want what's new, but at the same time they mock it.

"Do you think we'll ever feel at home here?" he asked softly.

Pelin squeezed his hand. "I guess it'll just take some time."

Before the trouble with the government, Kemal was the outgoing type, quick to make friends. Now, he was already missing his old life, the one he had left behind. Still, he was trying to adapt. Both he and Pelin knew things would never be the same here as at home, at least not anytime soon.

One evening, Pelin came home with a full shopping bag. Kemal raised an eyebrow. "Looks like you went big!"

"Yeah, I got a few things," Pelin said, a mysterious look on her face. "But my biggest investment isn't in the bag." She paused to watch his reaction. "Promise you won't be upset when I tell you what I invested in."

Kemal hesitated, curiosity growing. "I trust you, Pelin. What is it?"

"I signed a lease for a small office," she blurted out. "It's much smaller than the one I had in Istanbul."

"You did what?" Kemal sat down on a kitchen stool, shocked that she made such a big decision without discussing it first. Sure, she often acted independently, but this was a whole new level. "We haven't even been here for a year, and you've already signed a lease for an office? Seriously?!"

Pelin took a deep breath and adjusted her hijab. "Kemal, please understand. I need this. We finally have our own place, and it's nice and quiet. But I can't get used to working where I shower and sleep. This is a home, not an office."

She moved closer to him. "My book sales are booming worldwide. The suite is totally affordable. And since we don't know how long we'll be in the UK, I only signed a six-month lease."

With a frown, Kemal said, "Six months? Pelin, we don't even know if we'll be here in six days. What if we have to leave suddenly?"

"I can't put my life on hold forever. I need to get out. I'm much more productive when I'm not working at home."

"The office is in a lively business district," she added, her tone calming. "I'm so excited! It's on the eleventh floor of a cool new building overlooking the Thames." It reminded her of her suite back in Istanbul. She loved being near water. In Istanbul, she often watched the ferries going up and down the river, seeing the centuries-old towers of the skyline mix with modern skyscrapers.

Pelin patiently explained her reasoning to Kemal, and slowly, he started to understand why she signed the lease. He acknowledged she needed more space and a quieter spot to catch up on work and store her files. A recent government hack of her online accounts made her wary of storing documents online. And it pushed her to want a secure physical workspace.

Kemal nodded slowly. He remembered the panic they felt when they had discovered the hack. "I get it, but is it safe? What if they track you there?"

Pelin was quick to respond. "I've made sure they won't. I signed the lease under a different name, and Alyn agreed to co-sign with me. We did a Zoom call, and she signed electronically. It's just business—the leasing company only cares about the money."

Kemal stood up. "I just hope you're right."

Pelin didn't respond; she was already busy packing a few boxes for her new office. With nothing more to say, Kemal went back to his own office in the apartment and tried to focus on work. As he revised a column for Sunday's paper back in Istanbul, his thoughts drifted back to his home city. Who had been the mysterious caller who warned Pelin?

His thoughts were interrupted by an unexpected email—from Ismail. Kemal hesitated before responding, making sure not to reveal his location. He couldn't risk anyone else seeing the message. Instead, he kept it short, letting Ismael know he was ready to get back to work and would have his weekend column ready on time.

That same evening, Kemal received another email from his boss: "Kemal, my friend, it's great to know you're working again. Your last piece on the economic situation sparked quite a debate. But be careful. There are people here who are concerned about your safety, and Pelin's too."

The email left Kemal feeling uneasy. He pushed back from his desk and paced around the small office. Running a hand through his hair didn't help quiet his thoughts.

This wasn't working.

With a slight groan, he grabbed his coat and stepped outside, hoping the fresh air would clear his mind. As he walked, he kept wondering—should he tell Pelin? Would it help or just add to her worries?

By the time he reached the corner, he'd made up his mind. No. She had enough on her plate. This was his problem to figure out.

As the days went by, Kemal grew restless. The silence in their new home felt like a burden. Pelin was always working, often leaving him alone with his thoughts. He missed his life in Istanbul, the familiar faces, and all the things he used to do when he felt bored. He spent many evenings down at the coffeehouse and hanging out with friends. Having conversations with others felt so necessary for his work. How could he know what he was writing about if he wasn't conversing with his sources and his readers?

One evening, while Pelin was working late at her office, Kemal went for another walk. The streets of London were buzzing with energy. Laughter and loud music spilled out of almost every pub and coffee shop he passed. Couples, young and old and in-between, strolled down the street. Every now and then, he'd hear a few people speaking Arabic. Those familiar tones warmed his heart.

He ended up in a small park, sitting on a bench overlooking a pond. The colors of the sunset shimmered on the water's surface, reminding him of evenings spent by the Bosporus. A lump formed in his throat as he thought about Istanbul.

With his mind elsewhere, he hardly noticed when someone sat down next to him. It wasn't until the guy spoke that Kemal snapped back to reality.

"Beautiful night, isn't it?" the stranger said, speaking perfect Turkish. Kemal didn't know how to respond. He turned to face the guy and nodded.

The stranger smiled. "Aren't you from Istanbul? You look like someone I've seen in a picture on TV or in a newspaper back there. I just arrived in the UK for a special assignment," he said.

Kemal's mind raced. Was this just a coincidence, or was this actually happening? How could someone from a huge city like Istanbul recognize him? I'm not famous, he thought. Kemal didn't consider the small photo of himself next to his weekly column in the Istanbul *Daily Times*. To him, that was too minor for anyone to remember.

Who was this guy, and what was his assignment here in the UK? Kemal wondered. Then his mind shifted. Special assignment? What about Pelin? Was she safe? *What is going on?* he asked himself.

Kemal stood up. "Nice to meet you, but I have to go now." The stranger stood and held out his hand. "Nice to meet you too, and I hope we cross paths again soon," he said with a smirk.

Kemal turned and left, but the stranger trailed behind him at a distance, darting in and out from behind buildings and cars. As Kemal hurried away, he didn't notice the man trailing him. He was still getting use to avoiding strangers.

After making sure Pelin was settled, Kemal headed home and got back to work.

He wrote about the latest events trending in the news. His opinion pieces were supported by years of loyal readers, which were good for business.

Once Kemal finished his work and was about to shut down his computer, a notification pinged on his laptop. His heart raced as he opened an email from an unknown sender. The subject line read: "We know where you are."

$$—\ 7\ —$$

Pelin and Kemal were lying in bed, reminiscing about the person who rang their doorbell a couple of weeks ago. Neither of them made a move to answer the door; they just waited to see how long it would take for whoever it was to leave.

"I guess we can forget about that person at the door," Pelin suggested, since no one ever returned.

"Yeah, I agree. We've reached a milestone, Pelin!"

It had been a year since they moved to London, and they had managed to steer clear of any major trouble with Turkish agents or anyone else who could stir up chaos in their lives. During her first year in exile, Pelin mostly kept a low profile, worried about drawing attention to herself. Staying safe was her top priority, even though she didn't want to give up on her campaign against her government's cruelty toward its citizens. Just navigating public transport every day was stressful enough. When she got to the office, she took a moment to unwind before diving into work. She still managed to make progress on a book she hoped to send to her editor by spring. This one would be nonfiction, describing how her own life had been upended by political persecution.

"I know some people will be upset when my book comes out, but others will be happy," Pelin wrote to Aylin, her editor, in an email. Pelin planned to dedicate her book to those worldwide and to those who were silenced or persecuted for their work—especially by their own governments, like hers.

She wanted to raise awareness about how books were being banned and history erased, even in Western countries that had once championed freedom of speech. "There's a chapter about how I was threatened with prison or death by some government officials. That should explain why I had to go into exile," Pelin wrote in a follow-up email to Aylin.

Musing on this ongoing writing, she said, "Kemal, one good thing about living abroad is that I can express myself more freely, even if it's just in print." Pelin had decided to skip social media, fully aware that anything she posted could be twisted into false information. Instead, she chose to convey her message through newspapers and magazines.

Kemal agreed with Pelin about having more freedom to write what they wanted while living abroad. However, his situation was different. He was still working for the *Daily Times*, where his pieces went through an editor and required the chief editor's approval before publication. Still, he was happy to be back writing, publishing weekly editorials for the *Daily Times*.

"I have my ways of writing what I think is important, just in ways that won't jeopardize my job," Kemal told Pelin.

"Yeah, I know, Kemal. You're a gentle-hearted writer. You know how to please everyone," Pelin teased.

Kemal didn't see himself as a gentle-hearted writer. While he wasn't as outspoken as Pelin—she was a novelist and creative writer—he had a regular employer, one that could be endangered by what he wrote. Still, he sometimes published articles hinting at governments suppressing basic human values and free speech, though he never mentioned his own situation.

To vent his frustration about what was happening to Pelin, Kemal occasionally wrote short articles about how some citizens were harassed even while living on foreign soil. He didn't directly point to their experiences, but his overall message encouraged readers not to be discouraged by the crackdown on their freedoms.

Kemal was trying to inspire people worldwide to write about what mattered to them.

"Kemal, please don't risk your job or put yourself in danger by defending me publicly," Pelin warned.

"What nonsense, Pelin! I'm your husband. You come first in my life. It's only natural that I defend you, no matter the consequences."

Ismail Hasan had no clue about Kemal and Pelin's exact whereabouts. He felt entitled to know, since Kemal was one of their top journalists. Given that Kemal had to leave the country, he was still the newspaper's most popular writers. He had nearly two million followers. Hasan didn't push the issue, but it was a tightrope for both.

Most of Kemal's readers had no idea who he really was; he wrote under a fictitious name. Hiçkimse (Mr. Nobody). They were just loyal to his weekly column . . . and their interest was piqued by his obvious pseudonym. That was another reason Hasan didn't want to stir the pot. At one point, he considered sending an investigative journalist to track Kemal down, but decided against it, trusting Kemal to stick to his agreement with the newspaper.

Kemal understood his responsibility to his employer. That's why he kept in touch through emails and Zoom calls. It was easy for Hasan to trace Kemal's IP address and figure out that he and Pelin were in the UK. With everything going on, Kemal did his best to keep their location a secret. He limited the number of people he communicated with privately because it was too risky to trust anyone outside their immediate circle. That included some family members. He and Pelin worried about the harassment others might face from those trying to find them.

Even though some days felt normal, Pelin and Kemal were still living in dangerous times. They needed to keep their lives simple and quiet, taking every precaution to stay safe. Pelin constantly worried about her mother, who she feared was being harassed by security agents assigned to track her down.

"Hey, Mr. Korkmaz and Mrs. Korkmaz! Haven't seen you in a couple of weeks. I've been sick and out of work," the doorman in the lobby said.

"I noticed you were away," Kemal replied.

"By the way, there was a guy who stopped by to see you a day or so before I got sick. He had the same accent as you two and said he was a friend. He said you'd be surprised to see him. But then he started acting a little weird and insisted on going up. I only let him ring the buzzer."

"Well, that explains it, Kemal. I bet it was one of them, an agent snooping around," Pelin said.

"We can't be sure, so let's not worry," Kemal told Pelin. Still, the doorman's information brought them closer to figuring out who had been buzzing their door. Pelin figured the guy who rang the buzzer was Turkish, since the doorman said he had the same accent as her and Kemal. But they'd probably never know for sure unless he showed up again.

As Pelin and Kemal walked out of the building, her phone buzzed. It was the security company hired to monitor the building where her office was located. Her office had been breached. The two of them hopped in an Uber to go downtown to check it out.

When Pelin and Kemal reached her office, they found that someone had damaged her computer while trying to access its hard drive. The files she left on her desk were scattered all over the floor. "Thank God security responded quickly; otherwise, it could have been a lot worse," Pelin told the investigating officials.

— 8 —

It was another typical London morning—cool, foggy, and drizzling. Pelin stared out the window, taking in the unfamiliar streets of her temporary home. A wave of unease washed over her as she reflected on how her life had turned out. No matter how hard she tried to focus, two images kept invading her mind: the men who had attacked her and Kemal in the alley the day before. It was clear that when they left Istanbul, their attackers had followed them.

Pelin recalled everything that happened the day that they were attacked. Kemal was getting back to the routine of starting his day early. He had found a bakery close by and was eager to run out for fresh bread. He walked lightly on the creaky floorboards toward the door. Just as he touched the doorknob, she startled him as she walked out of the bedroom.

"Where are you off to?" she asked.

"I'm going out for fresh bread."

No longer able to sleep, she asked if it would be a problem if she could tag along with him. He hesitated, "Are you sure? It's awfully early."

Kemal and Pelin had completed their purchase of bread and were already out the door on their way back to their apartment. They were smiling and carrying warm fresh bread. Pelin remembered she was still hanging on to her large aluminum mug that she refilled at the bakery with fresh hot coffee.

Their peaceful morning came to an instant halt when two men emerged from a dark alley and blocked their path. Kemal froze when he spotted the handgun in one man's hand. Not wanting the attention of the pedestrians walking by. He ordered Kemal and Pelin into the alley behind the dumpster. "Move now!" the armed man said, with his eyes darting nervously. "I am not afraid to use this weapon I am holding."

From that point on, he demanded they do as he said. He told them no one would get hurt. The shorter bald man spoke low but clearly, not wanting anyone nearby to hear him. Pelin couldn't stop shivering. She squeezed her coffee mug with both hands, fearing that things were about to get ugly. Neither she nor Kemal had ever been in a such a dire situation before. It didn't seem real somehow, but it was very real.

As the men forced her and Kemal deeper into the alley, away from the streetlamp still blazing in the pale dawn, Kemal squinted his eyes, trying to get a good look at the two men. He thought he recognized one man as the man he met in the park a day earlier.

He cursed himself for not confronting the man earlier—and now, for not even remembering his face clearly. The man caught Kemal staring and suddenly lunged at him. He grabbed Kemal's right arm and twisting it behind his back in an attempt to cuff him. They fell to the ground. Kemal's face scraped against the pavement, and the man's knee pinned his spine, crushing the air from his lungs.

Then, out of nowhere, Pelin managed to slip the lid off her coffee and hurl the hot liquid into the face of the man holding Kemal down.

"Are you insane?" the man shouted, recoiling in pain and dropping to his knees.

Gasping for air, Kemal seized the moment. He forced his free arm upward, striking the man's hand and sending the weapon to the ground. He broke free.

"Run! Run!" he shouted to Pelin.

Though aching and winded, he pushed himself up and ran behind Pelin, were eventually they got away.

With the memory of the attack still on her mind, Pelin turned to Kemal, who was slumped over his desk. He wasn't the same energetic person she remembered from a year ago. Lines were etched across his forehead, dark circles under his eyes, his beard beginning to gray. It was such a drastic change from the man she used to know. She could see that the sleepless nights since leaving Istanbul, and the stress was weighing heavily on him.

"Kemal," Pelin called out, her voice barely a whisper. "Are you okay? After yesterday, I think we really need to talk about what's next for us." Coming to London for refuge wasn't working; the same agents they had tried to escape had tracked them down.

"We need a plan," she told him. He shut his laptop and rubbed his unkept hair, which hadn't been cut in months. A thick lock curled up above his ear, making him look like a boy again. Pelin's heart melted for him. How could she keep him safe, when she was the one putting him in danger?

"And what kind of plan do you have in mind? We're not citizens here. The police don't owe us anything. We're on our own," Kemal replied.

"Maybe not," Pelin said. "I think Tarek was right when he suggested we go to the police. You never know."

They sat in silence for more than a minute. As the seconds ticked by, Pelin couldn't help but think about how much Kemal had sacrificed to follow her into this life of exile—a life that wasn't working for him. He'd put everything on hold, trading freedom for fear, always glancing over his shoulder with every step outside. It broke her heart to see him like this.

"I'm sorry," she whispered, her eyes swollen. "I never meant for it to come to this. My book... I knew it would ruffle some feathers, but I never imagined it would lead to this."

After apologizing, she brought up going to the police again, even though she wasn't sure they would take any action. "Regardless of whether we belong here or not, we're human. They can't just stand by and let someone hurt us." She had no idea how the London authorities would respond to their complaint and their request for protection. But Pelin felt that going to the police was the right move.

"You might be right. But I don't have much faith in the police here—or anywhere," Kemal said. He wanted her to understand why he was hesitant. "Look at how many men and women who look like us are in their graves. Some of them even called the police. Tarek might have had a good idea, but staying alive is my main concern. Taking a chance with the police isn't. My faith comes from elsewhere."

His words didn't comfort Pelin much, but she respected his feelings. Kemal held back from sharing how he was really struggling to cope with what had happened to them the day before. He was trying to balance his commitment to her, his career, and keeping the two of them safe.

He wrestled with thoughts swirling in his mind. His worry about their safety, about the recent attack on their lives, showed in his agitated eyes. He was torn between love and his commitment to his career, which was a huge part of his life. He had spent years trying to climb the ranks as a journalist—more years than he had been married to Pelin. Love for one's work is powerful.

Kemal had no answers for Pelin or for himself; he was in a strange place. The only other person he knew well in the city was his brother Tarek, and he felt that Tarek had already done more than enough for them. The one thought that kept creeping back into his mind was to ask Pelin to tone down her grievances with the regime.

Pelin couldn't tell what was going through Kemal's mind. She knew he was agonizing and was obviously worried about him. "I guess we knew the risks before we left Istanbul," she said. Although she hadn't realized what the isolation of London would do to their sense of security, their grounded connections to the causality of place.

They hadn't had much time to focus on each other; most of their energy went into staying safe. Pelin knew that publishing her latest book would bring some trouble, but she had had no idea it would impact their lives this way. Making the decision to leave everything behind was the hardest choice she had ever had to make. She sensed it may have been even harder for Kemal.

"Kemal, is there something you want to share with me?" Pelin asked. "Have you thought about what I mentioned this morning?" She felt guilty about their situation. Kemal didn't respond right away. He walked over and grabbed his coat from behind the door. "I need some fresh air. We can talk when I get back."

He paused at the door for a moment, and Pelin thought he might turn back, but then he was gone, the door clicking shut behind him. Pelin sensed that the recent attack was a major trigger for him, but she felt there was something else troubling him too. She was upset about everything that had happened as well. She understood his feelings . . . but she knew, not all of them. She needed to know what was really bothering him. It was a tough time, and she couldn't shake her desire to talk to someone.

Pelin was in a strange place, with no contact except for Tarek and Kemal. She was desperate to talk to someone other than those two. Each time she tried to reach out to Kemal, he came up with an excuse, saying it wasn't the right time.

The only other person she could reach out to was her sister Shireen, who lived in New York. Knowing that Kemal would disapprove, she called anyway. Kemal was not comfortable with her discussing their private matters with anyone, including family members. The moment the door closed, she walked to the window and pulled back the curtain, watching Kemal until he turned the corner.

Despite knowing Kemal wouldn't approve, Pelin picked up her phone and dialed Shireen's number. As she waited for her sister to answer, her anxiety grew. When Shireen picked up, Pelin's voice trembled as she greeted her sister. "Are you okay Pelin?" Shireen asked.

The tears Pelin had been holding back finally spilled down her cheeks. "I'm just having a moment." All the unrest in her life had caught up with her. Among other things, she felt homesick. "I don't know what to do, Shireen. We're safe for now, but I'm worried about Kemal. I really think I've messed up his life this time because of my stubbornness." Pelin was lost in doubt about her book, and all other work she had published in the past year in magazines and newspapers.

The two sisters hadn't been in touch since Pelin's rushed departure from Istanbul. She was ashamed of the direction that life was taking her. But once they reconnected, Pelin shared everything that had happened in her life since then. "I thought leaving would make things better, but it hasn't. If anything, it's worse." It seemed that nothing had changed. The threats on her life continued.

In the past, Shireen had felt a little jealous of her sister, but now she was ready to put those feelings aside. "I never thought I'd say this, but Papa would be so proud of you right now," Shireen said. She mentioned that Pelin's campaign against the government's censorship seemed necessary, even though she knew it was taking a heavy toll.

"Pelin, you're up against a powerful regime that won't stop until they know they've silenced you."

In Shireen's eyes, and their mother's, Pelin had always been a fighter, an instigator and a troublemaker.

"I'm starting to wonder if it's worth it. I think I'm driving Kemal crazy. I know he thinks I'd be better off just keeping quiet and living a simpler life."

"Kemal could be right. Now that you've got their attention, maybe consider taking a break," Shireen suggested.

"What do you mean? Now that I've got their attention, I'm not quitting."

"I mean you've made your point. You've raised awareness about how people are being oppressed and punished for speaking out, or just for being creative," Shireen replied.

Pelin understood her sister's concern for her safety, as well as Kemal's. He was even more aware of how stubborn Pelin could be.

He feared something terrible would happen to her if she kept going. After years of covering stories for newspapers, he'd seen peers sentenced to years in prison for doing the same thing Pelin was now doing. He wasn't sure if she understood what the government was capable of. What he wanted was for her to step back and think about everything. Pelin tried to sideline this concern, to ignore it, but it was a constant quiet presence. And now it was getting louder.

* * *

Kemal had grown up under this iron-fisted rule and learned early on to be careful about what he said. He had always kept a low profile, whether in his actions, speech, or writing. He lived as if someone was always watching him, never crossing that invisible line that could get him in trouble.

Pelin had always been different. On one hand, he wished she would end her campaign, but he wasn't sure she knew how to stop. Fighting for her fellow citizens' rights had been her life's work. She moved through life with a fiery energy.

Pelin refused to be silenced, whether in her speech or her writing. Kemal was often amazed by her work, admiring her courage but also worrying about her. It was true that someone had to stand up to the regime at some point; otherwise, there would never be change. He just wished it wasn't his wife doing it.

— 9 —

Kemal was worried Pelin might be in more danger than she realized. It felt to him like her fight against the government was getting out of hand. The persistent fear they lived under was eating at him, and he could no longer push it away.

After thinking it over, again and again, he brought this fear to Pelin. "My darling, I admire your courage. But truly, it's leading us both into deadly danger. We need to make a plan. We can't live and create in a constant atmosphere of worry or terror." Kemal's biggest challenge was convincing Pelin that she had already done enough. Knowing how stubborn she was, he braced himself for a difficult conversation. But Pelin walked into his arms and cried. He didn't move. He stood and held Pelin until she was quiet, until she could speak.

She agreed, then, that they needed to come up with another plan. They had to find a safe way out of this chaos.

"When we left Istanbul, I promised myself I'd always speak for those who can't. But it's not just about me anymore, is it?"

"No," Kemal said softly. "It's about our lives. Our future. Together."

"And it's about protecting democracy," Pelin added. "My father warned me about times like these. He told me that there will come a time when history will be erased, if we the people allow it to be."

"Before you continue, is it okay for me to take a break to think things over. I'm going out for a short while."

Pelin gave him a tight hug, and said, "Let's make a plan together."

While out, Kemal hopped on a bus. Blocks later, he got off and stumbled upon a Turkish coffeeshop hidden away in an alley. It just so happened the owner met him at the door; he introduced himself as Emir. Kemal was served with a warm cup of coffee as he sat scoping the place out. In this coffeehouse he felt he could breathe again. It felt like part of his past, his home. The sound of Turkish being spoken—just simple news and idle chatter—was strangely calming, and yet painful. It took him back to his last evening of prayer at his mosque. And when he returned home everything changed.

He left the coffeehouse pleased that he had found such a place so far from his homeland.

On his way out he noticed a stand of international newspapers. He picked up a tabloid that he was familiar with, one that was published in Istanbul. He was shocked when he opened it and saw a full-page ad in the form of a wanted poster inside, with Pelin's picture on it. "Oh my God," he thought to himself. Now the whole world knows. He folded the paper and stuck it inside his jacket, with the intent of disposing of it in the wastebasket further down the street.

When Kemal returned home, he said nothing about the tabloid. He walked to the shredder and shredded it to pieces. He was ready to sit down with Pelin, to continue their conversation.

"In this world we live in, everyone should have the right to read, write, and speak without being threatened." Kemal heard Pelin's voice from the next room.

He was surprised when he realized Pelin was talking on the phone. He listened a bit longer before announcing he was home.

More than an hour had passed while Kemal was walking, thinking, drinking coffee. All while Pelin and Shireen were still catching up. They chatted about everything that had happened since Pelin arrived in the UK. Shireen wasn't surprised that Pelin had fled the authoritarian regime; she had heard of Pelin's flight from their mother. But she choked up when Pelin talked about how painful it was to leave their ailing mother, especially not knowing if she'd ever see her again.

"Kemal just got back; I need to end this call. I hope we can talk again soon,"

After the call ended, Shireen couldn't stop thinking about her sister. She had never thought that Pelin's fight for free speech would force her and Kemal to leave their home. Her sister's fight had been for the people of Turkey; it was heartbreaking that she had had to leave the people she loved because she was fighting for them.

Shireen remembered, with sorrow, her own reasons for leaving Turkey. She had had experiences like those that had affected Pelin. Months before her own departure, the government was preparing for massive changes, under political pressure. She knew those changes would significantly affect many people like her. In 2016, while she was working as a cartoonist, local officials pressured her about a drawing they found offensive. Although she didn't receive threats as severe as Pelin's, she decided she would be freer to express herself elsewhere . . . or at least that's what she thought at the time. And her expression—in images—could be universal. It wasn't tied to a particular language. It had felt then that the world could be her home. But it hadn't quite felt that way since.

"I understand what it feels like to leave your home," Shireen said to herself. But she couldn't imagine what it was like to have to grab a few things and *run*. It was a sad day for her and thousands of other citizens in Turkey when the parliamentary political system turned into a dictatorship. She watched as those in power dehumanized people, to erase their words.

Living abroad didn't stop Shireen from keeping up with what was happening in her home country. She read countless articles about the arrests of journalists, authors, artists, and even a close friend. She became quite concerned for Pelin's safety. She dreaded opening her sister's blog, fearing what she might find. Given what had happened to others who wrote blogs in their homeland, she was grateful that Pelin and Kemal had made it out.

Before the phone call, she hadn't had an intense conversation with her sister in a long time. Both her worry, and her residual jealousy of her father's support of Pelin's activism, had put a chilly barrier between the sisters. But this call, and Pelin's fear, had melted it. After reconnecting, they promised to stay in touch.

When Pelin told Shireen that Kemal insisted things would get better, Shireen wasn't so sure. She invited Pelin and Kemal to come to New York if things didn't go well in London. For Pelin, Shireen's invitation was worth considering, but she knew it would be a hard sell for Kemal. She promised Shireen she would keep the invitation in mind.

Pelin set her phone on the end table, thoughtfully, carefully. She remained seated on the sofa. "I hope you enjoyed your walk," she said. Kemal seemed more upbeat than before he went out. He gave her a curious look as he glanced at the phone. Lately, when Pelin talked on the phone, it was with Aylin. This time, he could tell it wasn't her. "Who were you talking to?" he asked. He knew it hadn't been another threatening call. No danger hung in the air.

Pelin didn't answer right away; instead, she looked at Kemal with a warm smile. That smile—it reminded him of days that were safer, calmer. It showed she felt better than before he went out.

"I hope it was a friendly call?" Kemal said, his voice curious.

Pelin let out a heavy sigh . . . of relief. Maybe resignation. "It was Shireen; I finally got around to calling her."

"I hope you didn't discuss private family matters," he said.

Pelin decided to share a bit about their conversation. "Shireen sends her greetings, and we caught up a lot." She told them that it had been a welcome though difficult conversation, that the sisters had shared much about the events of their new lives in exile.

Kemal stood with his arms crossed and rolled his eyes. He felt ashamed that Shireen knew they had to flee Istanbul out of fear. He worried she would judge him, that she would think he should have done more to protect Pelin. But he was also disappointed to learn that Pelin shared their private matters with her sister.

"I must look really weak in Shireen's eyes," Kemal muttered.

"If anything, Kemal, she sees you as stronger. Not every man would have given up their life to follow their wife," Pelin replied.

"How does being pushed to the ground with a knee in your back while your wife watches make you look strong?" Kemal asked.

Pelin felt this like a slap. How could she help Kemal understand that life wasn't some theater act, that reality had different rules? But it was hard to continue sharing the details of her conversation with Shireen in the face of his reaction. She stood and locked eyes with him. "If you don't want to talk, just listen to me. We're living in a different world, not a traditional Turkish world, and it's a world where I don't feel safe. Talking with Shireen helped me feel better; besides, you did everything you could."

What Pelin said was true. They were just two people up against a powerful government. She held back from telling Kemal how many times she wished she had left Turkey alone.

"Why are we even having this conversation?" she asked Kemal. "Isn't it more important to focus on who was behind that attempt to kidnap me? Who was the person who hurt you?"

"You're right, yes. Your sister has never threatened us, after all," Kemal agreed. Despite this agreement, he was still trying to understand why he felt so upset about Pelin calling her sister. He wrestled this question down; he'd think about it later. As the head of the household, he wanted to be the one to come up with solutions to their pressing problems.

"Shireen wants you to know that we are always welcome to come stay with her in America."

"Ha!... isn't that nice to know?" Kemal said sarcastically. He didn't say it outright, but in his mind, moving to America seemed like a huge mistake. He had pointed out to her, earlier, that the U.S. has the highest crime and murder rates of any Western country. Not to mention the political turmoil he saw overnight on the evening news and read about in newspapers every day. "No, Pelin, America wouldn't be good for us right now. Besides, they don't want us there."

He continued, "Americans are fighting about how to keep people who look like you and me out. They're building walls. But to be fair, I'll keep the invitation in mind," he said. In the meantime, he wanted to focus on what was happening in the UK.

An unexpected buzz on the door intercom interrupted them. Kemal didn't move to answer. "We won't get back to normal if you won't even answer the door," Pelin said. When he tapped the intercom, he heard Tarek outside the lobby door. He was late getting Kemal's message about their latest harassment incident while leaving the bakery.

After hearing it was Tarek, Pelin looked at Kemal and rolled her eyes. "Is it fair that you can talk to your brother about everything, yet when I call my sister, you have a million questions?"

"Please," Kemal whispered before opening the door. He had a funny feeling that Pelin was being influenced by Shireen. She had never questioned his decisions before, as she did after the phone call. He was curious about what was on her mind, but with Tarek on his way up, there wasn't time to continue.

Once inside, with his jacket draped over his elbow, Tarek started apologizing for what Pelin and Kemal experienced. "I came as soon as I heard. I hope what you went through doesn't limit your view of Londoners," Tarek said.

"It's not about 'limiting our view of Londoners'. We are grateful that they allowed us to enter the UK. We're here seeking asylum because we were not safe in our home country. Back there, Pelin's freedom of speech and physical safety were threatened. And those same threats have followed us here," Kemal told his brother. He went on.

"I'm not naive about what goes on in the UK, nor about Londoners," Kemal added, mentioning he had spent a few years covering London for his newspaper. They had offered him the job of chief officer at the bureau for the *Daily Times* in London a few years earlier. He had turned it down because of the enormous responsibility. Even then, Kemal tended to shun pressure; he wanted a quiet life.

"I know a bit about the UK and its citizens. They can be generous when they want to be, but they're direct about who they want living here. You're an exception, Tarek; you made it in and are doing well," Kemal told him.

Kemal felt that the citizens of the UK had never fully embraced immigration. Many people in the UK felt similarly to Americans about immigration, preferring most foreigners to stay out. Liberals saw this xenophobia as a campaign of harassment against non-white people.

But Kemal turned to Pelin, saying, "The citizens of the UK are not the threat; the threat comes from our own government."

— **10** —

Pelin woke up the next morning feeling a bit better, after the long interview she and Kemal had had with the English detectives.

They'd called to report their attack soon after Tarek had left their place. Despite their reluctance to expose their vulnerability, they finally accepted the need to call the police for their own protection. Pelin was still worried about what the Turkish government might do next regarding their stay in London.

Even before her feet hit the floor, she could smell the strong Turkish coffee drifting through the air. Rubbing her eyes, she stumbled into the kitchen and found Kemal standing there, rubbing his hands together and smiling. Pelin was surprised he had already made breakfast. He'd set the table with a white tablecloth and a vase of colorful fresh flowers. He wanted to celebrate a new beginning for both of them, especially on her first day back at work.

Pelin had taken a break from her office, from writing, to recover from the stressful events of the past few days. She and Kemal had huddled inside trying to stay safe. Now she leaned in to give Kemal a quick kiss on the cheek. This breakfast, so festive, it reminded her of how he used to make breakfast every Sunday back in Istanbul. "Thanks, Kemal, this is wonderful," she said, after lingering over the dark coffee, the crusty bread and fruit.

After breakfast she decided that she would return to work. She grabbed her bags and headed out the door. Lost in thought about

48

Kemal's sweet gesture, Pelin boarded a crowded bus where almost everyone was glued to their phones. She sat next to an interesting lady wearing a bright orange hijab, similar to the white one she had on. The lady was looking at a flyer advertising deals on produce at a nearby Turkish market. Pelin started organizing her handbag while the woman kept glancing at the ads.

After six stops, Pelin stood up to let the woman exit the bus. As the bus pulled away, she looked out the window and saw the lady walking toward a bakery and coffeehouse. A sign in the window read, "Fresh coffee, bread, and assorted pastries." Outside, a few men in service uniforms were gathered around a tall table, sipping coffee and smoking cigarettes.

Pelin stood again to let another passenger take the empty seat next to her. The bus swayed, and she gripped the bar, her eyes widening when she noticed the two men who had followed her days ago sitting in the back. Feeling scared, she fumbled in her handbag for her phone to call Kemal. The bald man stood up and flashed a smile that quickly turned into a hard stare, clearly wanting her to notice him. Just as she was about to tap the buttons on her phone, his partner leaned forward and whispered, "We know who you are." He barely moved his lips as he spoke in Turkish.

That sent a chill down Pelin's spine, and her heart started racing. In a panic, she pulled the cord to signal the driver to stop at the next stop. When the bus halted, she jumped off, not even knowing where she was. Looking around, she spotted a police officer on the corner. She quickly headed toward a nearby subway station, desperate to escape. She hopped on the first train she saw, not caring that it was going the wrong way. She just needed to lose those two men.

Too shaken to go to her office, Pelin made a snap decision to head home. When she got to her door, she rummaged for her keys in her handbag. The squeaky elevator door opened, making her step back defensively, clutching her bag in front of her. Her neighbor walked out, giving her a puzzled look as he passed by. Pelin shrugged, narrowing her eyes as he continued.

Finally, she unlocked the door and slammed it shut behind her. With her jacket hanging around her elbows, she dropped her bags and let out a sigh of relief.

"Kemal where are you?" she shouted before spotting him sitting at his desk. He was raising a steaming cup of coffee to his mouth. She couldn't tell if he was working or just staring out the window. Taking a seat on a stool next to him, she insisted he listen to everything she had to say. Holding her phone as if expecting a call, she recounted the terrifying experience on the bus. "It happened again; they followed me again! This time it was twice as frightening." Her voice trembled as she described how the two men in dark suits had hounded her. "One of them even came up close and whispered in my ear." That was the moment she felt the most fear—when his breath stirred the hair over her ear. "I was terrified it could be my last moment alive."

There was one silver lining from the whole incident. Pelin told Kemal how the man got close enough for her to read the name tag pinned to his jacket: Embassy of the Republic of Turkey. She couldn't help but shake as she detailed every horrifying moment to Kemal. Her eyes were darting around the room, as if she was expecting someone to burst through the door at any moment. Kemal could see the fear in her eyes and knew he had to do something.

"There was one good thing from all this," she said. "I saw his ID tag. But I didn't catch his name. Just that it said, Embassy of the Republic of Turkey."

"So, you're sure they were two guys from the embassy?" Kemal asked.

"Yes, I'm sure. They got way too close."

Kemal raised his arms. "This whole thing is getting messier by the minute." He admitted he didn't know what to do next, but he knew they had to act.

Suddenly, the door buzzer rang. Pelin jumped and placed her hands on her chest, feeling her heart race. "It's okay, I'm here,"

Kemal reassured her. When he opened the door, he was surprised to see the detective from the day before standing there.

"Remember me?" the detective asked. "I was in the area when a call came in saying a lady was seen running into the building looking frantic."

He'd worked the neighborhood for twelve years and had never received such a call. Pelin popped into his mind immediately, and recalling their long interview, he feared the Turkish agents had taken matters into their own hands. He rushed over to their apartment.

"We're okay, but thanks for checking," Kemal said through the half-open door. "Come on, guys, this is serious!" the detective insisted.

Pelin stepped in front of Kemal and opened the door wider. "That's not exactly true," she said, her eyes brimming with tears—not from fear, but frustration. She wanted this to end. If working with the detective would help, she was all in. Her actions made the detective feel like there was a lot more going on than they'd revealed before.

It surprised Pelin that someone had noticed her running into the building. After taking a deep breath, she explained her terrifying experience on the bus. She didn't mention to Kemal that she hadn't been able to sleep lately; she didn't want to add to his worries, especially after he'd done so much to help them start fresh. The detective listened intently as Pelin spoke. He pulled out a notepad and pen, jotting down things he thought needed further investigation. He sensed there was more to the story than they had shared during their first interview. "This is important. Are you sure the men who followed you were from the embassy?"

The more information he collected, the easier it would be for Kemal and Pelin to get asylum. They came to the UK to escape an oppressive regime, but now it looked like they wouldn't be safe anywhere. It was becoming clear that the Turkish agents wouldn't stop until they got what they wanted. Now that they were in the UK, it was the government's job to keep them safe. Things could get even messier if something happened to them on UK soil. The detective convinced them to meet at the police station the next day.

Pelin and Kemal kept their promise and showed up at the detective's office. The room was simple, almost empty, with just four wooden chairs and a table. There were no windows, only two bright overhead lights. To Pelin, it felt like a jail cell. Inspector Barber wore a crisp blue suit and matching tie. A smell of tobacco lingered in the air. Pelin was nervous and stuck close to Kemal. She jumped when the chair scraped against the floor as the Inspector moved closer to the table.

Although they had met twice before, DI Barber still asked permission to record their conversation, it was protocol etched into his routine. "Before we start, would you like anything to drink? Coffee, soda, or water?" he asked. He explained that he had received more intel since their last meeting. The Turkish government had been tracking Kemal for months, trying to figure out his influence on Pelin's writings. They claimed he was the mastermind and wanted to label him as a spy for foreign governments. However, they didn't have enough proof.

Not looking up, Barber tapped his pen on the table and read from his notes. He seemed more serious than he had been during their previous meetings. "I need more details about why you feel threatened by your government," he said in a stern tone.

"Did you take part in any protests or demonstrations? Did you receive any prior warnings from the authorities?" he asked.

"I wrote a book, for God's sake!" Pelin exclaimed. "It was like all hell broke loose when I exposed the tyranny our government inflicted on its people."

"I'm not here to take sides; I just want to get to the bottom of this," Barber said, sounding a bit frustrated. He felt he didn't know enough to trust them completely. He wanted to make sure they hadn't intentionally left out any crucial details during their first interview. If they had, it could mean they wouldn't be allowed to seek asylum and could be sent back to Turkey, to face persecution from the authoritarian regime.

The DI began to ask more questions, looking for discrepancies from what this couple had told him before.

—11—

efore heading to her office to write, Pelin checked out two letters that she received in the mail. One was from Detective Barber, and the other was from the UK immigration office. Unfortunately, neither letter brought good news about their asylum applications, nor was there any update on an arrest for the assault on Kemal. All they could do was wait, and it felt like the immigration office was dragging its feet on purpose. Pelin was really frustrated with the whole system. It was hard to wrap her head around how one of the biggest immigration agencies in the world could take so long to process just two applications.

She tucked the letters away in a small safe with her other important documents. Pelin knew the UK didn't have any legal obligations when it came to asylum seekers. International treaties laid out the framework for the UK's duty to protect refugees and asylum seekers, but there was nothing concrete that guaranteed she or Kemal could stay in the UK. The little hope she had was quickly fading away, thanks to all the never-ending bureaucracy surrounding her case.

Pelin was getting fed up with being treated like a pawn in a chess game by the authorities who held her future in their hands. But she refused to let them crush her spirit with their political nonsense. She wanted to take back her dignity, even as an asylum seeker. Her thoughts wandered back to the woman on the bus with the bright orange scarf. There was something about her that made Pelin feel alive. The woman reminded her of her own colorful life back in Istanbul. She remembered taking breaks from writing and standing by her office window, enjoying delicious Turkish food, coffee while daydreaming.

She would look out the window and watch the tourists strolling through the narrow cobblestone streets. It was always fun to see them popping in and out of the stunning mosques. Watching how non-Muslims reacted to the call to prayer blaring from loudspeakers for the first time it was very interesting to her. Most looked surprised and confused, stopping in their tracks to figure out where the sound was coming from. Then she'd gaze out over the Bosporus, watching sailboats glide across the calm blue waters with their big white sails catching the gentle breeze. Pelin often included many of these strangers, and the sights of Istanbul, in her novels.

But it wasn't just the good memories that came to mind. She also thought about the people she left behind and the promise she made to herself and them. She promised to let the world know how the regime abused its power over its citizens.

Even though she managed to escape her homeland, the threat was still there, and so was her fight. They were actively trying to roll back all the progress Turkey had made toward democracy. She vowed to do everything she could to stop the country from slipping backward. Now that she was living in exile, she realized similar things were happening in the West. Plus, the rise in book banning in other countries really worried her.

Pelin couldn't believe that the United States had banned more books than any other country. A place she once saw as a symbol of freedom was now trying to silence voices, erase stories, and rewrite history. How could a country that prided itself on liberty also be the one trying to control what its citizens read, think, or write? she wondered.

All these recent events reminded Pelin of the Sivas Massacre in July of 1993. On that day, 37 creative artists lost their lives because of other people's prejudices and hate. It was a wake-up call. The fight for freedom of speech was still going strong. Pelin knew that if governments didn't learn from their past mistakes, they were likely to repeat them.

Her thoughts were interrupted when Kemal walked into the sitting room. He noticed her intense look. "Are you okay?" he asked her.

"I'm fine," she replied, avoiding his gaze. Instead, her eyes drifted to the beautiful city outside the window, another ancient city, beautiful like Istanbul. But even as she admired it, she felt a suffocating pressure inside, as if the walls were closing in on her. She knew her enemies were lurking in the shadows, just waiting to silence her. She was a warrior, and she refused to be trapped.

Just like the woman in the orange scarf walking happily toward the coffeehouse, Pelin was ready to do the same. "I'm not afraid anymore," she said to Kemal. "I've got to do this on my own."

Still, Kemal felt it wasn't the right time for her to go out again, especially after everything that had just happened. He was more worried than ever after the latest incident. The look on her face when she told him about the guy who got close enough to whisper in her ear stayed with him. He couldn't shake it off. Along with that, he still wasn't ready to tell her that tabloids were circulating with wanted posters inside, and that the wanted posters had her face on them.

"Think about it, Pelin. You have a bounty on you for treason." He wasn't sure she fully understood the consequences if she was brought back to Turkey.

Pelin listened. She understood, she told him, what he was saying, what it meant. But she could not, would not, let the information in. Kemal's caution couldn't penetrate her single-minded purpose. "I promised my people I'd be their voice. I can't keep that promise by hiding away," she said as she grabbed her coat. "This is a big deal. It affects way more than just us."

Pelin hadn't always imagined herself as an activist. In another life she sometimes would dream about a bookstore with Kemal. That was before the arrest warrants were drafted on her. There were times when she would enjoy attending open mic and reading aloud. But now she devoted most of her life to speaking out for others. Mostly those others were authors, publishers, and librarians that were getting threatened or censored by school boards and local and federal governments.

"It's great to stand up for those things, but don't you realize you're putting your life at risk?" Kemal asked.

"I just want to remind people that we must resist the forces that try to silence us and erase our past. Don't worry, Kemal, I'll be fine."

Everything she said made sense to him, but she was still his wife, and nothing she said could ease his worry for her safety.

Looking stronger than ever, she walked out the door, knowing Kemal was watching her from the window. She hurried around the corner and took the path through the park. All Kemal could do was pray that she'd come back safe.

Pelin walked into the coffeehouse where she had seen the lady with the orange hijab. She caught a few looks from some guys and gals, but nothing too crazy. None of the chatter she heard was in English. This time, she didn't bother to disguise herself. She adjusted her favorite white hijab over her hair, leaving her face wide open. Before grabbing a seat, she stood for a moment, checking out the tables and the small crowd of fifteen or twenty people hanging out. One of the two women staring was the same one she had shared a seat with on the bus. Pelin was pretty sure it was her . . . since she was wearing that same orange scarf.

The lady was watching Pelin closely. She tapped her friend's arm to excuse herself and then walked over. "Hey, I think we met a few days ago. Well, not officially, but we shared a seat on the bus," she said in broken English, extending her hand. "I'm Elif." Pelin wasn't in a hurry to introduce herself.

"Nice to meet you, Elif. I'm… Korkmaz." She stuck with her last name, not wanting to use her full name and draw too much attention.

"Mrs. Korkmaz? That name sounds familiar. Like the novelist, right?" Pelin held her silence.

"No way you're the novelist, are you?" Elif tried to keep her cool. "Come join me and my friend at our table."

"Thanks, but I just popped in for a coffee to go, and I have work to finish." She headed to the counter, rummaging through her purse.

Behind the bar, the coffeehouse owner was watching her closely. It took him a few seconds to place her, but now, he was sure. Pelin. A memory kicked in. He hadn't seen her in person for years, and he noticed her appearance hadn't changed much. He recalled seeing her face on the cover of a magazine while he was on vacation in Morocco. And he already knew why she was in London.

"Aren't you a novelist?" he asked, curious.

Pelin paused. She had told Kemal she wouldn't be scared. "I've written a few things," she replied carefully.

A smile spread across his face. "I'm Emir. Selling coffee is what I do. Want a cup? It's on the house."

She looked at him, feeling like she knew him from somewhere, but she couldn't figure out where. "Thanks, but I can pay."

Emir shook his head. "Just this once. Think of it as a welcome gift."

He went behind the bar and whipped up her cappuccino like a pro. Once it was ready, he came around and set the cup in front of her. Pelin smiled and nodded in thanks, then turned toward the door, but Emir followed her like he had more to say.

"I read your work, and the coffee is just a small way to say thanks for what you do." He spoke in their native language, making Pelin blush a bit. It had been a while since she let a stranger into her space without feeling scared.

Knowing a little more about Pelin from the news, Emir didn't mention her by name; instead, he used her maiden name, even though she had introduced herself differently.

Emir wiped his hands on his apron and offered her a handshake. "Please come back; there's always room for a novelist here."

"Thanks," she replied, realizing he knew who she was. "Maybe I will take you up on that." With that, she turned and walked away.

Emir opened the door and stepped back inside, the bell overhead jingling lightly. He scanned the café. Two men by the front window stared too long at Pelin, their tabloid spread open like a trap. One of them leaned toward the other. "Isn't that the woman who…?" Emir was already walking toward them. "She's been through more than you'll ever know," he said, in a low voice. "And she's under my roof now. That means she's off-limits." He looked at the men, then turned and walked behind the counter. The room was suddenly quieter than before.

12

Meeting Elif was a breath of fresh air for Pelin. It made her realize how others managed to carve out their lives while living abroad. Sure, they were in the UK under very different circumstances than her own but seeing the joy on Elif's and her friends' faces made Pelin question her existence. She had been merely surviving, not living. It felt as though her fate was in the hands of others—strangers who knew nothing about her, and she nothing about them. They were unseen figures who dictated whether she remained safe or was thrown back into danger. It wasn't until she returned to the office and stopped by the coffee shop that she felt she could finally move on from some of her darkest days.

In a surprising twist, Pelin decided she wanted to know more about Elif. She thought, why not? They were both from the same homeland and spoke the same language. Perhaps they were both searching for the same thing: meeting new people or longing for something they had left behind. She recalled their brief encounter at the coffeehouse and thought that would be the perfect place to track her down.

Pelin looked up at Kemal and said, "Hey, I need to share something with you." Fidgeting with her fingers, she began her story.

"Do you remember that woman I mentioned a few times? The one I met on the bus and then again at the coffeehouse?" she asked.

"Yeah, I remember," he replied, his eyes wide. He lowered his Kindle in his lap and leaned forward in his comfortable chair by the window, eager to hear more. "Go on," he said. "You said she reminded you of a distant cousin."

"Exactly! She seems interesting, at least from what I've seen so far. I'd like to get to know her better and find out what brought her to the UK."

Kemal was taken aback. Just a few weeks ago, Pelin had expressed that she never wanted to be close to anyone in this strange city.

"Why the change of heart?" he asked. "You never said anything like this before."

"I know it sounds strange," Pelin admitted, a bit unsure herself. "I think it would be nice to be around others, after so much time alone. I bet she misses her home too. We could be good for each other," she told Kemal.

Kemal shifted in his chair, sitting on the edge to listen closely. He was trying to wrap his head around her sudden change in attitude.

"It's time, Kemal. Since I've been here, I've felt out of place. Whenever I go out, I'm too busy looking over my shoulder to enjoy anything," Pelin said, looking Kemal in his eyes. This time, she desperately hoped he would understand how lonely she had felt, with no one to talk to but him. "Now I'm starting to see that there are others out there like me. But I bet there's no one with government agents searching for them."

With that, Pelin got ready to head to the coffee shop, leaving Kemal worried. But by now, he no longer questioned her motives. "If this is what you think you need to do, then like always, I support you." Pelin breathed a sigh of relief. "I love you, Kemal. Thank you." His understanding meant everything to her.

Feeling more confident with Kemal's approval, Pelin prepared to go out alone. With only a few hours of daylight left, she slipped on a warm coat and grabbed her purse from the table. She opened the door to leave but looked back at Kemal and smiled. Stepping outside, she felt the cool wind on her face, sending a shiver down her spine. She quickly stepped back in to grab her white scarf. It wasn't as thick as her others, but it felt soft and warm as she wrapped it around her head.

Before stepping back out, Pelin checked herself in the mirror and smiled. The city was alive, despite the damp chill in the air. A light drizzle made walking on the cobblestones slippery and treacherous. She walked carefully, feeling confident. She followed a somewhat familiar route along the Thames that led to the coffeehouse.

The streets were a mix of century-old buildings and modern skyscrapers reaching into the low-hanging clouds. A red double-decker bus rumbled past, splashing through puddles, while cyclists zigzagged in and out of traffic. Pelin was just happy to be out, letting nothing dampen her spirits as she strolled through the city.

She walked along the Thames, with the London towers just a short distance away. Turning into a narrow alley, she glanced over her shoulder to make sure she was not being followed. The sounds of heavy traffic and city noise faded, replaced by the loud voices of men speaking in foreign languages, signaling she was getting closer to her destination.

The coffeehouse was tucked away from the bustling streets, known only to those in the know. It was a hidden gem in a secluded alleyway, lit up by a bright streetlamp. The building, once an old warehouse, had worn red brick full of character, with ivy climbing up one wall.

Pelin spotted it by a small wrought-iron sign hanging above a narrow cobblestone path that read, "The Scriptorium."

A picture of Elif's face flashed in Pelin's mind, sending a surge of nervous energy through her body. Her heart raced, pounding like an excited drummer. Even before stepping inside, she felt the walls of the coffeehouse closing in on her, increasing her emotions.

With the doorway just a step away, Pelin wasn't sure what she was walking into. What if Elif wasn't who she seemed to be? What if she was one of the special agents sent to track her? All the uncertainty was making her second-guess her reason for coming, but she pressed on, determined to reclaim her life. Soon she would find out if this was the right decision, after everything she had been through.

More anxiety crept in. Pelin started to think about everything that could go wrong. How would she approach the woman? Though Elif might know a little about her, Pelin considered her a total stranger. And what about the other patrons? How much did they know about her?

Pelin pushed open the heavy wooden door with a small square window in the center. The door creaked, announcing her arrival to everyone inside. She shivered as she stepped in and noticed folks scattered around the tables, all seemingly in their own worlds, sipping coffee and tea, deep in conversation. The men's voices easily drowned out the few women there. As a few quick glances were cast in her direction, conversations grew silent. After standing and surveying the patrons, she walked toward the coffee bar. Pelin smiled awkwardly, feeling like she was in the spotlight, as if her whole life was about to unravel. The warm aroma of coffee and pastries helped calm the butterflies in her stomach.

She had a feeling that most everyone inside knew she was the infamous novelist wanted by the Turkish government for treason. But she also wondered how many really knew her. How many knew her story? Her journey? And if they did know anything, what exactly did they know?

Because of the stories written about her, she had become an unintentional international figure. Pelin remembered what Kemal told her about a large photo of her in one of Turkey's national tabloids. Some copies had made it to the UK, and one had turned up in the coffeehouse. Along with the photo was a fabricated story trying to justify the alleged treason charges. Kemal couldn't be the only one who saw the tabloid; other customers who frequented the coffeehouse must have seen it too. Maybe the person who brought it was among the many who were there.

Months of feeling invisible made every step Pelin took inside the coffeehouse cautious and suspicious. She scanned the room for anyone she thought could be a threat. Despite the looks she received and her moments of anxiety, she focused on why she was there—Elif and wanting to learn more about her. She wanted to reclaim her life. Pelin stood at the coffee bar and scanned the room, hoping to spot her. During their first brief meeting, Elif mentioned she was a regular, but tonight she was nowhere to be found.

Doubts bubbled up. What if she had walked into a trap? And if she had it was to late, she was now in the middle of it. Or maybe Elif was a journalist eager to score an interview with her?

After lingering in the coffeehouse for a while, Pelin looked around, focusing on the table where she last saw Elif. She wasn't there, but two women who had been with her the last time Pelin saw her were. They were whispering softly to each other.

"That's her! She's back!" one of the women said. "I think she's that famous author everyone's been talking about," the woman said. Pelin's self-imposed exile was a hot topic of hushed whispers among the women. Even if they suspected the charges against her were bogus, the news stories had sparked curiosity.

Pelin turned away when she caught the women looking at her. They seemed engrossed in their conversation. As she turned to leave the coffeehouse, she bumped into Elif coming out of the ladies' room. "Oh my, it's you!" Elif exclaimed, leaving Pelin speechless. "You remember me? I'm Elif, Elif Alsan. You were here a few days ago."

"Sorry, I remember you. It's just been one of those days," Pelin replied. There was no way she could forget Elif; she was the reason Pelin came back.

Elif placed a hand on Pelin's shoulder, causing a shiver to run down her spine. With her other hand, she waved toward the table where she had been sitting with the two other women. Despite her reluctance, Pelin joined them. The other two women seemed excited to have her there.

Though feeling uneasy, Pelin maintained her composure, sitting with her back against the wall. It was no secret anymore that she had fled her home. She knew most Turkish citizens had heard something about her from the media. Once Pelin settled into her seat, she was acutely aware that most eyes in the coffeehouse were on her. Elif leaned in close to whisper something in Pelin's ear. Whatever it was sent a chill down Pelin's spine and revealed a truth that would change everything.

13

Elif had welcomed Pelin with a warm smile and led her to the corner where her two friends were seated. "This is our spot while the husbands are at work," she said, pointing to the steaming cups and her friends. "Sometimes they spend hours on some secret assignment at the embassy." Elif boasted to her friends about having Pelin join them. What kind of secret mission could their husbands possibly have here in the UK? Pelin thought. The evening wasn't going as she'd hoped. Sitting with these three strangers and hearing the words "secret mission" made her feel uncomfortable. She felt out of place, even though she had just arrived; she wanted to leave. Elif was eager to hear the story about why Pelin came to the UK.

"I just got here. There's not much to say," Pelin replied. She couldn't blame Elif or her friends for being curious, especially after months of her photo being all over Turkish TV, and the various imaginative stories written about her. They probably already knew more than she could share. She just hoped they could distinguish the fake news from the truth.

Elif flashed a quick grin, clearly disappointed that Pelin wouldn't open up more. She and her friends wanted to know more about Pelin's background and why she was in the UK. But what Elif really wanted to know was if Pelin was really the famous novelist from Istanbul—the one wanted by the Turkish government for treason.

This couldn't be her.

Elif stared at Pelin. No—impossible. She wouldn't have made it this far, not with everything stacked against her.

Unless...

Unless Elif had underestimated her all along.

Pelin sipped her tea and occasionally glanced around to see what was happening. Being in a foreign land and a crowded coffee-house full of unfamiliar faces made her uneasy. Elif and her friends' curiosity stirred up as much suspicion in her as it did in them. Pelin had come out hoping to meet someone she could connect with, especially since they all were from Istanbul, but these connections, Pelin sensed, could not be trusted.

Elif eventually gave up trying to get Pelin to share more about herself. She figured she'd learn more through simple conversation, chatting over the lively chatter and laughter that buzzed throughout the room. Pelin quickly redirected the conversation by asking, "Hey ladies, what's there to do around here in the city?"

Maryam, with her bold dark mascara circling her eyes, jumped at the chance to answer. "Oh, there's tons to do in London! I totally recommend checking out the museums—the British Museum, the Victoria and Albert Museum. There's so much cool stuff about British history and culture," she said.

Sarah, the third friend in the group, nodded in agreement. "And the music scene is lively! How about the three of us set a date to go out and enjoy some live music?" she suggested.

Pelin was glad for the change in topic as she sipped her tea. She found Maryam and Sarah much more interesting than Elif. "Maybe one day," she replied but secretly thought it was a bit too soon to hang out with three new people.

Just then, she looked up and spotted a guy she recognized walking through the doorway. Her words were cut short as she watched him, her shoulders tensing and her smile fading. She quickly grabbed her phone from her purse. "Sorry, ladies, but I just got an urgent text. I really have to go."

Pelin was no longer interested in having a conversation with the women at the table. She was trying to figure out how to leave without being noticed by the man she was trying to avoid. She stayed seated for a few more minutes, hoping he wouldn't see her. Once she felt it was safe, she stood up, grabbed her things, and rushed to the door. She left without making plans to meet up with the women again or exchanging contact information.

Outside, she called a taxi and plopped down in the back seat, giving the driver her address. She felt a wave of relief when she finally reached her apartment. Happy to be home, she tipped the driver generously, grabbed her handbag, hopped out of the car, and dashed into her building. She rushed past the doorman, who noticed something was off when he saw strands of hair slipping out from under her hijab. She didn't bother fixing it; Pelin just wanted to get inside and lock the door.

The elevator dinged and stopped at the ninth floor. As she fumbled for her keys, she caught a glimpse of herself in the hallway mirror. She looked nothing like the cheerful woman who had left just a few hours earlier, the one excited for a fresh start. Instead, she saw someone worried, cautious, scared. Before unlocking the door, Pelin took one last look around to make sure no one was following her. When she stepped into her apartment and saw Kemal sitting in his chair, she finally felt safe.

She started to rethink the whole situation. The experience at the coffeehouse had brought back all the fear she had been carrying since that phone call. No matter how hard she tried to shake off her worries, moments like the one she had experienced with Elif reminded her that she wasn't safe. She couldn't stop thinking about how a powerful government was after her, and it felt like agents were popping up everywhere she went.

But now, in the comfort of her apartment, her worries started to fade, easing some of the tension inside her. She walked into the living room where Kemal was sitting, his head buried in a newspaper.

"Kemal," her voice came out shaky and a bit odd. He closed the paper, set it down on the coffee table, and looked up at her, noticing the frightened look on her face.

"Pelin, what's going on?" he asked, pushing the paper aside, seeing her distress. "Did someone do something to you?" He remembered the strangers following and harassing her. Pelin let out a heavy sigh and looked straight into Kemal's eyes. "It's my fault, Kemal," she said, leaving him speechless. "What do you mean it's your fault?" Kemal pressed, wanting her to share what was on her mind. "I just assume that whenever a stranger looks at me, they're up to no good," she explained. He bit down on his lip, holding back what he really wanted to say. It felt so unfair. He could not wrap his head around why Pelin's night, which had started off so well, had gone downhill. He could see the strain in her eyes and knew that something was troubling her.

"It's okay, Pelin. After everything you've faced, it makes sense to feel that way."

"I won't give up," Pelin promised. "I'm in the middle of a fight, and I can't just back down, especially if my enemy won't."

Pelin started pacing the room. She took off her hijab and ran her fingers through her hair. Kemal watched, worried. He got up and walked close, placing his hand on her shoulder. "Pelin, you don't have to stress about what upset you earlier. You're safe here at home. No one can get in; I checked with security, and they assured me no one can come up the stairs without being challenged."

"I know," she replied, but his words didn't ease her anger, and her disappointment that her evening hadn't gone as planned. "But there was a guy at the coffeehouse, Kemal… I recognized him. He wasn't a stranger. I've seen him before."

"Who was he?" Kemal asked. Pelin shook her head. She didn't want to say too much and risk upsetting him or letting her panic take over. She knew Kemal deserved the truth; he was the only one who had stuck by her through everything.

"I don't know his name, but he was one of the guys in the alley the night of the attack. He's also one of the guys I bumped into on the bus."

Kemal's expression turned serious. He bit his lip, trying to hold back his anger. "One of them? And he showed up at the coffee shop? Are you sure?"

Pelin nodded, struggling to keep her own anger in check. "I'm sure. Thank goodness he didn't see me. But as soon as he walked in, I felt it. That same cold sinking feeling in my stomach that I had when he bothered me on the bus. I knew I had to get out of there."

Kemal stepped closer and reached for her hand. "Why didn't you call me?"

"I wasn't sure if I needed to. Maybe I was just being paranoid. So, I made up an excuse to leave because of a text I got."

Before she left the coffeehouse, Pelin was certain it was him. "I took one last look at him before I walked out."

Kemal stood quietly, deep in thought about what Pelin had just told him. He felt a mix of anger and concern. "This changes everything," he said, stepping away. "If they've tracked you here, we're not safe. You can't go back to the coffee shop . . . even the office could be a risk."

Pelin took a deep breath after hearing Kemal's suggestion. "You mean go back to hiding? No matter where I go, they'll find me. They always do."

"I thought coming here would keep us safe, but things like this keep happening. It looks like we're not safe here," Kemal replied.

"Kemal, hiding isn't an option. I'm done with that. I can't keep doing this. I'm tired, Kemal. Tired of running, tired of looking over my shoulder."

"I get it, but we've got to be smart about this. Just look at who we're up against," Kemal said, before deciding to step outside for some fresh air, as he usually did every evening. As he walked out the door and onto the sidewalk, he was still thinking about the conversation he just had with Pelin. The streetlights flickered as he moved further away from the building. He glanced around, feeling much like Pelin, skeptical of everyone he passed. He saw them as potential threats. He knew they couldn't keep living like this—always on edge and scared. Something had to change.

Back inside, Pelin paced the room, her mind racing. She had to shake off this fear. Time was running out. She and Kemal needed a new plan, one that would help them take back control of their lives.

She peered out the window, hoping to catch a glimpse of Kemal. Nothing. He'd vanished around the corner into the darkness. With a deep breath, she clenched her fists. No more. Fear had held her back long enough.

Before she could second-guess herself, she sprang into action. She walked through every room, yanking cords from the walls—smart lights, the Alexa, even the TV. They were listening. She was sure of it.

—14—

Kemal rushed to get home. On one hand, he couldn't wait to tell Pelin about meeting Emir. On the other, he was not sure how she would react to him having a conversation with a wealthy businessman from Istanbul, after emphasizing that they should trust no one.

He had started out walking and then sprinting through the alleys, and back streets of London. He weaved in and out of the crowds of pedestrians as he made his way to the main streets. Kemal found himself out of breath and ended up flagging down an Uber. He thought for once he was able to give Pelin some positive news, after her visit to the coffeehouse didn't go well.

At first Kemal found it difficult to believe that Emir Sahin was the owner of the Turkish coffeehouse he'd visited before. Emir was an average-looking guy who wore a black T shirt and blue jeans without a belt. In Istanbul, that wouldn't have been the garb of a coffeehouse owner . . . but this was London.

Emir knew almost everything about Pelin and Kemal's situation, as well as their problems with the Turkish government. Everything that he knew was not from newspapers, tabloids or TV. He had a relationship with an insider, one of the counsellors to the regime.

Kemal was happy to meet Emir but kept a careful distance. It was something about him being from Istanbul and now being in London that puzzled Kemal. Kemal had learned the hard way about trusting strangers these days, especially those from Turkey. However, the two of them spoke as if their meeting was a reunion.

Emir told Kemal that like a few others from their homeland, he had some idea of what Pelin might be going through. "I have heard a few rumors, and I am sure that this is a difficult time for you both. But please know, the coffeehouse is a safe place," he said. He told Kemal that he left Istanbul some years earlier under similar circumstances.

Emir told Kemal about his decision to open the coffeehouse. He wanted to create a haven for those who were like himself, trying to escape the oppressive regime. He wished to give them a place to be accepted without judgment and to provide them with support.

Kemal thanked Emir Sahin for his kindness and for understanding his wife's situation. He paused for a moment, taking a deep breath, somewhat relieved that he had found a place where he and Pelin could visit and would feel comfortable and welcome.

This act of kindness was a relief to Kemal after being in the UK for all this time, knowing no one but his brother. He couldn't wait to tell Pelin all about his conversation with Emir, how the man made him feel welcome to the small Turkish community in London.

Before entering their apartment, Kemal stopped to take a few deep breaths. He walked inside. "I am home." He looked into Pelin's eyes and smiled, hoping the news he was about to tell her would bring her some comfort.

"I met the owner of that Turkish coffeehouse today. His name is Emir Sahin," Kemal told Pelin. Her eyes opened wide, and a light went off inside her head. That's him, she thought, I now remember him from university. That's why he seemed familiar. It had been years ago, and they both had changed, but she knew he had recognized her as well. She gave Kemal no clue that she met Emir earlier, that she knew him from home.

"I felt a few positive vibes after having a conversation with him," Kemal said with a fresh look on his face as he spoke. His eyes were wide open, and his face seemed brighter. She listened as Kemal continued to talk about being at the coffeehouse—an experience which differed from her own.

"He knows about your situation. He knows your work, and he's read most of the news articles from back home that mentioned you. Emir Sahin wants you to know that you are always welcome at the coffeehouse. He assured me you would be safe there," Kemal said.

Pelin looked at him as if she didn't believe a single word he said. She wondered to herself, how could Kemal out of the blue trust the first person he meets, and someone from Istanbul? She knew that Kemal preferred to be trusting, but was this foolish?

She was still a bit shaken from her own experience of meeting with strangers there. Pelin had been looking over her shoulder for so long that it seemed she had forgotten what it was like to trust anyone, especially someone from Istanbul.

"So, this Sahin tells you he knows my story, and he welcomes me to his coffeehouse. Tell me, Kemal, what do you know about him?" Pelin asked Kemal.

Kemal thought for a moment, as he tried to recall the most important details of the conversation he had with Emir.

"Well, he mentioned he moved to London a few years ago because of similar circumstances to our own," Kemal replied. "He also said that his experiences and his move to the UK inspired him to open the coffeehouse as a haven for people like us."

Pelin nodded her head, trying to understand. "What else do you know about Emir Sahin? Tell me, how do his experiences back home relate to ours?" She wanted to know more about why this man was being so generous to Kemal. Maybe he too was working for the Turkish government and the agents who were after them. She couldn't help but wonder. After all, the owner of a coffeehouse would be ideally placed to ferret out dissidents. Kemal was on his high, and probably never considered these things. He was just excited to meet someone from his home that he could connect with, after having no friends in London.

"Pelin, what I gather is, not only does Emir Sahin seem passionate about his work, but he also seemed to be a generous man."

"And?" … she asked, wanting to hear more.

Emir had told Kemal that he felt obligated to provide support to newcomers who are in need. He promised Kemal that he and Pelin would be safe at the coffeehouse. He also said that they could count on him for whatever they needed.

"We need nothing. We just need to be left alone, so we can live normal lives again. Another thing, Kemal, the story you are telling me about this Emir Sahin sounds good, but I am not too convinced."

Kemal could understand that she was reluctant to trust Emir, or anyone else right now.

"I know a large part of your reluctance is my doing Pelin." He had repeatedly suggested that she not trust anyone. He was always telling her to be cautious of her surroundings when out. And so far, she had been doing a pretty good job of it.

"I think we should take Emir at his word. I believe he is sincere in offering us his friendship."

Kemal's recommendation about Emir had Pelin puzzled. She looked at Kemal. "That takes time."

Kemal did his best to paint Pelin a vivid picture of Emir Sahin. He reiterated Emir's passion for freedom and expressed his belief in Emir's dedication to his work providing support to those in need. He made every attempt to get her to see things his way.

"I am still not too keen on trusting anyone just yet," Pelin said.

While Pelin had many questions after her own experience, Kemal thought it was time to move on. He had been cautious with strangers as well. During his visit at the coffeehouse, he watched the men interact. In that moment, he realized he was ready to ignore his own advice. Pelin understood that Kemal missed meeting up with friends in teahouses and coffeeshops. After all, he had left his friendly and sociable life behind to support her. She promised Kemal that she would think more about it. Her plan was to revisit the coffeehouse again, when she was comfortable enough to do so.

It was apparent that Pelin hesitated to place her faith in the coffeehouse owner or any other Turkish individual. It began the day she received the phone call. Since that day, she had gone through a series of disappointments and betrayals, which had shattered her trust in people. Her fear intensified when she thought about someone snatching her off the street and taking her back to Turkey to stand trial for treason—which was not an unfounded fear. It was real.

Given the political instability, and the corruption in the Turkish judicial system, Pelin worried that if that happened, she wouldn't get a fair trial. Her fear was not irrational; stories of individuals forced to stand trial in hostile territories were common. These stories often ended in harsh punishments, even death.

Being afraid had become a part of Pelin's everyday life since she left her home. That feeling had created an overwhelming sense of dread, constant anxiety. Simple tasks, like going to the market or meeting friends became daunting. Every time she stepped out of her home, she had to consider the possibility of being recognized, kidnapped, and taken away against her will.

She felt that her social life was over. She lived behind walls; and her mistrust extended to everyone she met. It was overwhelmingly difficult to maintain relationships and build new ones. That included her recent meeting with Elif and her friends.

The nagging thought about Kemal's demeanor change never left her mind. Was this the same Kemal? That same man, whenever he left the house, was suspicious and trusted no one." Pelin noticed a stark difference in him when he returned from the coffeehouse. It seems he saw a glimmer of hope in the coffeehouse owner's intentions. Was Kemal's change born out of loneliness, or was there something more? Was he longing for a companion from a world that he left behind? Searching for a friend who might understand him better, and one who spoke his native tongue?

Kemal was asking Pelin to lower her defenses. Even though she listened, she stayed resolute. She stood with her arms crossed, and her body stiff with determination. She had reached the limit of her patience and felt an urgent need for the conversation to end.

"Kemal, I appreciate your concern, but after all I have been through, I have to trust my gut feelings," Pelin said. She turned away from him and walked towards the kitchen. There was a mix of emotions flaring up in her. Pelin had a lot of doubts and questions about Kemal allowing Emir to get too close in his life.

"Why would Emir be so kind?" she wondered aloud. Was he truly a kind-hearted person, or was something more sinister lurking beneath his friendly disposition? Was it safe for them to trust him? With all the murky waters surrounding those in power in Turkey, who knew what kind of man Kemal had met?

Kemal's phone buzzed, interrupting her thoughts. To her surprise, when he answered the call, she heard him say, "Emir Sahin, no, you are not interrupting."

Kemal walked into the kitchen, looked at Pelin. He was smiling and making hand gestures, trying to inform her who was on the other end of the phone.

The call caught her off guard. Just as she was trying to tone down her thoughts about Emir, here he was—calling out of the blue.

Pelin watched as Kemal walked around the kitchen with an amused expression on his face. He whispered something to her, but she couldn't quite make out what he was saying. He continued to gesture towards his phone, trying to communicate some kind of message to her.

"He wants to invite us to dinner tomorrow night, at his home. He says his friend can't wait to meet you." Kemal ended the phone call and stood with his hands folded together, waiting for Pelin's response. She looked him in the eyes and asked, "Kemal, Emir Sahin is still a stranger. Are you sure you want to go to his home?"

—15—

Pelin walked quietly into the kitchen with dark circles around her eyes. She paused and watched Kemal as he stood at the counter preparing a fresh pot of coffee. With his back turned, he hadn't yet noticed her. She opened her mouth to speak but hesitated. Finally, she murmured, "I'll skip breakfast today."

Kemal spun around. His concern was evident when he saw her standing there with her eyes barely open.

"Do you need more sleep?"

"No," she replied, as she brushed her hair from her tired eyes. "I barely slept; I was thinking about everything you said about Emir. I need to clear my head. I think a walk in the city might help."

His coffee cup froze halfway to his lips. "A walk in the city? Pelin, you never leave this early unless it's for work."

"There's a first time for everything," she said, managing a slight smile. Something had changed in her overnight. Maybe it was the urgent need to start her life over.

Kemal pushed the barstool toward the counter, its legs scraping across the tiles. Pelin winced slightly at the sound. "I need this, Kemal. I just need some fresh air. I need to walk through the city."

He didn't argue further, though worry creased his forehead. Over the past few days, he'd gotten used to seeing her safe in their apartment, shielded from the city's chaos. He expected her to stay indoors, healing from the bus incident and her experience in the cafe. But clearly, she had other plans.

"The city center?" he asked cautiously. "Are you sure that's where you want to go?"

"Yes," she said firmly, slipping on her coat. "I need to feel part of the world again, even if it's full of chaos."

Kemal sighed but knew better than to argue. "Be careful. Call me if anything happens."

"I promise," she replied gently and walked out the door and into the morning chill.

As the bus carried her downtown, Pelin felt unusually calm, even as the crowded streets came into view. Once off the bus, the city's noise surrounded her, vibrant and alive. She moved through the crowds easily, a newfound confidence guiding her steps. Even all the noise and energy of the financial district brought her peace, something unimaginable just days earlier.

Buildings towered over her, their mirrored windows catching sunlight. The smog from traffic didn't bother her today. Approaching Canary Wharf, with its towering steel and glass structures gleaming, something else drew her attention.

A young woman stood by the Starbucks entrance, distinctly out of place. She was perhaps in her mid-twenties, modestly dressed, a worn hijab covering her head, an oversized coat hanging from her thin frame. Around her, well-dressed patrons sipped expensive coffees, oblivious to her presence. The contrast was stark.

Pelin watched quietly as the young woman repeatedly asked passersby for change. Each plea was urgent. Ignored by those absorbed in their phones or music, the young woman's courage struck Pelin deeply. Without a second thought, Pelin reached into her purse, walking over to press a 100-euro bill into the woman's cold hand.

The young woman's eyes widened in shock and gratitude. "Shukran," she whispered, staring down at the unexpected gift.

"What's your name?" Pelin asked gently.

"Leila," she replied softly after a brief hesitation. "I'm from Syria."

"Leila," Pelin repeated warmly. "That's a beautiful name. Please, join me inside for coffee and something warm to eat. You don't need to stand in the cold."

Leila glanced nervously at the Starbucks entrance. "I can't," she admitted, her voice barely audible. "They won't let me inside. The manager said I'm bad for business."

Pelin felt her heart tighten at the harshness of the situation. She glanced through the glass at customers who were inside, not paying any attention to what was happening just outside their comfortable space.

"There's another café across the street," Pelin offered gently. "Come with me?"

Leila hesitated, with her eyes wary, but chill and hunger pushed her to trust Pelin. She followed quietly, relieved to escape the cold. They found a small cozy café a block away. It was warm and welcoming, with the smell of freshly baked bread filling the air. Seated across from each other, sipping hot coffee and nibbling toasted bread, the two women shared pieces of their lives.

This was Leila's first time comfortably sitting in a public place since arriving in the UK three months earlier. She opened up about fleeing Syria with her elderly mother and teenage brother, and their hard journey through Turkey and Greece. She also talked about the harsh realities of life as undocumented refugees in London. Pelin listened intently, her own memories of exile resonating deeply. Yet Leila's story carried a weight Pelin hadn't known.

Nearly an hour later, Leila suddenly became nervous, aware of the attention she might be attracting. Her father's last words echoed in her mind: "Trust no one." She quickly thanked Pelin for her kindness and slipped on her oversized coat and headed for the door. Pelin watched her small figure disappear into the bustling street, feeling an aching responsibility. She knew she needed to do more.

Sitting alone, her coffee long cold, Pelin replayed their conversation, thinking about Leila's struggles, the camps, deportations, and her living under constant fear. She felt ashamed of her own worries in comparison. The urgency to act grew inside her.

Reaching for her phone, Pelin hesitated. Kemal would be furious. He'd see her actions as dangerous and reckless. Yet she realized her fear had kept her trapped too long. She decided then that she had to act.

Determined, Pelin wrapped her coat tighter around her shoulders, left a generous tip on the table, and stepped back out onto the street. She would find Leila again and the next time, she won't let her disappear.

After this meeting with Leila over coffee, Pelin was reluctant to return to the apartment. The entire point of her outing had been to clear her head, yet her thoughts were more twisted than ever. She had yet to do what she came out to do, and that was to clear her head! Wandering deeper into the heart of the city, she found herself standing outside the Turkish coffeehouse again. The last time she was there, she had rushed out the door after a close encounter with a Turkish agent who she thought was tracking her. She took a deep breath and thought about it for a moment. 'Why not?' a voice inside whispered.

Despite knowing Kemal would disapprove of her returning to the coffeehouse; afraid that some of the customers might be the very ones tasked with bringing her back to Turkey, she went anyway.

Looking through the window, she saw only a few customers scattered about. It seemed safe enough, she thought. Before she could change her mind, she pushed the door open and stepped inside. She sat at a small table in a corner by a bay window. A few sips of fresh warm Turkish coffee calmed her nerves. She looked around the room, making sure no one she knew was there. Then she took out her phone and began looking over emails from Aylin, her editor. One line stood out.

"The intelligence I gathered suggests the Minister of the Interior's brother might own the coffeehouse in London that you mentioned to me. His name is Emir."

Pelin looked closely at her phone. "Could it be?" she asked herself. After comparing her investigative notes to Aylin's email, the pieces seemed to fit. Aylin's suspicion was confirmed. Emir Sahin was indeed the Turkish Minister's brother. The Turkish Minister was the same man who disrupted her life. He was the one who ordered her arrest because he did not like her condemnation of the Turkish regime in her fictional novel. And Emir was the man she met in university so long ago. They both had changed so much, almost beyond recognition.

She felt nauseated. Just thinking about Kemal praising Emir earlier felt surreal. Her thoughts were sinking in while she sat alone inside the coffeehouse. She knew there was a possibility that she might have walked straight into danger. She took a sip of her coffee and tried to remain calm, not wanting to show her fear. Still, she couldn't shake the thought that the friendly face who welcomed her on her first visit to the coffeehouse might be tied to his brother's political schemes. She didn't have all the facts, but she was becoming very suspicious, even without concrete evidence.

Out of the corner of her eye, she saw an old weathered wooden door open, and Emir walked out of it. She immediately recognized him. There was no way she could forget him after her first visit there.

He walked toward her table with a smile on his face. His entire demeanor was a stark contrast to that of his brother. Still, Pelin remained wary after the email that Aylin sent, warning her about the minister's relentless desire to have her brought back to Turkey.

"Mind if I join you?" Emir asked. Not sure how to respond, Pelin nodded and gestured toward the empty seat across from her. She felt surprised when he asked if he could join her. She also felt trapped in a corner, with no way to escape. Even if she did, she had no idea where to run. The notion of escaping quickly left her mind.

By staying, she would get to know more about the brother of the man who was out to get her.

As they spoke, Pelin calmed down. Emir's presence helped her relax the nagging doubts that persisted about him. The two of them engaged in a polite conversation, one that she hoped would lead to more information about him and his brother. She recalled Kemal had told her that Emir had said she was always welcome and safe in the coffeehouse.

With several unanswered questions still lingering, she was pleased that she decided against leaving. She didn't want to reveal her intentions or give him any idea that she remembered him. Neither did she want to let on that she knew he was the Minister of the Interior's brother.

She listened to Emir share stories about his life before coming to the UK. In many ways, they were similar to her own. He spoke with pride about the photo hanging behind the counter, in a solid mahogany frame. The man in the photo looked like a guardian watching over the place.

"It is a nice photo," Pelin commented.

"Thank you, that's my father," Emir told her. "My father always wanted to build a space abroad for people like us—to meet others who'd also left their homelands behind." Emir smiled. "That was also my wish, or at least I tried to fulfill my father's wishes by opening this place. It's a place for people to come together to share their hardships."

Pelin nodded as she listened to him, finding herself drawn to Emir's kindness. She was on the verge of revealing that they had met several years ago at university but held back. It didn't matter; she sensed that he already knew and was about to say the same thing.

Instead, Pelin shared a few things about her work and how much she missed home. But her nagging doubt persisted. She was careful not to reveal too much about herself, knowing that she was having a conversation with the Minister of the Interior's brother. Pelin chose every word she spoke carefully, while in the back of her mind, she knew she might be in danger.

Emir sensed Pelin was reluctant to trust him because of who he was. "I know what you're thinking," he said. He tried to reassure her that he was not involved in his brother's political schemes. Still,

Pelin wondered if she could trust this man who sat across from her—the brother of the man who was out to destroy her life.

Finally, Pelin spoke up about the obvious issue that was bothering her. "I believe you know the reason I'm here, as well as the legal challenges I'm facing because of your brother."

Even as she spoke, Pelin could sense that Emir was different, but she needed to hear it from him. "You don't have to answer or explain anything," she said while watching the expression on his face. She was looking to see if he was being truthful.

"I need to know the truth. Are you anything like your brother?" The second question she asked was what else he knew about her or her situation.

Emir hesitated. He ran his hand through his hair while searching for the right words. He was surprised she would compare him to his brother.

Her questions were not easy for him to answer. Emir had been asking himself similar questions ever since his brother was appointed to the office of Minister of the Interior.

"We are brothers, but we couldn't be more different. The quest for power did something to Yilmaz. It corrupted him, and he eventually aligned himself with the wrong people."

Pelin felt sorry to hear him say those things about his brother. But just as she was about to ask another question, Emir's phone rang. When he looked down at the screen, his face contracted into a frown. He stood and asked to be excused for a moment. He stepped into his office without completely closing the door. Because of the look on his face when he answered the phone, Pelin leaned with one ear toward the door. She could hear snippets of what sounded like a heated conversation.

During the phone call, Emir repeated his brother's name, Yilmaz, several times. His name surprised her when she heard it. Her pulse started beating much faster.

"The agents are closing in on Ms. Korkmaz. They've tracked her to the coffeehouse," Yilmaz told his younger brother. His words sent Emir's blood rushing through his veins.

"Do not interfere," he warned Emir. Those were the last words that Yilmaz spoke before ending the phone call.

The call ended abruptly. Pelin sat back in her chair, still hearing the name Yilmaz echoing in her ear. The agents knew she was there, and they were on their way to capture her.

When Emir returned to the table, his face was pale. He no longer looked like the same man he was before the phone call.

Emir could not look Pelin in her eyes. He looked out the window for a moment, trying to collect his thoughts. Pelin knew something was wrong but had no idea what. She hadn't been able to hear what Yilmaz had said on the phone. Emir contemplated his next move, wondering if he should tell her about the conversation that he and his brother had just had. Would the bit of trust they had built between them be broken? He wondered.

He took the risk. "There's something I need to tell you."

He spoke in a more somber voice than he had before going into his office. Emir told her everything that his brother had just shared with him about the agents. Pelin's instinct was to grab her handbag and run; instead, she asked, "Why are you telling me this?"

"I want you to trust me," Emir replied. "I've never been a part of Yilmaz's world, and I promise I won't let anything happen to you here."

Pelin was speechless. Could she believe him? Could she trust the brother of the man who was out to put her in prison? She wanted to believe Emir was sincere. Looking at him, she saw a man in the middle of fighting his own battles.

"Our father believed in family and honor. I've tried to hold on to those values." He hesitated. "My brother chose a different path, a darker one. Yilmaz's quest for power and his alliance with the conservative wing of the government was not what our father would have wanted."

"I am sorry for all the harm that he's brought into your life. I wish I could undo it all. There is a lot more I wish to share with you, and I will at a later day. But for now, I want us to be friends and maintain contact. And again, just as I told Kemal, you are safe here."

She gathered her bag and thanked him for sharing what she knew had to be difficult for him. The reassurances that Emir gave her about not being involved in his brother's political schemes and having no connection to the regime meant a lot. His honesty and courage also profoundly touched her, but she didn't think there was any way she could be friends with the brother of the man who was out to destroy her.

She left the cafe, glancing around as she did, heading for home.

Now she felt guilty for sitting with Emir Sahin, the estranged brother of Yilmaz, and the man she met before she knew Kemal. By doing so, she had gone against Kemal's advice. Now she had to go home and reveal to Kemal that she met with Emir, their conversation, and what she had discovered about him and his brother. Especially about Emir. Her relationship with him in Turkey, at university, was not something she'd told Kemal about. She didn't look forward to telling him now.

Her phone rang interrupting her thoughts. "Are you okay?" Kemal asked. "You've been gone for most of the day. Where are you?" he asked.

"I'm just around the corner, making my way home."

"Good, I've been worried. I had this strange feeling that you were in trouble," Kemal said.

Pelin kept silent for a moment, not saying what she was thinking. "Yes . . . or not. Kind of."

Kemal was happy to hear her voice and decided against sharing with her the text that he had just received. A text from an unknown number that read: "Watch your back. Not everyone you sit with is who they seem to be."

—17—

Sometime before, Emir Sahin had been alone in his office, sitting with both hands firmly wrapped at the back of his head. He had just received another disturbing phone call from Yilmaz. Yilmaz had received an intelligence report sent to him from a team of Turkish special agents. The report confirmed that Pelin was not only in London, but that she had recently set foot in Emir's coffeehouse. Yilmaz's warning to Emir had been stern: "Don't interfere with the agents who are there in the UK to arrest Pelin and bring her back to Turkey."

The agents reported that Pelin had visited the coffeehouse in London more than once. They also reported the two of them had met during her last visit.

Yilmaz called a second time, warning Emir again not to interfere with the agent's secret operation. The phone call was difficult for Emir to digest, it left him confused. He looked up at an old snapshot hanging on the wall, a shot of him and his brother. It was taken back in their younger days, back in Istanbul. They took the photo when they were inseparable siblings who shared a life, and who had similar dreams. Now things were different, they both had gone their separate ways. Ways that neither of them could have imagined.

Emir's eyes drifted toward another frame. This one was older and more faded, it was a picture of their ancestors, the Sahin family. A family known for how they would help those less fortunate, whether through monetary donations or volunteering to build shelters or schools. In Emir's later years, before leaving Istanbul, he would often open his home up to those in need. He was full of kindness and understanding, always ready to welcome a stranger.

The Sahin family had always believed in fostering love, not fear, not division, but unity. But over the years, Yilmaz deviated from this path, only to honor the greedy and corrupted regime who was now ruling Turkey.

He gained more power as he entered his second term as Turkey's Minister of the Interior. Emir saw his brother flexing his political muscles, for the sake of pleasing his conservative constituents.

A bitter taste filled Emir's mouth as he remembered the phone call in which Yilmaz revealed his next step to get Pelin back to Turkey. Emir was ashamed that his brother was the one who ordered the arrest. He felt that Pelin was an amazing woman. His brother's actions hit him like a punch in the gut.

The last time he'd spoken to Yilmaz was when their mother died, and Yilmaz showed up for the funeral. The conversation between the two of them was not personal. They only discussed showing up at the family attorney's office the next day to go over their mother's will.

During the phone call about this attorney visit, Yilmaz asked Emir to tune into a broadcast playing on the Turkish State TV news channel. Which Emir found to be rather strange. But he tuned in anyway and saw his brother standing before the cameras announcing that Pelin was living illegally in the UK. He promised the citizens of Turkey that it was only a matter of time before the special agents would arrest her and bring her back to Turkey.

Watching Yilmaz was a vicious slap in his face—his brother had known of his friendship with Pelin. His wish to arrest her was a betrayal of their family's values, and the bond that the two brothers once shared. Emir sympathized with Pelin; he thought of her with affection. He saw her as a brave individual standing up for her beliefs, as well as advocating for her people. He deeply enjoyed reading everything that she wrote, and now he watched one of his favorite writers and former friend become a target of his brother's political schemes.

Their brotherhood was now poisoned by power and Yilmaz's ruthless political ambitions. Emir could feel his pulse quicken. He was desperately searching for an explanation—anything to help him understand why his brother had abandoned all traces of his former self. Why had the brother he once knew and loved vanished?" Why had Yilmaz turned into someone else. Someone Emir didn't want to or couldn't recognize?

Emir had always been drawn to Pelin back in their university days. He remembered her vividly, her laughter, her intelligence, and the way she carried herself with such grace. Though he had hoped for more than friendship, he never acted on his feelings. Now, seeing her in this situation, he felt a mixture of anger and a strong desire to protect her.

His brother's arrogant actions had put him in an awkward position, but he was determined not to let it affect the cordial relationship he wanted to reestablish with Pelin.

Despite his feelings, Emir put on a smiling face that day, when he saw Pelin walking into the coffeehouse. He hoped she hadn't seen his brother's press conference announcing to the nation that she had fled the country and had now been found to be living in the UK.

As he did with many of his customers, when Pelin returned to the coffeehouse, Emir approached her again.

"Mr. Sahin, she said.

"Oh no, call me Emir." He did not want her to call him Sahin, like some of the others do. The moment the name 'Sahin' slipped from her lips, Pelin's heart stopped. It didn't matter that Kemal had told her a lot about him already. Seeing him in front of her was different. He welcomed her back to the coffeehouse and showed her the perfect place to sit. It was a quiet place away from those who rushed in for a coffee to go, and more important, it was away from the satellite tv that was tuned into the Turkish news channel.

Emir then excused himself and went back to his office to finish a few things and try to pull himself back together.

Pelin closely watched his every move before he disappeared behind the door that read Office. She remembered it was Aylin who had first uttered the name Sahin to her. Aylin's exact words were, "The Minister of Interior, he's the one who issued the warrant for your arrest. He's also pushing to have your latest book banned."

Pelin sat inside the Sahin's coffeehouse quivering with urgency and fear. She was trying to make sense of it all—how Emir, who seemed kind and ethical, could be connected to the Minister of the Interior, a man she considered one of the most dangerous figures in the Turkish regime.

She tried to hide her shaking hands and recompose herself by gripping the sides of the table. Why was this man, Emir Sahin, so keen on introducing himself to her for a second time? Had he forgotten that he had already done so during her first visit? Was it a mere coincidence, or was it a trap? Was he involved in his brother's political scheme? Pelin tried to keep a neutral expression on her face, even though she felt for sure she had walked into a trap.

—18—

Pelin woke early, and before getting out of bed she watched a clipped video of Yilmaz's speech on her phone that Aylin sent her. He was speaking harshly of her and her future. She skipped breakfast and told Kemal she needed to go to the office to wait for a call from Aylin. None of what she told Kemal was true. Her real destination was back to the coffeehouse. This time Emir had asked to meet with both her and Kemal. However, she did not mention that to Kemal. Withholding the truth from Kemal about where she was really going was painful. But she believed it was necessary, given all the worry she had already caused him.

She didn't want Kemal to know how much she feared for her life after hearing the Minister of the Interior's press conference. Her priority was not going to the office. Now Pelin's priority was meeting with Emir to learn more about his brother Yilmaz. She couldn't comprehend how he could spread such treasonous lies to the nation.

To avoid the heavy morning traffic, Pelin took an unusual route. As she walked along the quiet narrow street of the old neighborhood, the fog gradually lifted, changing to a steady rain. The moisture made walking on the slick cobblestones treacherous, requiring her to tread carefully to avoid slipping while trying to maintain a steady pace.

Though she had mustered the courage to go out alone again, she remained vigilant, especially after her previous encounter with the men who had followed her. Every noise and shadow felt like a potential threat. As she hurried past the rows of identical brick houses, she kept replaying the Minister's words from the press conference in her head. Yilmaz had called for her arrest on live television, and although she was in London, the danger from Turkey felt closer and almost suffocating. She couldn't shake the feeling that someone was always watching her, even in this quiet London neighborhood.

When a cyclist passed by splashing through the puddles, it startled her. She instinctively turned to look behind to check if anyone else was following, but the street was empty. It was just her, the rain, and the soft hum of the city waking up. She pulled her raincoat tighter, feeling the chill in the air seep into her bones.

The rain intensified, pounding against her umbrella like steady pebbles falling from the clouds. Despite her efforts, she was unable to prevent her anxiety from flaring up. She hadn't told Kemal about the meeting with Emir, but she knew he had every reason to be worried. Now that the Turkish Interior Minister had revealed to the citizens of Turkey that she had been spotted in London, she and Kemal were on edge once again.

The more she contemplated their complicated situation, the more anxious she became. Yilmaz's influence was extensive, and his power even greater. Pelin knew his ruthlessness all too well. This was no longer just about politics; it had turned personal. He wanted to see her destroyed, and the worst part was that she didn't even know why. Was it merely because of the book? Or had she unknowingly crossed some invisible line long ago?

Amid all these thoughts, she couldn't stop thinking about Kemal and how she felt she had betrayed him. Pelin was starting to notice some changes in Kemal. She could see it in the way his once calm demeanor had been replaced by a quiet, restless energy. Now she felt guilty about not being upfront with him regarding her meeting with Emir.

Kemal had been making phone calls, reaching out to his contacts back in Istanbul. It was his way of staying informed about the situation there. His sleepless nights were becoming frequent, and Pelin could see the worry on his face. She couldn't bear the thought of adding more stress to his already difficult life, which is why she had chosen to meet Emir alone. She wanted to shield Kemal, at least for a little while longer. But deep down, she knew she couldn't keep the truth from him forever.

As Pelin approached the coffeehouse, she slowed her pace and took one last look around. Her stomach tightened. The windows were fogged up, and she noticed the lights were dim. The sign on the door still read 'Closed.' She saw two workers moving around behind the counter, tidying up for the day ahead. She hesitated for a moment before tapping gently on the window. One of the workers looked up and recognized her. The worker immediately unlocked the door.

When the door opened, the aroma of freshly brewed coffee filled Pelin's nostrils. Stepping inside from the pouring rain was a relief, but it did little to calm her nerves. Emir was already seated at the table by the window, the same one they had shared during their previous meeting. As she approached, he stood, though not with the same demeanor he had displayed last time. This time, a slight frown marked his face—a look of concern.

"Are you alone?" he asked, glancing behind her as if expecting Kemal to appear out from the rain at any moment.

"I didn't tell Kemal about this," she replied, adjusting her damp hijab. Guilt and regret washed over her for not including Kemal. "He's been through enough already. I need to hear what you have to say without dragging him into this."

Emir frowned, his deep concern evident, but he didn't argue. Instead, he gestured for her to follow him to the back of the café. They entered his office closing the door behind them, ensuring their conversation remained private.

His office was spacious, with a mahogany desk positioned near a large window overlooking the distant skyscrapers. Bookshelves lined the walls, filled with an array of books and magazines.

"I see you have a copy," she said. "The one that started all this."

Emir glanced at the book and nodded. "Yes, I read it," he said, his voice dropping to a whisper as he leaned closer across the desk. "That scene on page 94—the one where the minister destroys evidence in the basement of the capitol building—that actually happened."

Pelin raised an eyebrow. "Emir, it's a novel. Fiction."

"But it happens to have been true."

Pelin suddenly realized why Yilmaz had a vendetta against her, and her writing. Some of what she had written as fiction was truth. At that time, she had felt a duty to expose the criminal actions of Yilmaz and the regime. Never mind if only through story. Pelin hadn't realized that her imaginative picture had been as real as a photograph for Yilmaz and his allies.

Her novel inadvertently put her in danger. It opened Yilmaz to an investigation and a possible arrest.

Emir pulled out a chair and motioned for her to sit. He handed her a warm cup of coffee he had already prepared. "I figured you might need this."

Pelin wrapped her hands around the cup, hoping to warm them as she settled back in the chair. Emir pulled up a chair beside her, took a sip of coffee, and looked directly into her eyes.

"Like I told you earlier, I haven't spoken to Yilmaz in years," Emir began, speaking in almost a whisper, not wanting his voice to travel outside the door. "Pelin, he's gone too far. He's ruthless, and he's obsessed with power. I know my brother well enough to say that he won't stop until he gets what he wants."

"What do you suggest I do? Is it no longer safe here?" Pelin asked, trying to hold back her anger. She felt let down by the British authorities; in some ways she believed they may have been colluding with Yilmaz and his agents.

As she posed those questions, she recalled her phone call with Shireen, her sister in New York. It was the last option she had to consider, but time was running out, and the walls felt like they were closing in. Leaving the UK now seemed the only choice she and Kemal had for staying safe. Yilmaz's agents knew exactly where she was, and they were waiting for the right moment to strike.

"I don't know how much longer we can keep running," she whispered, more to herself than to Emir.

Emir sat on the edge of his chair, bowing his head and exhaling deeply. "You're right." He shared her thoughts. They had both believed she would be safe in the UK. "It seems my brother has a connection here in London; the police have turned their backs, allowing him and his agents to operate freely."

Emir began searching through his contacts for a trusted friend who could provide Pelin and Kemal with a safe place to hide until the situation improved. "It's no longer a question of *if* they'll come for you; it's a matter of *when*," he told Pelin.

Pelin stood and said to Emir, "I have to go; I don't have much time." She took a moment to look out the window, checking the area to ensure it was safe before she walked out the door. Time was running out, and she needed to get home to inform Kemal of how serious things had gotten.

Feeling as though he wasn't much help, Emir reached for his phone. "I can call you an Uber to drive you home."

"No, I'd rather take the bus; it will give me time to think everything over." She was afraid to take the chance with an Uber, worried that the driver might be a Turkish agent posing as an Uber driver.

Once she stepped outside, the rain began to pour. Her umbrella offered little protection from the gusting wind. After taking only a few steps, she was drenched.

Having walked only a short distance, she noticed someone standing across the street out of the corner of her eye. It was someone in a long dark coat, standing inside a doorway and watching her. Before breaking into a fast pace, she took another look and prayed that whoever it was would not follow her.

Was it one of Yilmaz's agents? Were they ready to make their move? Amid the storm, with few people on the street, it would be perfect timing, Pelin thought.

Fearful that it might happen, she hurried down the street, rushing toward the bus stop.

Finally, she was sitting on the nearly empty bus, where she was able to relax. Her conversation with Shireen came back to mind. She was glad she hadn't mentioned her name while meeting with Emir, not wanting her to get caught up in the chaos. However, it was likely that he knew about Shireen, considering how much he knew about her and Kemal.

When she stepped off the bus across the street from her apartment, she knew her work was cut out for her. The first thing she had to do was be honest with Kemal. The second was to try to convince him that they must leave; there was no other way to escape the agents.

If they remained in London, it would be just a matter of time before Yilmaz sent his men after them. Their only option seemed to be to flee and abandon everything once again. The memories of their last escape were still fresh—not to mention the long nights filled with uncertainty and fear. Pelin hated to tell Kemal that it was happening all over again.

If Kemal refused to go to America, where else would they go? She thought, "We have already run twice. How many more times can we keep doing this?"

Kemal was worried; she was out in the storm, and he wasn't sure if she was safe. When he heard the keys at the door, he ran to open it.

"Look at you, you look like you just swam in the Thames," Kemal said.

"I'm just happy to be back in the warmth of our home," Pelin told him, but in her mind, she knew it was only home for a short while longer. She disappeared into the bedroom to remove her wet clothes and change into something dry and comfortable. Before going back out to face Kemal, she sat on their bed, her face in her hands. She needed to reflect on her conversation with Emir.

Finally, she felt ready to be honest with Kemal about why she hadn't gone to the office. Unsure of where to begin, she promised herself that she would tell him everything. After all, Emir was right; she and Kemal needed to prioritize safety above all else.

—19—

When Pelin walked back into the room, Kemal wrapped his arms around her, pulling her close. He wanted to warm her cold body. "I was worried something happened to you," he whispered in her ear, feeling both anxious and relieved.

Pelin felt a wave of guilt and stepped back from his embrace. She took a deep breath, gearing up for what she had to say. Kemal could tell she was nervous, but he had no idea why. For Pelin, this was a big moment. She knew she had to come clean. After all, Kemal was her partner, her confidant, her rock, and the love of her life. She couldn't help but wonder if he could ever forgive her for the situation they were in and for her meeting with Emir.

"I went down to Birch Street," Pelin started to explain.

Kemal looked confused, thinking she had gone to her office. "You went to the Turkish coffeehouse?"

"Yeah, I went back to the coffeehouse." She looked up at him and added, "I met with Emir. We talked for a bit, and I lost track of time."

Kemal's expression shifted, and he grabbed her by the arm, pulling her close. "What did you talk about with him?" His voice was tense, showing his frustration.

Pelin cleared her throat, trying to stay calm. "I wanted to find out more about his brother. We also talked about the homeland."

Kemal's grip on her arm loosened a little, but his frown deepened. The idea of Pelin going to the coffeehouse alone again didn't sit right with him. It felt too risky, especially given their situation.

And now he remembered her long-ago friendship with Emir when they attended university together. He didn't know much about how or how close they had been. Was something else going on?

"After meeting with Emir today, I think he's honest," Pelin continued. "You said similar things about him after you first met." She paused and looked him in the eyes.

"Are you sure you can trust him?" Kemal asked, sounding doubtful.

He let go of her arm and stepped back, still frowning. He sensed there was more to the story; Pelin's vibe made it clear she was holding back. "Is there more you need to tell me? You don't seem like yourself."

"I know, I'm sorry." Pelin recounted her conversation with Emir. He had been through some of what they had experienced, sharing that he had also left Turkey because of harassment from government officials.

Kemal's expression softened a bit. He took a deep breath and ran a hand through his hair. That was a sign Pelin recognized when he was processing his emotions. They both fell silent.

"Two hours, Pelin," Kemal finally said. "I was worried sick. You didn't answer my calls or texts."

Pelin felt bad for leaving him hanging. She could tell he was disappointed, and he had every right to be upset. She stepped closer and touched his arm, her fingertips grazing his skin. "I know, Kemal. I'm really sorry. I should've let you know."

Kemal nodded, agreeing but holding back his concerns. Even though he was relieved she was home safe, a new worry nagged at him. It was the consequences that might come from Pelin's meeting with Yilmaz's brother? He was a relative stranger, and Kemal thought about the potential risks. It was so frustrating thinking about it.

After a long moment of tense silence, Kemal asked Pelin, "What's your impression of Emir?"

Pelin sank into a nearby chair, leaning back. "I'm not sure what I think of Emir yet," she replied. "It's tough to figure out what kind of person he really is behind that smiling face. He seems alright, but it's too early to tell." She sat up in the chair. "But I can tell you what I think about his brother if you want to know."

"I think we know enough about him," Kemal said, raising his eyebrows.

As they kept talking, Pelin realized it had been smart not to share too much about her or Kemal's personal life. Instead, she had asked questions of Emir, digging deeper into Emir's life and his relationship with Yilmaz.

"Sounds like you did a good job investigating," Kemal said. He wondered if she had thought about the fact that Emir came from a powerful family, which probably made it easier for him to leave Turkey. Having a billionaire brother likely helped too.

Pelin felt a twinge of guilt. She lowered her head, second-guessing her decision. "Maybe I shouldn't have gone to the coffeehouse."

A moment of silence passed between them.

"But meeting with Emir taught me a few things," she told Kemal. "After all, it wasn't Emir who issued the arrest warrants for me. I left knowing that Yilmaz is unpredictable and dangerous. Emir told me his brother's goal is to become Prime Minister, and he'll do anything to achieve it."

Kemal nodded. "Yeah, he's unpredictable and ruthless. We need to do whatever it takes to protect ourselves. I'm not sure what that involves, but we don't have much time."

The recent news conference didn't help. They both knew they were in a dangerous situation, and their safety in the UK wasn't guaranteed. Yilmaz seemed to have bought off some part of the British security services, and his agents could come after them at any moment. They didn't know how corrupt the police were here . . . or if they were. They were truly strangers in a strange land.

Pelin stood and walked to the window, looking down at the street below. "The situation we're in is bigger than us. Back home, people are punished every day for speaking out. Their names get added to that so-called Blacklist, and arrests happen daily."

Pelin was trying to remind Kemal of Shireen's offer by comparing their lives to those stuck back home. She didn't dare mention Shireen to Kemal right now, but she wanted to pave the way to do so. "Things aren't looking good back home, Kemal. You won't read about this in the news, but my contacts tell me that more and more people are disappearing without a trace."

Kemal listened closely to Pelin, taking in every word. He replied with empathy. "Believe me, I can't even imagine what's going on back home. Hearing you describe it is alarming. I wish it were different. I wish we could've stayed and fought this battle on our turf, but that would've been a losing fight."

Pelin nodded, blinking back tears. "We're the lucky ones. We have another chance."

Moments like these reminded Kemal why he loved Pelin so much. Even in the face of danger, her heart was always with those she left behind. He knew she wouldn't give up the fight, no matter where she was. Sometimes he wished she hadn't come this far, but he admired her commitment.

Pelin turned to face Kemal, letting out a long breath. "Kemal, our future is uncertain." He agreed, baffled. "Who knows where we'll go from here?"

"I wish I could tell you, but I can't," Kemal replied.

"I can," she said without realizing it.

Kemal was surprised to hear that. "Where? Tell me where!" he urged, raising his voice not out of anger but out of worry and confusion. "Did you make a deal with Emir to hide us or something?"

Pelin shook her head, realizing she needed to clarify her statement quickly. "No, no. It's not about Emir. Kemal, do you remember when I told you Shireen invited us to come to America if things got bad here?"

Kemal's expression shifted to skepticism. He looked directly at Pelin, his voice softer. "Pelin, please. America?" he responded sarcastically. "Wherever we go, it has to be safe. I'm not sure America is that safe for people who look like us."

For a moment, Pelin was taken aback by Kemal's response. Then she crossed her arms and looked down, surprised by his dismissiveness. She understood he was concerned, and his protective instinct had only grown stronger after everything they'd been through together. Now she wondered if she was losing his support. Did he still doubt her judgment after all they'd faced?

"I get it; I know you're trying to keep me safe," she murmured, forcing a smile. She didn't want to argue; it would only lead to them blaming each other for their situation. "Pelin..." he started. He wanted to express his regret, but the words wouldn't come.

She turned away before he could finish, taking a deep breath to steady herself. "It's fine," she said quietly. "But before we go any further, the answer is no. Emir didn't suggest or offer me a safe place to go. The idea of America was my own."

Kemal nodded. "I think it would be best if we kept our distance from Emir until we learn more about his relationship with his brother. You know blood is thicker than water."

Pelin reached out and gently touched Kemal's arm, acknowledging that mistakes had been made by the two of them. They agreed to be discreet about whom they trusted moving forward.

"I understand that time is running out," Kemal said, his tone softening. "But I really need to think. Going to America requires a lot of planning."

Pelin opened her mouth to respond, but a loud knock at the door interrupted her thoughts. Her mind raced, wondering who it could be and how they had made it to their floor. She and Kemal exchanged worried looks before he cautiously approached the door.

To their surprise and relief, the doorman from the lobby stood there holding a note for Pelin. It had been left by an unknown person. Following strict protocols, security had denied the individual entry into the building.

"It was a man," the doorman explained. "He asked me to deliver this note to you. I don't think I'm breaking any rules by doing so," he said. With that, he handed over the note and disappeared behind the closing doors of the elevator. Kemal was left holding the note, looking at Pelin, both of them confused.

They stared at the envelope in Kemal's hand as the tension in the room mounted. They were hesitant to open it, fearful of what its contents might reveal, adding uncertainty to their already precarious situation.

With her hand shaking, Pelin reached for the note, considering various possibilities. Whatever it contained, they both knew it was time; they had to leave London.

"Wait," Kemal said, gently catching her wrist before she could take the envelope. His eyes scanned the hallway beyond their door, still ajar. "Let me check something first."

He stepped into the hallway, looking both ways. The elevator doors had closed, but something felt off. It was too quiet, sending a chill down his spine.

"Kemal?" Pelin called softly from inside.

He quickly returned, locking the door behind him and securing the security chain. "Did the doorman say who this man was? Any description?"

Pelin shook her head. "Just that it was urgent."

Kemal turned the envelope over in his hands. No name, no markings—just plain white paper. "This could be anything," he said quietly. "A trap. A warning. Or nothing at all."

"We have to know," Pelin insisted, her journalistic instincts kicking in.

Kemal nodded, carefully tearing one end of the envelope. He took out a single folded sheet of paper. As he unfolded it, a small photograph slipped out, landing face down on the carpet. Pelin bent to pick it up while Kemal read the note, his face draining of color.

"What does it say?" Pelin asked, still holding the face-down photograph.

Kemal began reading the note, as Pelin waited nervously to hear what was written on the note.

"Read it out loud, Kemal."

"Okay, brace yourself." It was upsetting for Kemal to read the contents of the note, which read, "We know exactly where you are and it's only a matter of time, you will be in our custody."

The sound of Kemal speaking excitedly on the phone jolted Pelin from her sleep. She couldn't quite catch what he was saying or who he was speaking to. The only words she made out were, "That is good news, sir. We'll leave for your office as soon as we're dressed."

His conversation was brief, but it was enough to stir her curiosity. When she walked into the kitchen, Kemal was plugging in his phone. He turned abruptly and almost bumped into her; a wide smile stretched across his face.

"Who were you talking to?" she asked.

"Finally! Finally, some good news," he beamed. "It was Attorney Johnson, you know, the immigration lawyer. He called to let us know we've been granted asylum."

Pelin blinked, stunned. Asylum? Already? She had heard horror stories of endless backlogs and drawn-out battles in immigration courts. "How is it possible we were granted asylum in less than a year?" she asked, disbelief settling in.

The news lit up what had long been a dark uncertain future. For once, something was going right. But Pelin couldn't shake the feeling that something didn't add up.

She sat at the kitchen counter, burying her face in her hands. Kemal was ecstatic, already envisioning their new life. But Pelin was uneasy. Her instincts told her this was too fast, too easy.

Kemal struggled with English. Pelin feared he had misunderstood the attorney. Could it be a mistake? Why had their case moved ahead of so many others?

Kemal shrugged. "They granted us asylum. Let's just be happy."

To him, it was a moment of liberation. For the first time in years, they could plan beyond tomorrow. The dread of deportation had finally lifted.

Pelin approached him, tears of joy and uncertainty trickling down her cheeks. Kemal embraced her tightly. "Let's get dressed and go see the attorney. Let's make it official."

Though she stayed quiet, Pelin's mind was racing. She still had questions, and she intended to ask every last one of them, just not to Kemal. She would save them for Mr. Johnson.

When they arrived at Mr. Johnson's office, the air smelled faintly of stale coffee. He was standing in the middle of the room, holding a TV remote as a heated debate between two members of Parliament blared from the wall-mounted screen. Embarrassed, he quickly turned it off and gestured toward the long walnut conference table.

As Pelin settled into one of the high-backed leather chairs, she noticed a crooked British flag in the corner and an oil painting of Margaret Thatcher hanging above the desk.

For over an hour, they signed document after document. Finally, Mr. Johnson collected the papers and asked, "Any questions?"

Pelin wasted no time. "Why was our case approved so quickly? I've heard it usually takes years."

Mr. Johnson, always composed and confident, leaned back in his chair. "It's hard to say with certainty. The Turkish government didn't provide much information. The board believed you were in grave danger if returned. That urgency likely fast-tracked your case."

Pelin straightened in her seat. "Isn't that true for everyone applying for asylum?" Her tone was sharp, skeptical. She felt he wasn't telling them everything.

Kemal's foot tapped anxiously on the floor.

Mr. Johnson exhaled and tried to elaborate. "Each case is different. But yes, in your situation, the board was likely influenced by a recent press conference held by Turkey's Minister of Defense, where he told the citizens of Turkey that you would be arrested and brought back and put on trial. The charges related to free speech carry serious weight in Turkey. It made clear that returning you could be dangerous."

That gave Pelin a bit of relief, but not enough. She remembered their first meeting, when Mr. Johnson had warned them that they were up against a powerful government. Back then, he'd seemed doubtful about their chances.

"Are you sure that's the only reason?" she pressed.

"Well," Mr. Johnson said, "you were lucky to have a judge who understood your situation. Before joining the bench, she was a novelist herself. And a respected immigration attorney in this very city."

Pelin was taken aback.

But Mr. Johnson wasn't finished. "More surprisingly, a team from the prestigious firm Wembley Pathways volunteered to assist. Their involvement was requested by a Turkish businessperson."

"A Turkish businessperson?" Pelin echoed, with her eyes narrowing.

"Yes," Mr. Johnson nodded. "They covered the costs too. Wembley Pathways isn't cheap. I was shocked myself."

"At what cost?" Pelin asked, her voice now low and steady.

Leaning in, Mr. Johnson whispered, "The businessperson insisted on paying everything. They even requested that Kemal's case be included alongside yours." He paused, then added with a faint smile, "Money can sometimes move things along."

Pelin couldn't make sense of any of it. Why would someone she didn't know care this much?

The attorney continued, "This person also sat in on two of your hearings but asked to remain anonymous. Before we go any further, we should begin your applications for work permits and other documents. The benefactor left a note offering continued support."

Pelin stared, her thoughts spinning. She looked at Kemal, who was shaking his head slowly. He was just as lost as she was.

"But why?" she whispered. "What was in it for him?"

Kemal looked at Mr. Johnson for answers.

Clearing his throat, Mr. Johnson replied, "It's too early for me to share more."

"That's not enough," Pelin said, her voice rising. "This is my life. I deserve to know who's taken such an interest in me."

Kemal placed a hand on her shoulder. "Pelin, please. Let's not fight. Let's be thankful."

He turned to Mr. Johnson and apologized, but he, too, was curious.

Mr. Johnson removed his glasses, dabbed his nose, and repeated, "My hands are tied."

Just before they left, he said gently, "Mrs. Korkmaz, please don't worry about who helped. Consider it a gift."

Kemal and Pelin walked out in silence, the attorney's words echoing in their minds. Outside, as they approached a taxi, Pelin shook her head.

"A gift?" she muttered. "No one spends that kind of money out of kindness."

Kemal sighed. "Does it matter? We're safe now. That's what matters."

Pelin turned to him, her eyes sharp with suspicion. "It matters if we owe someone. It matters if they expect something in return."

Kemal hesitated. "Maybe we'll never know. Maybe that's for the best."

She exhaled sharply. "And what if it's not? What if this is just the beginning of something we're not prepared for?"

He opened the taxi door but paused. "We can ask all the questions in the world. But we're here. We're safe. Isn't that enough?"

Pelin didn't answer. She stared out toward the horizon, the sun dipping behind gray buildings. It should have been a moment of celebration. Instead, uncertainty clouded everything — and the mystery behind their salvation refused to let her rest.

— 22 —

Just one day after visiting Mr. Johnson's office, Pelin and Kemal were eager to move on with their lives. Before dawn, Kemal quietly slipped out of bed. Still half-asleep, he bumped into walls on his way to the kitchen to brew a pot of coffee.

When the coffee finished, he felt the urge to clear his mind with a short walk. He scribbled a note on a sticky pad: Going for a walk. Will be back in time for breakfast and left it on the counter. Outside, the morning fog was lifting, pink streaks coloring the sky.

He took a familiar shortcut through the apartment complex. A parking lot toward the paved trail leading to the park. But something made him pause. Parked in a "Residents Only" spot was a sleek, black mini-Mercedes bus with Turkish government plates. A stream of cigarette smoke drifted from the half-open passenger window.

Kemal frowned. He had walked this route a few times already and had never seen anything like it. Curious, he moved in for a closer look.

The bus had no side windows, just a large front windshield, two front passenger windows, and heavily tinted ones in the back. But inside, bright overhead lights revealed a wall of communication equipment. He saw two men up front and a third at a computer in the back.

Crouching for a better view, Kemal crept closer, until his knee struck a metal trash can. The lid clanged loudly against the minibus. Pain shot through his knee as the vehicle's interior lights went off.

The doors burst open. Two large men jumped out. A third emerged from the back. One of them spotted Kemal's silhouette as he took off, limping. With his heart pounding, he ran. Pain stabbed his knee with every step, but he didn't stop. He didn't have a destination, only one goal: get away from the men who were chasing him.

He crashed through the entrance of a towering apartment building, knocking over a floor lamp and shattering a ceramic vase. The door attendant jumped up, startled.

"Hey! You don't live here!" he shouted, fumbling for his phone and grabbing Kemal's sleeve.

Kemal broke free, dashing into the lobby, ignoring the damage behind him. What he didn't know was that the chaos he'd caused and the scene with the attendant would be the very thing that saved him. The three men chasing him stopped short of the entrance, watching silently through the glass.

Minutes later, flashing red and blue lights could be seen lightening up the building's windows. Two police cruisers pulled up. Four officers entered with caution.

Kemal, breathless and with his hands raised, pleaded, "I did nothing wrong. They were chasing me!"

But to the officers, all they saw was a disheveled man in a messy lobby with no one else in sight. "Clear evidence," one officer said, waving his hand at the broken vase and lamp.

Kemal was handcuffed, read his rights, and led out stumbling over his untied shoe, confused and desperate. "Why won't anyone believe me?" he shouted as they placed him in the back seat of the cruiser.

From behind a privacy fence, the three men watched. Once the police left, they slowly walked back to the minibus and drove toward the Turkish Embassy.

Though their hands were tied, and they couldn't legally arrest Kemal on UK soil, their presence sent a chilling message. Meanwhile, whether intentionally or not, the local police kept their distance, dismissing it as a foreign affair that didn't concern them.

At the police station, Kemal sat in a holding cell, with his voice hoarse from trying to explain. "I offered to pay for the damages. I didn't mean to break anything."

"You can tell that to a judge," the booking officer said. "Right now, calm down."

"Calm down?" Kemal snapped. "How am I supposed to calm down in here?"

***

Back at the apartment, Pelin paced like a tiger in a cage. Every few minutes, she stopped to look out the window. It had been ten hours since Kemal left his note.

Where is he?

No calls. No messages. Nothing.

Her instincts kept telling her that something was wrong. Tears ran down her cheeks as she sank onto the sofa. Yes, it's true, Kemal could be impulsive, but he would never stay away this long without calling.

At 6:15 PM, she grabbed her phone with her hands trembling and called Tarek. He answered on the second ring.

"Tarek!" she cried. "Kemal hasn't come home. I think something's happened to him!"

Sobbing, she explained the note, the silence, and the mounting fear. Tarek promised to find him. And two agonizing hours later, he called. "I found him, Pelin. He's okay. We're in a taxi, on the way."

Pelin was relieved to hear that Kemal had been found and was okay. She collapsed back onto the sofa, crying again. When the elevator doors opened, Kemal stepped out. His back was bent, his clothes torn, his face was full of anger.

Pelin rushed to him. "Oh, Kemal! What happened? Where were you?"

He gently pulled away. "Jail," he said bitterly. "They threw me in jail for no reason."

Her face went pale. "Jail? One day after getting asylum?"

Kemal sat wincing from pain. "I'm sorry, Pelin. I shouldn't have gotten close to that minibus. But I had to see. Something's up, I believe the ones in the minibus were Turkish agents. And now… the same system we're supposed to trust turned its back on us. They were allowed to come here and spy on us."

He explained everything, the van, the chase, the arrest. "I tried to explain, but no one would listen."

Pelin sat at the kitchen counter, shaking her head. "This… this is worse than I imagined."

"I know. It feels like we brought the danger with us," Kemal said, clutching his ribs. "Those men were there for a reason."

Pelin reached for his hand. "Kemal, we must leave. It's not safe here."

"We can't," he said. "Not with a court date coming."

"Then go, pay the fine, and we're done. We have to go."

Kemal looked away. "The officer said I might serve jail time."

Pelin's voice was calm but firm. "We can't wait. We have to go." He moaned deeply with his body aching, and his spirit was exasperated. "Maybe you're right. Maybe it's time."

"I'm not saying run. I'm saying do it the right way, pay the fine, then we should be free to leave."

He nodded slowly. "Maybe it's time to go back home."

"No," Pelin said, her voice trembling. "We can't go back to Turkey. You know what'll happen the second we step off the plane."

Kemal gave a nod, his face full of dread.

"What about America?" she asked. "We just got our asylum here. We can use the travel documents and disappear, somewhere quiet, just for a while."

Kemal's brows furrowed. "America? That's... way far. And I don't know. It doesn't feel right. They don't exactly welcome people like us."

"But we can't stay here," she pressed.

Kemal rubbed his temples, the pain in his head competing with the bruises on his body. "You think running will fix this? They found us here. What if they find us again?"

Pelin turned, gripping the back of a chair. "I don't know, Kemal. But we can't just sit here, waiting for them to knock on the door."

— 23 —

Pelin and Kemal were stuck wondering if their newfound freedom was a blessing or a trap. Was that anonymous businessman pulling them into some shady situation? The threats, the mystery businessman, the Turkish surveillance van, all those thoughts swirled around in her head. For her, their dream of a new life in the UK was unraveling. It was time to face the tough reality.

After meeting with the attorney, they felt uneasy. Looking back on everything, they both agreed that the UK wasn't safe. But amid all the tension, Kemal was starting to think she might be right.

That morning, Kemal stepped out of the bathroom, looking fresher than he had in days. His beard was neatly trimmed, which was a rare sight. Pelin raised her eyebrows. "Hey, don't forget we have that 10:00 appointment with Mr. Johnson this morning," Pelin reminded him before he got too caught up in his newspaper deadline.

Since arriving in the UK, Pelin had learned one thing above all: nothing is ever as simple as it looks.

At the attorney's office, Mr. Johnson was smiling as they walked in. He finished a phone call and gestured for them to sit.

"So, you've got questions about your immigration papers?" he asked, waving them over to sit down.

As Pelin settled into her chair, her eyes locked on an open folder on the desk with her name scrawled across it. Her heart skipped. In bold red ink was a word she didn't expect to see: DENIED.

She nudged Kemal with her knee, trying to catch his attention, but he didn't notice. He kept chatting with Mr. Johnson, they both were unaware of her actions. Leaning forward, Pelin glimpsed inside the folder. There, tucked neatly, was a check — 10,000 euros — her name typed neatly in the memo line. A sticky note clung to it; with a smiley face scribbled in one corner.

The signature on the check was upside down and barely legible, but she could still make out a line of handwriting beneath it: *Thank you for handling their hearings.* From that moment she knew something wasn't right.

Mr. Johnson notice Pelin eyeing the folder. While still speaking to Kemal, he slowly closed the folder and slid it into his desk drawer. Pelin's stomach twisted. She barely heard anything between Mr. Johnson and Kemal after that. Her mind was stuck on that file she had just seen on the desk.

"So, you're thinking about taking a vacation. You wanted to double-check a few things about international travel and find out about the details of reentry?" Mr. Johnson asked.

Kemal was about to ask more questions when Pelin signaled that she'd heard and "seen" enough. It was time to go.

Kemal wrapped things up. He stood up and shook Mr. Johnson's hand. "Thanks, sir. I think we have all the info we need." Mr. Johnson smiled politely and reiterated what he thought was important. They left the office, the door clicked shut behind them.

Kemal looked puzzled. "What just happened back there that made you want to leave so quickly?"

She didn't answer, holding back everything until they got home. She just sat quietly in the back seat of the cab, staring out the window watching the rain trickle down the glass, with a knot in her stomach.

Kemal, sitting next to her, was worried and confused. He noticed her red watery eyes and took her hand, giving it a gentle squeeze to help her relax.

As soon as they got into the apartment, Pelin jumped right into it. She told Kemal about what she'd seen on Johnson's desk-- the file and the check. "Why would a rich businessman care about our immigration case? I really want to know, and as you can see, Kemal, Mr. Johnson isn't being helpful." She couldn't shake the feeling that the businessman's involvement was more than just a financial thing. She sat at the kitchen counter, firing off questions like bullets. "What if the Minister of the Interior is behind all this? What if those extra lawyers were part of a setup? What if they're trying to track us when we travel?"

Pelin was starting to think that traveling outside the UK could be too risky. She felt like they might be too dangerous.

Kemal knew that immigration approvals didn't happen overnight. He took out his phone and googled "immigration approvals." What he found differed from what Mr. Johnson had told them. "All the pieces do not seem to fit. We need to do a bit more research before we pack."

Pelin wished Kemal could've seen the file before Johnson tucked it away. "We weren't supposed to see it, but I did." She told him that what she saw made her even more curious. She couldn't stop asking herself why their case moved so fast through the courts, and why Johnson had said their request was approved when the folder had been stamped "Denied." And who had written that check? That concerned her, and that seemed to be directed to Johnson.

Looking at Kemal, she hoped he understood why it was so important for her to figure out who had gotten involved in their asylum process and why. "It's not just about getting approved," she said, her concern showed on her face. "Someone, whether it's a member of the immigration board or someone from the law firm, seems to be really interested in my case. It gives me a creepy feeling, like there's more going on than we know."

She paused, trying to get her thoughts straight. The fact that others were involved left her feeling very uneasy. "Again, Kemal, we need to figure out who's behind this."

She noticed the look on Kemal's face. It was like he was silently telling her to chill out. To him, it was done, they had their official asylum papers. Pelin wanted to feel that way too, but her suspicions just wouldn't let go.

Walking away wasn't really her style. There was no way she could ignore that file she saw at the lawyer's office. All her worries were just thoughts, but that file with her name on it was real. She'd seen it with her own eyes. The check was real too . . .although Pelin hadn't seen who it was made out to.

After the incident with Pelin seeing the file, Mr. Johnson rushed to complete it and close it out.

"I agree there's no point in trying to change anything. But I want copies of our file," Pelin told Kemal. "I plan to send Mr. Johnson a check for 10,000 euros."

Kemal rubbed his face in disbelief. "10,000 euros! What's the deal with that?"

Pelin's eyes narrowed slightly. "This stink. I don't take handouts, Kemal. I 've always paid my own debts. And by the way, there's no reason to celebrate."

"Pelin, you can't prove the Minister was involved."

Before Kemal could finish, his phone buzzed on the counter, cutting him off. He saw it was Mr. Johnson calling. Pelin stood up and moved closer to him. "Put it on speaker," she whispered. "I want to hear what he has to say."

"Hey, Mr. Korkmaz, you might be interested to know that after you left, I looked at your and your wife's files. Everything seems to be in order, so you should be getting the official documents in the mail any day now."

"What does that mean?" Pelin couldn't help but jump in. She squeezed Kemal's arm, eager for more info.

"Please, Pelin, our papers are coming. I just want this over with," Kemal whispered.

Mr. Johnson was caught off guard by her voice, and replied, "That's all I can share. I can't go into more detail."

Pelin's anxiety grew at Mr. Johnson's vague response. She knew Kemal wanted to move forward, but she wasn't ready to let it go.

In a softer tone, she said, "I get that you want to wrap this up, but I can't just move on without knowing everything."

Kemal checked his watch and then turned to Pelin. "I need a break. Remember, I still have a job that I'm getting paid to do." He had a deadline for a piece he was working on for the newspaper in Turkey.

"Go ahead and take your break, but don't be mad at me just because I'm not cool with the idea that some random person is poking around in our private business."

Kemal shook his head and laughed. "If sending a check to Mr. Johnson to pass along to some rich Turkish guy is what it takes to close this chapter, then fine by me."

Pelin was itching to know more. She bit her lip to keep from saying anything else about their asylum case. Still, she couldn't shake the feeling that it wasn't just about some wealthy businessman or immigration officials being interested in her situation. She had this nagging sense that something much darker was going on, and it was driving her nuts.

She couldn't ignore the unsettling thought that the Minister of the Interior might be involved. He could have set up the quick hearings and possibly even the results. If that was true, then the whole process was a sham. That would mean their immigration papers were bogus, which could lead to all sorts of issues when traveling or getting caught in the UK illegally down the line.

Her main reason for going back to the attorney was to get some clarity on her concerns. Every visit seemed to create more chaos and anxiety. As far as Kemal was concerned, the issue was settled, but she felt the complete opposite. She really needed to figure this all out. Outside of some government agencies, why would anyone besides a close friend or family member care about her immigration status? She knew her family wouldn't cover any costs without telling her.

Kemal walked off to his corner to work on his article for the Sunday *Times*. Pelin couldn't just push her thoughts aside. So, while Kemal was busy, she decided to call her sister, Shireen, in America.

Pelin pressed the phone tighter to her ear. "Shireen, I think it's time for us to leave the UK. The hearings went well... but there are still a few things that don't sit right."

There was a moment of silence before Shireen asked. "What kind of things, Pelin? Are you in danger?"

"Not exactly. Just...some questions we don't have answers to just yet," Pelin said. "I'll explain everything later. For now, I just wanted you to know that Kemal and I are planning to buy tickets. We'll start packing in the next day or two."

After the call, Pelin felt relieved about their decision to leave the UK. She felt much better after talking to Shireen, but she also knew her worries wouldn't just go away.

She was eager to escape a place where she had struggled to take charge of her life. Pelin was determined to get back to advocating for people like her. She thought that moving to America for a while would help her reach more people and make a bigger impact in her campaign for free speech. Still, she knew that even in America, things wouldn't be all smooth sailing. There were politicians there who opposed certain forms of free speech, and the banning of books was a big concern.

Pelin had mixed feelings about leaving the UK. She hoped it was the right choice, but with a sense of despair. She realized some things might never improve. Despite that they were not going back home, she was relieved to be leaving the place where she had been trying to get her life sorted out. For time being, it was still full of chaos.

Neither she nor Kemal had any idea what they'd be up against when they got to America, but they agreed, although reluctantly, that it was worth the gamble. "I'd rather take the leap and be wrong than stick around and regret it," Pelin told Kemal, even though she knew he couldn't hear her because he had his noise-canceling AirPods in.

As soon as Kemal sent off his editorial column to the newspaper, he hopped onto the travel agent's website to finalize their plans for the trip to America.

That night, Pelin stood in the window watching the lights of London gleaming in the rain. Kemal joined her. They were a couple of Afro-Turks caught between worlds.

"Do you think we'll ever really belong anywhere?" she asked quietly.

Kemal squeezed her shoulder, "In Turkey, our skin made us feel out of place. In London, it's our names that did it."

"And what about America?"

"Who knows? All we can do is look ahead and hope for a welcome, whatever kind it may be," Pelin said.

24

Kemal had seen New York City in movies, on postcards, and through his computer screen, but it felt nothing like the reality of being there. It was like stepping onto another planet. For years, he had written about the city with passion. He wrote columns with sweeping descriptions of neighborhoods he had never walked through. Kemal had always admired the towering buildings he had only seen in photos. New York had always been a city he dreamed of visiting, but not in the way he ended up coming.

Now he was here, but not the way he had imagined. Not as a traveler, and not as a journalist chasing a story. But as a man running for his life.

None of the things he wrote or dreamed about the city could have prepared him for the reality of what was unfolding right in front of him. Standing on the crowded sidewalk, he felt the ground rumble beneath his feet as a subway train roared below. The air was heavy with unfamiliar scents—a mix of warm pretzels and roasted chestnuts coming from food carts nearby.

Kemal's heart quickened as he tried to take it all in. It was difficult for him to maintain the grin on his face. He was so excited to be walking along the same streets that had always fascinated him. Whenever he researched anything about the history of the boroughs. Kemal was amazed at how so many people could walk on the sidewalk without bumping into one another. He wondered if he looked as much of an outsider as he felt. He was totally lost in the moment. He was constantly looking up at the skyline, head tilted back like a tourist. He was gawking! He chuckled to himself.

He took a deep breath and felt the city's air rush into his lungs. This was New York, the New York he'd written about many times. He was most impressed by the literary history of the city, especially the works of authors of color who told their stories in that setting. Writers like James Baldwin, Paule Marshall, Jami Attenberg, and Jacqueline Woodson, all had inspired him. Their words wove through his thoughts as he walked the same streets they once did. Their influence had even played a part in his decision to choose a novelist as his partner for life.

These streets were now his to explore. Stepping onto the cobblestone streets of Brooklyn, Kemal felt a sense of wonder. The brownstones with their stoops and iron railings were a reminder of his home, Istanbul.

Walking down the tree-lined avenues, he passed many mom-and-pop shops and cafes, imagining them as the birthplaces of successful literary works. He pictured Pelin, hunkered down at a table in one of the cafes, writing her own stories about her journey to America and how she ended up here.

Kemal's face lit up and his eyes opened wide when he spotted a small Turkish coffeehouse just a few feet ahead. He had been craving a decent cup of coffee after several days of traveling, so he went inside. The cafe with its cozy atmosphere, warm tones and mismatched chairs, welcomed him. Finding a seat by the window in the corner, Kemal looked over the menu and was delighted to find a variety of Turkish coffees and desserts, all brewed and baked right there in the kitchen.

Sipping his coffee and enjoying the sweetness of the baklava, Kemal felt a sense of peace wash over him. He could hear conversations between customers throughout the room speaking his native language. Hearing the Turkish music playing in the background gave him the feeling that he had stepped back into his homeland. He was astonished that he had found such a place in America.

After finishing his coffee and dessert, Kemal signaled to the server that he was ready for the bill. The server assumed Kemal was Turkish and thanked him in their native language. They exchanged brief greetings, but Kemal refrained from engaging in a deeper conversation.

Kemal stood and left a couple dollars on the table. Before walking out, he turned and looked at the shelves filled with Turkish books, newspapers, and magazines. As a journalist from Istanbul, these publications he saw weren't just ink on paper to him; newspapers were part of his life. He recognized all the papers from his country.

Looking closer at the headlines of one of these newspapers, Kemal saw printed in large bold letters, "National Unity Prevails: Government Strengthens Security Measures for a Prosperous Future."

Kemal recognized the names of the reporters, the editors, and the photographers. Some were his peers; others were his adversaries. In Istanbul, he worked for the third-most-popular paper. He stood there with a flat look in his eyes. He took offense at two of the papers for their distorted news.

The content published in the papers, and the power and intent of the publishers, was to shape public opinion. The newspapers represented the government's voice, a voice that was eroding freedom of speech. He was glad that he did not introduce himself to anyone in the cafe as a journalist from Istanbul, who had just arrived in the city.

While sitting in the cafe, a flood of memories and emotions surfaced about why he had come to America. Still, he enjoyed the atmosphere, the conversations spoken in his native tongue. It was seeing the Turkish publications that stirred a mix of nostalgia and caution in Kemal. It was also a reminder that he could take no one or anything for granted.

Stepping back onto the street, Kemal's mind was still on the newspapers and magazines. He also had concerns over some customers whose conversations he could not help but overhear, like the two men who sat near him. They spoke a lot about the Turkish government. They sounded like staunch allies. They praised the regime and how they wanted to remain loyal and serve their leaders from afar. Their words gave Kemal a very uneasy feeling.

He meditated over the likelihood that the cafe's patrons were aware of Pelin's situation. They probably knew that the government wanted her for treason. Even here, oceans away from Turkey, the long arm of its politics and social divisions seemed to reach its supporters.

The thought that Turkish citizens who lived and worked in America knew about Pelin dampened Kemal's spirits. He had hoped that moving to America would ease his worries, but now he wondered if such hope was only a dream. Was coming to America the right thing to do, or was it just a relocation of their problems? Pelin's status as an activist, being wanted by the government, might have followed them.

Walking among the crowd rushing toward the subway, he picked up his pace. With his head down, he boarded a train. The fascination he had with the city, the people, trendy boutiques, art galleries, and independent bookstores had now faded into the background.

Kemal was lucky enough to find a seat on the crowded train during one of the busiest hours of the day. As the train left the station, his thoughts went back to the Turkish men who were discussing politics back in the coffee shop. He wondered how they or other like-minded people might react if they discovered Pelin was right here in New York, living in the same community where they lived and worked.

Thinking about the ads placed in the tabloids worried him. The papers were advertising a monetary reward for anyone who had information that might lead to Pelin's arrest. Those were the same paper that denounced her after her book was banned.

Kemal looked at his watch and realized that time had slipped by. He had been gone for hours. He felt guilty and worried about Pelin. Never mind that she was safe with her sister . . . or was she? She had to be, she was with her sister, after all. He had grown accustomed to calling whenever either of them was away for long periods of time. But being caught up in discovering his new environment, he forgot.

A voice in his mind tried to erase the comfort he was feeling by replacing it with a haunting question: What if something happened to her while he was away? She had a target on her back. If anyone who considers themselves a loyalist sees her, recognizes her, it could be dangerous. Never mind that they were in a foreign land miles away from where the nightmare began. No matter where he and Pelin went, the presence of those in power loomed over them. He believed they would do whatever it took to capture Pelin, or something far worse. Anyone who spoke out against or disagreed with the way the country was being run was the enemy of the people. He and Pelin needed to always be on guard, even in America, which they had hoped was safe.

It all was a reminder to Kemal that Pelin's fight for freedom was far from over. Although the world they were now in differed greatly from their own, the threat against them was real. Kemal knew he and Pelin had to steer clear of the misinformation and propaganda spread by conservative media in New York. He had spent nearly the entire day exploring Brooklyn, visiting Prospect Park and the Brooklyn Museum, but the highlight of the day was undoubtedly the discovery of the Turkish cafe. He was hesitant about discussing the cafe with Pelin; he didn't feel as if it was the right fit for her.

The atmosphere had a Turkish feel, but it didn't match the style of the Turkish environment that he and Pelin were accustomed to. The coffeehouse in Brooklyn leaned a little too far to the right. It's likely that if Pelin visited the cafe, the negative experiences she had in the Turkish coffeehouse in London would resurface. That was something Kemal did not want to happen. Not when they were attempting to start over.

Kemal hurried back to Shireen's with a lot to share about the city and what he had discovered, but his excitement faded when he opened the door and found no one home.

Walking into the kitchen, he saw a note on the counter, left by Pelin. "I went out for a short walk, will be back soon," the note read. She ended her note by saying she hoped he had a wonderful day.

Kemal read the note again, this time more slowly, trying to make sense of it. Why would she wander off into Brooklyn alone? In a city like this, there was no telling where she might end up. It seemed reckless, especially considering the news had reached America about her being a fugitive from her government. Not to mention there was a ransom attached.

The chime of his phone broke his chain of thought. Kemal picked up his phone off the counter and saw that it was a text from Pelin. "I am fine, enjoying the sights and sounds of the city, will be back soon." The text ended with a smiling face emoji. Pelin's message was meant to reassure him; still, he worried she might end up in harm's way. Strange things had happened in the past year and a half.

"Where are you?" He hit send and waited. The message showed as delivered, but no typing indicator appeared. No response came.

25

Pelin returned from her stroll through the city, she was exhausted. "I saw your text, but I was unable to respond." She had to catch a crowded bus, and there was standing room only.

When Kemal asked how her outing was, she responded with one word: "Interesting."

Tell me what you saw that made it interesting?" She walked over to the sofa and flopped down. "First, allow me to catch my breath." Pelin was overwhelmed by her experience in the city, but she was unsure where to begin sharing it with Kemal. She was also uncertain of how he would respond.

"I'm glad you had an interesting outing, and now I'm happy that you returned without incident," said Kemal.

They both sat silently for a few moments, waiting for the other to speak first about their adventures in Brooklyn, as well as in Manhattan.

"I decided to do something very brave and very foolish." The only words Kemal heard were "brave and "foolish." He rubbed his face with the palm of his hand and walked over to sit near her.

The words *brave* and *foolish* had him eager to hear what she'd done. He took a deep breath to steady his heartbeat and listen to what she was about to say.

Pelin began by sharing how exciting she found her journey around the borough. "Oh my God, Manhattan! I only saw a little of it, but there's so much action on those streets."

"Why did you travel so far?" Kemal asked.

"I know it was a crazy thing to do, but I took a cab to the Turkish embassy."

Kemal paused for a moment; his eyes widened. He shook his head in disbelief.

"I had to see it for myself," Pelin told him.

"You never cease to amaze me," Kemal said, not wanting to dampen her mood after what seemed like a nice outing. "Taking a cab across New York City was a bit much, and to go to the Turkish embassy? You know Pelin, most people, especially those in your situation wouldn't go near that place."

"I needed to see it. There is a significant difference between viewing an image online and standing there in person." Pelin knew that Kemal would not understand why she took a cab to the embassy. For her, being in front of the embassy made her feel close to home, a feeling that seeing it online could not evoke. The thought of being in danger never crossed her mind. Her eyes and thoughts were focused on the building's architecture and the sight of the Turkish flag waving in the wind.

Pelin closed her eyes, recalling how the smell of spiced coffee mixed with the rich smoky scent of grilled kebabs, were drifting from the food carts by the gates. She told Kemal that she could almost hear the hum of Istanbul's crowded streets.

"Despite the false accusations against me and being forced to leave my country, I lifted my shoulders and held my head high in front of the embassy. In my heart, I felt proud to be a Turkish citizen." She explained to Kemal that she felt she had every right to be standing there and thought of her family and friends she had left behind.

Pelin didn't believe she was being reckless. She viewed herself as upholding her commitment to freedom of speech, a right she cherished and fought for both at home and now abroad. The very act of being there and standing in the shadow of the embassy was a testament to her refusal to be silenced. Standing across the street from the embassy was a way to extend the fight, to stand in solidarity with those she had left behind. Before getting back into the cab, Pelin took a moment to pray. She prayed that one day she would be able to return to the only home she had ever known.

"If only the people inside knew my story," she murmured. "If they understood the real reason I had to leave, why my books were banned, and why I am being called a traitor. I never wanted to overthrow the government, never. All I wanted was change, a better future, one built through democracy and not destruction."

Still, Kemal was troubled by why she went to the embassy alone. "You could have been arrested, or worse."

Nodding her head in agreement, Pelin said, "I know. But I was careful, Kemal. Look at me; I am here in front of you, unharmed." She assured him that she did not get too close.

Kemal reminded her of the chilling incident involving Jamal Khashoggi, the journalist who entered the Saudi embassy in Istanbul in 2018 and never came out. The memory of that gruesome event sent shivers down his spine. Kemal did not want to see Pelin make the same mistake. Venturing even an inch past the threshold of the Turkish embassy would be dangerous for her.

Pelin's eyes lit up like stars as she described the embassy and her emotions while she stood there. "I was standing at a safe distance," she reiterated. "I saw people going in and out. I assumed they were workers and visitors. I could hear the guards speaking our language, along with some of the others who walked through the gates."

As Pelin recounted her story, Kemal sat back in his chair and listened, absorbing everything she said with a mix of fascination and concern. He couldn't help but wonder if some of the people Pelin described were the same ones he saw entering and exiting the coffee shop.

Their journeys into the city were very different. Kemal went out for a casual walk to explore the community, while Pelin specifically set out with the intention of seeing the Turkish embassy.

"Yes, what you did today was both brave and dangerous," Kemal told Pelin.

"I know, but it was something I had in mind to do once I knew for certain that we were coming to New York," Pelin replied.

Kemal understood that once she had set her mind on something, there was almost nothing he could do to stop or discourage her. She was the most stubborn human he had ever met.

"To be honest, Kemal, I almost felt like walking right through those gates; if it weren't for the small-minded people working there who feared an outspoken woman, I would have."

"I can see you doing that," he acknowledged, recognizing Pelin's fighting spirit. "You have in the past, and it seems you continue to take grave risks."

Pelin smiled. "Standing across the street from the embassy was a pivotal moment for me. I felt as if a weight had been lifted off my shoulders." It was a moment she had not experienced in some time.

For Kemal, it was reassuring to hear Pelin say that. Her visit seemed to have stirred something within her—perhaps a newfound determination, a willingness to disregard fear. He hoped that one day she would be able to walk through those gates and be cleared of all accusations.

Kemal looked Pelin in the eyes and saw her yearning to return to the past. He wished they could go back, reclaim the life and the places they had known, even if they were blindfolded. But here they were, stranded on foreign soil, bound by a slow-moving justice system. If they returned now, they would be walking into a rigged trial with phony judges and jurors. Their fates would be sealed before they even spoke a word. Kemal was heartbroken, knowing that all he could do was stand still. There was nothing he could do.

"Kemal, thank you for your patience and understanding." His willingness to listen provided her with relief and a deeper understanding. Coming to America was a significant turning point for her. It wasn't just a new beginning; it was a distinct chapter, one different from what she had known. In this new and unfamiliar world, Pelin's immediate goal was to find a place where she could pursue her passion for writing and continue publishing her truths about the struggles she and her peers were experiencing.

She faced Kemal. "If confronted by anyone, I won't back down," she said, speaking with clarity and confidence. Her words were not just a promise to him; they were a commitment to herself. Pelin felt she had spent too long hiding and running. She felt she had made too many sacrifices in the process. She was ready and determined to move forward and reclaim her identity. After all, that's why she came to America.

They were both startled and sat up straight when they heard footsteps. They turned their heads to see Shireen standing in the hallway. Shireen noticed that they both looked confused and curious. Pelin felt a twinge of guilt, wondering if her sister had overheard any of their conversation. They quickly composed themselves and welcomed Shireen home.

"I hope you two are starving; I made reservations for dinner. We can catch an Uber to the Greek restaurant, which isn't far away." Kemal rubbed his belly at the mention of the restaurant. Shireen was excited to go out with her sister and Kemal. It would give her the chance to show them the world she had been living in for the last five years.

Before Pelin closed the blinds on the bay window, she glanced out at the cityscape, taking in the twinkling lights. She had no idea what she might discover as the three of them prepared to leave the house together for the first time. The city itself was a place where everyone was from somewhere else. Full of immigrants, all seeking safety, opportunity, a new way . . . like she and Kemal.

The Uber ride to the restaurant was filled with laughter. The driver wore a Yankees cap and shared jokes and stories about the city and the people he had met as a driver. He had a tale for almost every street corner they passed, mentioning that the late-night customers were the most entertaining.

The driver looked at Pelin and Kemal through the rearview mirror with a grin, "I once picked up a Wall Street investor right outside that dive bar back there — as I drove a little way down the street he started swearing. He just invested in Bitcoin and now he was crying' about losing twenty grand before we even reached the next block."

The driver laughed, but Pelin and Kemal felt bad for the investor.

"See that deli on the corner?" The driver pointed as they drove by. "Met a lady in there last winter. Bought me a coffee and told me she was a 'retired magician'... then *disappeared* on me when it was time for the check."

When they arrived at the restaurant, the aroma of grilled meats and fresh herbs melted all bad feelings. Traditional Greek music mixed with conversations in various languages. The place radiated warmth and energy, much like the city itself. Pelin felt herself relax.

Dinner featured a blend of Greek and Arabic dishes, accompanied by stories. The restaurant was one of Shireen's favorites, so she had a story about each dish, some of which reminded her of the beloved foods she had enjoyed back in Istanbul. When the lamb stew arrived, Shireen told them about when her mother had tried to teach her how to make it and she burned the onions three times in a row. Finally they made the stew without onions. Her reason for bringing them to this restaurant, was because she knew that both Pelin and Kemal would appreciate this taste of home.

Kemal was surprised by some of the things Pelin and Shireen discussed during their meal. Pelin leaned in closer, she spoke low and shared her dreams and fears more openly than she had in year. Sometimes, she said, tracing the rim of her glass with her fingertip, "I wonder if I'll ever feel safe enough to write everything I want to say."

Shireen smiled gently. "You will," she said. "Look at me. When I first got here, I wasn't sure if I would find a job. Now, look, I am teaching at NYU."

They both stood and hugged each other while full of laughter even as they prepared to leave.

While waiting in the coat room, Kemal worried that the couple next to them could hear the conversation between the sisters. He leaned in slightly and whispered, "Excuse me, ladies. I just thought you might want to know that your voices are louder than you realize." He was asking them to lower their voices. "Not everyone in here needs to know about your lives." He was curious why two people nearby were looking at them and whispering to one another in Turkish. Kemal was unsure who they were or what their business was in New York.

Pelin and Shireen's laughter faded as they slightly turned their heads to look at the couple Kemal had noticed. The man and woman stood close together, speaking in hushed tones, their expressions unreadable. But there was something about them—an air of familiarity—that unsettled Pelin. The man's sharp features and the woman's poised demeanor reminded her of officials she had encountered back home.

The man wore a dark long overcoat that looked a little tight over his broad shoulders, the kind government officials favored back home in informal settings. His brown shoes were highly polished and gleaming. The woman with him was equally well dressed. She wore a sheer black scarf tied neatly over her hair, framing her pale face. Her long wool coat was buttoned up to her throat. It looked quite expensive and designed to blend in rather than stand out. They didn't appear to be husband and wife, and everything about them—their stillness, their immaculate dress—showed discipline, control, and authority.

Pelin took a steadying breath and reached for her coat. "Let's not overthink it," she murmured, forcing a casual smile. "Maybe they're just tourists."

Kemal nodded, though his jaw remained tight. "Maybe," he echoed, but he didn't believe it.

—26—

Kemal couldn't help but be curious about the Turkish couple who were nearby as they grabbed their coats. He wondered if it was just a coincidence that they were checking out at the same time as him, Pelin, and Shireen. He also thought it was a bit strange that they ended up on the same train.

As they took the escalator up and out of the subway station, Kemal glanced around to see if anyone was following them. "Thank God, no one's behind us," he muttered to himself, but he kept looking back whenever he could. Pelin was excited to explore the city, but she noticed that Kemal seemed a bit uneasy.

She took a deep breath, letting the cool air fill her lungs. She turned to Kemal with a small smile. "Do you smell the roasting chestnuts?"

Kemal wrinkled his nose and looked over at the line of yellow taxis idling at the curb.

"Chestnuts? I smell diesel, three kinds of street meat, and possibly a guy who hasn't discovered deodorant."

He gave a half-shrug. "But I guess that's what New York smells like."

Shireen looked over at her sister, who was craning her neck, gazing up. Her eyes were fixated on the towering skyscrapers. Her face lit up like a child's as she watched Pelin. This was the exact vision that Shireen had imagined Pelin and Kemal would have as

136

they walked through the streets of Manhattan. As they turned the corner onto 42nd Street, Pelin nudged Kemal. "Isn't it amazing?"

"Sort of," he muttered.

Pelin hoped that Shireen could not hear Kemal's comment, not wanting to ruin her sister's night because of Kemal's mood. "Come on, Kemal, it's New York. There's no other city like it in the world."

She wanted to share her enthusiasm with him. However, he was looking around with a guarded expression. His eyes were darting around, trying to look at everyone who walked by. It was almost impossible for him to relax and enjoy the city. While still waiting for him to respond, she could sense that his mind was elsewhere, preoccupied with looking for potential threats.

Kemal had always pictured himself as a man of the world, at ease in any city. But the frenzy of New York, especially after the note suggesting that someone might be following their every turn, was getting to him.

Pelin recognized the signs: his restless movements, the way his confidence frayed at the edges, worn thin by an anxiety he could no longer hide.

Kemal still wasn't smiling like he usually did. She leaned in closer and whispered, "If I didn't know you, I probably would think you're from New York." She had read somewhere that people in New York hardly smile when out in crowds.

Pelin did her best to cheer him up. But she wasn't about to let his mood bring her down. She kept chatting with Shireen. The sisters had been talking about a night out in the city ever since Shireen invited Pelin to New York. Shireen was doing her best to make Pelin and Kemal feel welcome. More than anything, she wanted to make up for lost time.

Pelin paused again, trying to help Kemal relax and enjoy the city. But she could see he was still on edge, keeping an eye out for anyone who might be following them.

Pelin walked back over to her sister. Shireen had stopped at the edge of the sidewalk. She was looking up at the Empire State

Building. Someone dressed as Spider-Man was scaling it. Pelin's heart was filled with warmth as she watched her sister, now forty-two but still with that unmistakable spark of wonder in her eyes. A soft smile came across Pelin's face as she saw Shireen this way. It was in that moment that Pelin thought back to the days when their parents used to walk with them through the city of Istanbul.

"Look at her," Pelin whispered to Kemal, nudging him again. "That's what I wanted. This is how I remember her, always smiling. Isn't it nice to be with her again?"

Kemal's expression softened a little as he looked at Shireen, but he still seemed tense. He hesitated before answering, as if struggling to find the right words. "I know this means a lot to you," he said quietly. "And I am glad you are happy. But..." He ran his hand through his hair, and looked at the chaos, honking cabs, and crowds of people streaming past them. "It's just... it's a lot, you know?"

Pelin sighed, forcing herself to stay calm. She tried to imagine what New York might look like to someone like Kemal, who had spent most of his life in more familiar places. For her, the crowds and the noise were exciting and a constant reminder of what her life used to be. But for Kemal, it felt overwhelming; he was worried.

The city was a crazy mix of lights, sounds, and people—some just hanging out while others zipped by. Kemal had never really been comfortable with all this chaos.

"Don't overthink it, just... be here," Pelin said softly. "Let it wash over you. It's totally okay to feel a bit overwhelmed."

But Kemal just shook his head and gave a hesitant smile. "I don't know, Pelin. It's hard for me to see what you see. Everyone's in such a rush. It feels like they're all running from something."

Shireen noticed the tension on his face, like he was bracing for something to happen. She reached for his hand, squeezing it gently, hoping her touch would help calm him down.

"I used to feel the same way when I first moved here," Shireen told Kemal and Pelin. "I thought everyone looked so weird, always rushing by. But that's just how it looks on the surface. If you spend enough time here, you'll start to see it a little differently. There are moments of kindness; believe it or not, some people even hold the subway door open for each other. If you pay attention, you'll see how some people nod to strangers, trying to make them feel a part of this immense, busy community."

Kemal's expression softened, but he still looked skeptical. "Maybe," he said quietly, looking at his sister-in-law. "I just don't get how you can live alone in a big city like this."

Shireen didn't push him to explain why he thought she couldn't handle New York; she grew up in Istanbul, which is pretty big too. But that was just Kemal's way. He'd always been cautious and protective, not the type to get excited like she and Pelin did. That had been true long before they had to leave their home country.

He and Pelin were so different in many ways. But that was part of what attracted her to him: the calmness he brought to her life, how he could ground her when she felt overwhelmed by her own feelings.

Now, though, she wished he could just let loose for a bit and see New York like she did. She wanted to enjoy the city with him, hoping that he would fall in love with it. But maybe that was too much to hope for, she thought. Not everyone sees things the same way.

Noticing how Pelin was feeling, Shireen looked at Kemal and said, "I know it's a lot to take in, but just keep an open mind; you'll be okay."

As they walked down the crowded sidewalk, Pelin slipped her hand into his, hoping her warmth could ease his tension. They passed street vendors selling pretzels and hot dogs, the delicious smells mixing with the scent of roasted nuts and the occasional whiff of garbage from a nearby alley. People brushed past them, and conversations floated around in all sorts of languages.

To Pelin, it felt like music, a symphony of lives coming together. But when she glanced at Kemal, she could see he was still struggling to find the beat, still feeling out of place in this sprawling wild city.

For now, she decided to keep her excitement in check. After all, this was the happiest the two sisters had been in a while. For Shireen, strolling through New York City with her sister, arm in arm, felt like a dream come true. It was hard to believe it was really happening. This was a moment they'd been waiting for. Both sisters felt a warm joy in their hearts, thrilled to be together again, and they regretted the time they had missed. They promised each other they wouldn't let so much time go by without seeing each other again.

Shireen was playing tour guide for Pelin and Kemal. As they made their way up Fifth Avenue, Shireen suddenly stopped, grabbing Pelin's arm and pointing ahead with a grin. "Look!" she exclaimed, pointing at the iconic triangle-shaped building up ahead. "There it is, the Flatiron Building!" She could hardly contain her excitement as she watched Pelin's face light up. Kemal pulled out his phone and snapped a photo. "And Madison Square Park is right nearby, where all the cool kids hang out," Shireen added.

Pelin caught her sister's vibrant energy and couldn't help but smile back. She realized this trip was Shireen's way of showing her a good time and reminding her that life wasn't just about battling challenges. Shireen wanted Pelin to take a breather, to try new things, and to rediscover the carefree joy that had been buried under her struggles.

As they weaved in and out of the busy street, passing street performers and jazz clubs, Kemal was reminded of Istanbul. Pelin stopped to grab a bag of roasted chestnuts from a street vendor. She couldn't leave without trying them. The warmth seeping into her fingers as she enjoyed the tasty snacks.

Kemal felt as if he were stepping into another world. The city stretched endlessly before them, a sea of lights and movement that left him breathless. For a moment, he was reminded of home, but not exactly. But rather in a large city that felt so different. Shireen hung back, giving them space. Pelin slipped her hand into Kemal's and, with a soft smile, leaned in to kiss his cheek. They stood together, taking in the sprawling cityscape, each were in their own quiet thoughts.

Pelin thought about the possibilities that might be waiting for them. For a moment, she felt a flicker of hope, believing that maybe she could find her place here. But Kemal still wasn't sure if coming to America was the right move for them. He was struggling to adjust to the chaos of the city. Still, he didn't want to dampen the joy he saw in Pelin's eyes.

Shireen stepped back up and linked her arm with Pelin's, her eyes sparkling with excitement. "Come on, sis," she said, pulling her forward. "Let's find a rooftop bar and watch the sunrise. We've got the whole night ahead of us!"

Pelin glanced at Kemal, looking for his approval about going to a bar so late. Not wanting to ruin her fun, Kemal nodded, giving her the green light.

For the first time in a long while, Pelin embraced the enthusiasm of the night. With Shireen pulling her forward, a sense of renewal washed over her.

"Come on, Kemal, let's do it," Pelin said, her voice carrying the hopeful determination of someone finally ready to let go of their fears.

But as they prepared to move, Kemal suddenly stiffened. He saw the Turkish couple's shadow in a shop window. Now he believed that they weren't simply appearing in the same places by coincidence—they were deliberately tracking them. He noticed the man leaned in closer to whisper something to the woman, their eyes were fixed directly on him. A cold sensation crept along his spine, validating every suspicion he'd had had.

"Pelin," he said quietly, trying to sound calm. He grabbed her elbow, pulling her closer while keeping his eyes on the strangers. "Don't look now, but we need to get out of here. Like, right now."

The woman from the couple reached into her coat pocket, and Kemal's heart raced. Whatever they thought they had left behind had somehow tracked them down to New York, thousands of miles from home.

— 27 —

After a late night out, Pelin and Shireen woke early the next morning, moving slower than usual. Shireen headed straight to work, while Pelin left, looking for a quiet spot to do research.

For the first time in two years, it felt like normalcy. She had wandered into the New York Public Library almost by accident. Outside, the lions stood guard, they reminded her of the stone lions she'd seen as a child, perched outside old mosques and fountains in Istanbul. It made her smile, giving her a small connection to home.

Inside, she moved through the vast marble halls, and up the worn stairs, the high vaulted ceilings, and even the scent of old books told of age and how they had survived time. She found a quiet corner on the second floor, tucked between rows of tall windows, and settled in.

For a few hours, she lost herself in her work, struggling as she had for months to complete her novella set in the Ottoman Empire.

She was on a roll, fully engaged in her work. Hours slipped by until she looked up at the clock and realized she was running late. Grabbing her things, she rushed out the door, heading straight for Washington Square Park. She needed to find the Lillian Vernon Creative Writers House, where she planned to meet Shireen for lunch.

When she arrived, she was surprised to see that Shireen wasn't alone. At the table sat Dr. Lisa Jones, a distinguished-looking woman in her mid-fifties.

142

She stood as Pelin approached the table. Dr. Jones was tall and elegant. She wore her short gray hair in a curly afro and had on blue-framed glasses that matched her navy-blue suit and pearl necklace.

"I'm so sorry I'm late," Pelin apologized, catching her breath.

"Don't worry at all," Lisa said warmly, rising to shake her hand. "Shireen's mentioned you often. It's wonderful to finally meet you."

Pelin smiled shyly. "Thank you for joining us, Dr. Jones."

"Call me Lisa, please. And by the way, I've read your novels. They're powerful. How is the new one coming along?"

They settled and jumped right into a conversation, Pelin opening up about her struggles and how much her life had changed since fleeing Turkey.

Lisa leaned forward intently. "It must have been terrifying, a shock, to leave your home in the dead of night with almost nothing."

Before the meal ended, Lisa surprised everyone with an offer: "Pelin, I'd love you to share your story with my journalist students, and perhaps we could open it to the public. Americans need to hear voices like yours, especially now, when democracy and free speech are under threat worldwide."

Shireen smiled proudly, knowing how significant this moment was for her sister. Pelin, however, felt her stomach tighten with nerves. Yes, speaking openly would give her a louder voice, but it would also paint an even bigger target on her back.

On one hand, Pelin felt honored to be asked to speak at a major university in America. This was a rare opportunity for a woman of her background. She thought about the backlash and criticism she might face. Especially from those who opposed her views and her very existence.

Not every American familiar with Pelin's case agreed with her. Some thought she should be sent back to Turkey. Some aimed to silence her voice by imposing their own version of history on citizens. Some politicians in both America and Turkey wanted to reshape public perception, forcing everyone to think like them. Erasing history and banning books were just some of the tactics they used.

Taking a deep breath and clenching her fists, Pelin knew she had a story that deserved to be heard. She decided not to let fear hold her back. She would accept the invitation and speak to the students and anyone else interested, no matter the consequences.

When Pelin shared the news later that night, Kemal's reaction was immediate. "Are you out of your mind?" he blurted.

Pelin looked straight into his eyes and replied, "It's not…"

"Not what?" Kemal interrupted. "You're already walking around with a target on your back. Don't you think this is a bad idea?" He couldn't stay still; he paced the room after Pelin revealed that she would be speaking on the NYU campus about international human rights abuses and freedom of the press.

He turned to Shireen, disbelief on his face. "Does Pelin really think the Turkish authorities will just stand by while she rips them apart?"

It was hard for Kemal to accept that after everything they had sacrificed, Pelin would risk it all. He groaned and said, "This public stance could undo everything." He stared out the window, lost in thought.

Shireen, who was usually unshaken, felt her heart racing after hearing Kemal express his disapproval of Pelin speaking publicly.

Pelin stared back at Kemal, her eyes were red. "I'm going to do it."

Kemal doubted Pelin had considered that her speech would be recorded and shared online for everyone to see. "The Turkish authorities are sure to love it. You're setting yourself up for failure. We're not citizens of this country, and we're fugitives from another. We have few legal rights to protect us from them."

Pelin stood and walked over to the window where Kemal was looking out. "Kemal, why are you so afraid? This is exactly what I need to reclaim my identity. You have to understand."

Kemal cracked his knuckles and spoke quietly to the glass instead of directly to Pelin. "I know you're driven to do this, but I'm not ready for you to take such a big risk."

"This is a new life, Kemal; we have to start living it. We might never get this chance again." She paused; her determination was clear. "This is the biggest stage in the world. I've always dreamed of speaking before a large audience, just not about free speech."

Kemal worried for Pelin's safety in front of such a big crowd. He understood her books were sold internationally, but he saw that differently. "Now the world will discover the real Pelin, not Aysia Basar, the pen name she has published under for over a decade."

Exhausted, he leaned his head against the cold window. Kemal remembered why they came to America: to start over. He wanted to believe that in this new land, Pelin would eventually end her fight with the regime. But it was clear she was picking up where she left off by going forward with the speaking engagement.

"I hear you, Kemal; but you know I can't walk away from my dreams. I've worked too hard to get here. And besides . . . some celebrity can be protective. I'm not 'nobody' . . . I'm a dissident writer! In America, that can mean people care about you, protect you."

Kemal lifted his head from the window. He understood her bold vision, realizing there was no use in trying to change her mind.

"Okay, I will accept the reality before me. Reluctantly." He knew Pelin was determined to follow through with her commitment. She was waiting to hear from Lisa about a date and time. Her window to the world was about to open.

The news that Pelin would be speaking in America was like a spark igniting a fire. It spread quickly across the ocean, reaching many eager to hear her voice again.

The date was set, and leaflets announcing Pelin's talk were being handed out all over campus and around the city. Lisa Jones wanted her students, as well as everyone connected to journalism, to be there. She believed the literary world should become more familiar with how the rights enshrined in America's First Amendment differ across borders.

In a few weeks, Pelin's name would be splashed across news outlets internationally. Some media outlets owned by the Turkish government were tasked with smearing her name before she even spoke. It was a tactic to persuade the president of NYU and board members to cancel Pelin's engagement. Agents working out of the embassy in New York were also put on notice to use whatever limited powers they had and meet with local authorities. They wanted to emphasize that Pelin was a criminal. They wanted her deported back to Turkey.

The buzz was building, and the agents' tactics were backfiring. It was reported within days of the announcement that the event had sold out.

Kemal struggled to keep it together; his nerves were shot. Both he and Pelin had never seen anything like this. Shireen was also taken aback by the news of a packed house.

"Tell your sister not to worry; she'll be fine," Lisa said during a phone call with Shireen.

Seating wasn't the only thing selling. Pelin's inbox pinged, and she felt a rush of anxiety upon seeing it was from her publisher. Her books were flying off the shelves in the U.S., especially in New York, selling out as soon as they came off the printer. The latest sales summary from her Turkish publisher was shocking; the demand had tripled in just a few weeks. But then came the catch.

Her publisher warned her to brace herself. Rumors were swirling that the government was considering a harsh crackdown on controversial voices, and Pelin's voice was at the top of the list. If they moved forward, they could freeze both the printing and shipping of her books at any moment. The message was clear: print and ship as many copies as possible, at least while they still could.

Pelin grew more worried as she read the last line. Kemal looked over her shoulder, reading the email with a frown. "You need to consider publishing options here in the U.S.," he whispered. "Big or small, it doesn't matter. You need to make your move now."

Kemal was right; he had read that the window to break into the American market was wide open, but it wouldn't stay that way for long. He feared the Turkish government would find a way to shut her down before she even got the chance.

Pelin closed her email and let out a sharp breath. Her hands shook a bit as she placed her phone on the table.

"They're trying to shut me down before I even get a chance to speak." Her voice was calm, but there was a spark in her eyes.

Kemal rubbed his face and sighed. "We saw this coming," he said. "They're scared of you, Pelin. That's why they're doing this."

Shireen leaned in, worry on her face. "What do we do? Can they really stop you?"

Pelin shook her head. "They can try."

Kemal wasn't convinced. "They're not just trying to ban your books, Pelin. They're watching you. That's what worries me."

Pelin looked at him, "I won't let them silence me."

Shireen reached for Pelin's hand. "Kemal has a point. You've been through so much already—"

Pelin pulled her hand back gently, her voice firm. "This is exactly why I can't stop now. If I back down, they win."

Just before stepping onto the stage and approaching the podium, Pelin took a deep breath. The roaring applause gave her goosebumps. She looked out at the sea of diverse faces; she saw that every seat in the auditorium was filled. "Wow… this is unbelievable," she said softly in the microphone.

As the applause died down, Pelin began her speech by reminding everyone of their right to live freely. She explained how the First Amendment protects fundamental freedoms for everyone, and how many people across the world model their hopes on it.

Pausing briefly to let her words resonate, she continued, "But the world is changing fast. There are people in power trying to rewrite our history and our rights, trying to keep free speech unavailable to most of us."

The audience leaned forward, captivated. With a confident smile, Pelin said, "Let me give you a glimpse into my life as a writer and an artist. In my novels, fiction often carries the weight of hidden truths and sometimes exposes corrupted governments.

After fifty-five minutes, Pelin concluded to enthusiastic applause. To the audience, she was a fearless woman of color unafraid to challenge authority, a voice for the voiceless.

But not everyone had come to hear her speak. Four rows behind Shireen and Kemal, sat half a dozen Turkish agents. Their plan was to abduct Pelin. These were the same agents who had tracked her too New York. They were aware she was staying with her sister.

"This is our target, Pelin Korkmaz." The senior agent distributed copies of Pelin's photo to his team. "We will not let her slip away again," he declared. An eager young agent nodded, determined to prove himself worthy of being on this assignment.

* * *

As Pelin and Dr. Jones approached the dressing room, Pelin noticed a suspicious man lurking nearby. Before she could react, the man jumped in front of her. Dr. Jones stepped swiftly in front, shouting, "Run, Pelin! Get inside and lock the door!" Security guards rushed toward the intruder, who escaped through an emergency exit, triggering alarms.

Inside the dressing room, Dr. Jones checked Pelin over carefully. "Was that someone you knew? He spoke your language."

"No," Pelin replied shakily. "And I doubt he was here for a book signing."

"Follow me, Mrs. Korkmaz. There's an emergency exit down the hall. It's useful when the crowd gets a bit wild. I'll have security inform your husband and sister that you're okay."

"Thank you. You saved me," Pelin said.

"I had no choice; I won't let anyone hurt you."

Dr. Jones quickly arranged security measures, reassuring Pelin that authorities would investigate. Moments later, an announcement apologized for the canceled book signing. Disappointed attendees lingered briefly, their confusion soon turning to anger when they learned someone had attempted to kidnap Pelin.

As Pelin settled into the safety of her hired car, frustration and disbelief surged through her. "How did he even get backstage?" she exclaimed angrily. Kemal comfortingly wrapped an arm around her.

"It must have been an inside job," Shireen speculated anxiously. "We should file a police report."

Despite her anxiety, Pelin felt a renewed determination. She refused to be forced into silence. "I think I'm getting used to the harassment," she sighed defiantly.

To clear the stress, Pelin suggested stopping for late-night tea.

The security team carefully checked the café before allowing them inside. Still, the guards' presence was a stark reminder of the threats Pelin faced.

Pelin sipped her tea, and the three of them reflected on her speech. Two women recognized her from the event. One approached eagerly, only to be stopped by a guard. She called out, "Can you believe a state down south banned the dictionary over a few words some parents found offensive?" she shouted to Pelin before going back to her table.

"Yes, I can. I heard about that outrageous incident," Pelin shouted back. She hoped her message would inspire more people to stand up for freedom of expression and fight against censorship.

As she turned to take another sip of tea, she noticed Shireen looking at her phone with a puzzled expression. "What's wrong?" Pelin asked.

Shireen handed Pelin her phone, showing her a text from an unknown number. It read: "I saw you on the news. You think you're so smart, don't you? You believe you can expose our secrets and get away with it? You're mistaken. We're coming for you, and we won't stop until you're silenced forever."

Pelin felt a chill run down her spine as she looked around the café, wondering who could have sent the message. Was it someone inside? Or outside?

She realized she wasn't safe—not even with the guards around. Someone was after her, and her government was desperately trying to stop her from telling the truth.

Kemal and Shireen were staring at her with concern. Whoever sent that text had hacked into Shireen's phone. Kemal was right; whoever was after them would follow them anywhere.

Once again, Pelin felt terrible knowing she had put the two people she loved most in danger. A decision had to be made on how to move forward, now that the harassment had followed them to New York. She had to choose between her life and her career. Taking a deep breath, Pelin said, "I think we should leave."

Pelin's words hung in the air, her voice steady despite the knot of anxiety in her chest. Shireen and Kemal exchanged worried glances.

"For now, let's just get out of this cafe." Shireen whispered.

"Where would we even go if we left this city?" Kemal asked.

"Anywhere but here," Pelin said, lowering her voice. "They've already found us. What if they're watching us right now?" She glanced at the café window, where streetlights flickered against the dark glass.

Kemal let out a sharp breath, gripping his teacup as if it would help calm him. "Running isn't a long-term solution. If we just disappear, they'll find another way to discredit you. To silence you."

Shireen tapped on her phone, her fingers trembling slightly. "I can call the police. Show them the message, maybe they can trace it."

Pelin shook her head. "And what will they do? A police report won't stop them. You saw how easily that agent got past security tonight."

The café door chimed softly as a man in a long coat entered, scanning the room. Pelin tensed, gripping her chair. Was he just another late-night customer—or something more?

"We need a plan," Kemal said quietly but urgently. "Not just an escape, but a way to fight back."

Pelin met his eyes. "And how do you fight an enemy you can't see? One who hides in the dark and strikes when you least expect it?"

"You shine a light on them," Kemal simply replied.

— **29** —

Exhausted from everything that happened the previous night, the three of them welcomed the chance to sleep in late. The sun was already high in the sky, shining brightly through the window of the cozy kitchen. Its rays bounced off the dangling crystals that hung from the ceiling, creating colorful rainbows on the walls and a magical atmosphere. However, the mood around Pelin was anything but magical. She lay in bed awake, staring at the ceiling and the red digits on the alarm clock—a reminder that she had to get up and face the day.

She dreaded doing so, haunted by the chilling encounter with the man who had attempted to kidnap her at NYU. It felt like a dream, but it had really happened. She tossed back the covers and eventually eased out of bed, placing one foot at a time on the cold hardwood floor. The scent of coffee led her to the kitchen, where she joined Shireen and Kemal. Pelin took a seat at the kitchen counter, somber, trying to avoid looking directly at either of them. She was shaken. Last night's events had taken a toll on her.

Kemal and Shireen were engaged in their own conversation but paused and looked over at Pelin. Kemal lowered his head, staring sightlessly at the floor. It was difficult to see her like this. He hated that her night had ended this way, especially since it had been two years since she had spoken in public. This should have been a day of celebration for her, a moment that he and Shireen viewed as a great success. But Pelin's thoughts were different; she saw it as a nightmare come true.

From her past experiences with the agents, she knew they were still up to their devious tricks. To think they were brave enough to cross borders and operate in the "Land of the Free" was infuriating. Kemal watched his wife sitting at the counter, her fingers tracing the rim of her coffee cup, lost in thought. The usual sparkle in her eyes was absent. He knew she was grappling with what had happened and wanted to talk about it but was struggling to find her words.

"You know we're here for you, don't you?" Kemal asked.

"Yeah, sis, like everything else that's happened, we will figure this out together." After hearing their reassurances, Pelin broke her silence. "I suppose it's time I accept the truths of the world." She began to share her sleepless night, explaining that the thought of being back under the agents' radar was suffocating. She thought she had left her troubles behind in London. Pelin recognized that her close encounter with the man at NYU was the opening of another unwanted chapter in her life. The agents didn't care that they had no authority in America; they refused to back down.

"There are a few billionaires in the world who spend significant wealth trying to rule it. Their goal is to spread their ideology and persuade others to follow, think, and live by their rules. Not only do they spend millions to influence, but they also use their money to punish politicians who do not play their games."

After the events following her speech at NYU and the threats to her life, Pelin understood that something needed to change. Feeling her pain, Kemal agreed. The thought of being back under the agents' radar was troubling. "America is a wide-open country," Kemal said, a spark of hope in his eyes." Why don't we get out of here for a while?" He suggested renting a car and going on a road trip to explore other parts of the country, something he had always dreamed of doing. "We can lose ourselves on the open road. We have nothing to lose by getting away."

Shireen looked uncertain, not believing it was a good idea. However, she held her tongue, wanting the best for her sister while worrying that this spur-of-the-moment plan could place them in unforeseen danger. There was already enough uncertainty and imminent danger in Pelin's life without adding further unknowns.

Caught between concern and reluctant understanding, Shireen felt uncomfortable but remained silent. She didn't want to be seen by Pelin or Kemal as interfering in Kemal's decision, but she was genuinely upset by his sudden suggestion.

Pelin wasn't sure she could trust Kemal's idea either. She had come to America seeking safety and security, but after the kidnapping attempt, she felt more exposed and endangered than ever. She raised her eyes to look at Kemal's face, the face she trusted. Perhaps putting some distance between herself and this latest incident was exactly what she needed.

The incident at NYU was behind them, and there was nothing they could do to change it now. Supposedly, the authorities were investigating what had happened, and her worrying was a waste of time. Although she wasn't sure how a road trip through America would ease her mind, she was willing to try. If nothing else, it might provide a break from those who were tracking her. But her problem was bigger than the agents. Their job was to find her and bring her back to Turkey; her battle was with those in power who had signed the order for her arrest.

"They see me as a threat to their authority," Pelin said, growing angrier as she spoke. "I refuse to be silenced by oppressive hands." It wasn't just about governance; it was about their changing the rules, their make-believe ideology. She spoke with a mix of determination and weariness, understanding that her struggle was part of a larger global issue, a fight against oppressive forces that was spreading.

She knew well that camps of right-wing governments were growing globally, with the agenda of silencing dissent. "They portray those like me as the enemy of the people." Pelin saw the Minister of the Interior and his circle as nothing more than power-hungry opportunists. Their true mission wasn't governance but control—silencing dissent by dictating what people could say, learn, read, and watch. Even the arts weren't spared; if creativity threatened their narrative, they were more than willing to starve it out of existence.

After a lengthy discussion, Pelin and Kemal decided the benefits of a road trip outweighed any risks. She felt a little of her old self returning; the thought of exploring unknown places wasn't a bad idea. It would provide a mental break from constantly looking over her shoulder.

Although Kemal's idea was spontaneous, Pelin looked at Shireen and nodded. "A road trip is probably just what I need right now. From my years of writing and researching about this country, I know America is vast, with so much to offer and countless beautiful things to discover."

Shireen wasn't convinced and could no longer remain silent. She didn't think it was wise for the two of them to drive alone in unfamiliar territory. "Are you sure about this? The country isn't as safe as it used to be. The news is full of troubling stories."

"No need to worry; we will be okay. I think getting away from the city for a while would give Pelin some peace of mind," Kemal insisted, determined to make it happen.

He loaded the black rental VW SUV with only the necessary luggage and showed Shireen an atlas where he outlined their planned route. He had circled Washington D.C. in red, indicating it was the highlight of the trip. His excitement was visible, a stark contrast to the concern in Shireen's eyes. No matter what, she continued to believe that it was too soon for Pelin and Kemal to go on a road trip. With a bittersweet farewell, Pelin embraced her sister tightly.

"Maybe this will be better." Shireen handed Pelin a new phone that she added to her account.

"Thanks, I'll call at every stop," Shireen said, tears streaming down her cheeks as she waved goodbye, watching her sister and Kemal drive off. "Please be safe," she shouted as the black rental SUV disappeared.

Shireen hurried back upstairs to research the places they intended to travel through. Though her worries didn't completely dissipate, seeing the destinations and knowing Pelin's and Kemal's determination gave her a glimmer of hope. The journey south on Interstate 95 could provide not just a physical escape, but also a chance for Pelin and Kemal to find some peace. She hoped they would rediscover themselves amid the vast landscapes and the changing colors of fall.

Shireen had only spent one full day alone when the doorman's buzz surprised her. He came to inform her that two visitors were inquiring about her sister's travel documents. They identified themselves as Customs and Border Protection Officers, claiming they were there to correct a mistake on Pelin's and Kemal's travel documents. "The mistake might affect their stay in America," said the doorman.

Shireen was alarmed to have two men claiming to be border patrol officers come to her home. That was a red flag for her; nevertheless, it heightened her concerns for her sister. Why had the men come here? Shireen quickly gathered herself and hopped on the elevator to speak with the visitors. When the elevator door opened, Shireen's gut tightened. Two men in dark suits stepped inside, smiling. When she saw the Turkish flag pins on their lapels, she almost fainted, *Not Americans. Not hotel security.* She said.

"Aren't you the sister of Mrs. Korkmaz?" one asked, "Just a few questions." She gave a small, uncertain laugh. "Sure. Is something wrong?"

"Are your sister and husband staying with you?"

"Yes. Vacation," she lied easily, shifting her bag onto her shoulder.

The men inched closer, boxing her in.

"Can we see your identification?"

Shireen smiled wider, tilting her head. "Of course, I can grab it from my apartment," she said, then she spoke louder, "Or we can ask the doorman to help."

Down the hall, the doorman had been chatting with another guest. When he heard her voice, he straightened up and looked their way. The two men hesitated just a second too long. Shireen slipped out of the elevator before they could block her and ran in the direction of the doorman.

Her quick thinking, along with the doorman's help, prevented a potential disaster. She hurried to call a former student and now ally who owed her a favor. Johnny Stewart was not only a trusted friend but also the mayor of Weavers Valley. It was a mountain town bordering North Carolina and Tennessee. Johnny assured Shireen that Pelin and Kemal would be welcome in his town until things cleared up in New York.

Pelin gripped her phone tightly, her pulse quickening as she listened to Shireen's urgent voice.

"Go to Weavers Valley and ask for the mayor. Stay there until it's safe."

"*Safe…*" The word felt almost foreign to her now. Could a town in the mountains truly protect her from the long reach of her enemies?

Pelin glanced at Kemal, his grip on the steering wheel turning his knuckles white, his jaw clamped. He was trying to be her rock, but she knew he was just as anxious as she was.

"What did Shireen say?" he asked without taking his eyes off the road.

"She said to go to Weavers Valley. The mayor is an old friend of hers," Pelin replied, staring out at the blur of city lights fading behind them.

Kemal nodded, but the crease in his brow deepened. "That means they've already been sniffing around. If they showed up at Shireen's place, they know we're on the move."

Pelin swallowed hard. "They don't just want to scare me anymore, Kemal. This is something bigger. If they get their hands on me, I don't think I'll ever see daylight again."

The words felt like lead leaving her lips, each syllable heavy with truth. Kemal's fingers flexed around the steering wheel, his knuckles whitening. "That's not going to happen," he said firmly. "I won't let it."

— 30 —

Pelin's face lit up with a smile as she watched Kemal navigate the busy streets of Brooklyn in their rental car. It was his first time driving since they left Istanbul.

The city they were leaving was buzzing with the sounds of honking horns, blaring sirens, and people weaving in and out of traffic. In the rearview mirror, Kemal saw the tall skyline getting smaller behind them. He grinned and pressed the gas as they merged onto Interstate 95 South, ready to leave the chaos behind.

"The next rest stop is fifty-six miles away," Pelin reminded him, checking her phone. She had promised to update Shireen at every stop, as Shireen worried, especially since this was Pelin and Kemal's first road trip in America.

It was obvious that Shireen wasn't herself during their first call. Just moments after Pelin and Kemal left her place, two guys showed up looking for them.

"Are you okay?" Pelin's voice rose in panic as Shireen shared what happened.

Kemal tightened his grip on the steering wheel as he listened on speakerphone. He accidentally let the car drift onto the shoulder, sending vibrations through the vehicle. He quickly jerked it back onto the highway and glanced at Pelin. "What's going on?"

"She's okay, Kemal," Pelin said, though her expression told a different story. "I'll fill you in, but for now, just focus on the road."

Kemal pulled into the next rest stop and turned off the engine. Pelin turned to him. "Two guys came to Shireen's place asking for us. They said they were with Customs and Border Protection or something. But they weren't. They were Turkish agents."

A single tear rolled down her cheek as she felt sad that those men would come to her sister's home and threaten her.

Kemal almost choked before asking, "How's Shireen? Is she okay?"

Pelin's eyes filled with tears as she nodded. "She's safe but shaken. She got rid of them by saying we had already left for California. They even had photos of us from as recent as my speech at NYU."

Kemal gripped the steering wheel tight, his jaw tense. "It's a good thing that we left, if not they might have tracked us down too."

Pelin bit her lip, holding back tears. "What do we do? We can't just run forever."

Kemal took a deep breath to gather his thoughts. "We stick to the plan. We're driving to North Carolina, but we've got to be more careful."

"Tell me exactly what went down when they went to see Shireen," Kemal asked.

"The guys approached her in the lobby. The security guard got suspicious and stopped them. He wouldn't let them get to the elevator. Thank God he was there; otherwise, she wouldn't have made it to her apartment."

Kemal bit his lip and shook his head. "Yeah, thank God we weren't there."

Pelin nodded but felt uneasy about the whole thing. They had left Shireen alone, not thinking someone might come looking for them.

Shireen must have sensed Pelin's worry because she called again before they left the rest stop. This time, she sounded lighter and amused. "You should've seen them," she laughed. "Two guys in cheap suits, wearing Turkish flag pins, pretending to be U.S. immigration officers. What a joke."

Despite her worries, Pelin chuckled. "What if they come back?"

Shireen laughed too but then got serious. "I've got a plan if they show up again."

"A plan?" Pelin's eyes widened. She bounced her knees together, eager to hear what her sister had in mind.

"I already talked to the police. If those guys try anything again, they won't get far."

Pelin breathed a sigh of relief, glad to hear her sister had contacted the police.

"And listen," Shireen said, lowering her voice, "My friend, the one I told you about, he is reliable. He lives in a small town in North Carolina. We met five years ago when I started at NYU. He knows everything and is cool with taking you in until things chill out."

Pelin frowned. "How do you know we can trust him?"

Shireen paused, then chuckled. "Because he's the mayor of his town."

Kemal, who had been listening, raised an eyebrow. "The mayor? Isn't that the guy in charge of the village?"

"Yep," Shireen confirmed. "He's waiting for you in Weavers Valley. Just ask for him. He'll keep you safe."

Pelin held her stomach with one hand and exhaled slowly. Their road trip had taken an unexpected turn—one that could mean the difference between staying hidden and getting caught.

Kemal started the car again, and as they merged back onto the highway, Pelin felt grateful they had left the city when they did. What had once been a simple getaway was now more of an escape.

As they crossed from New York into New Jersey, the four-lane highway narrowed, and the landscape changed. Brooklyn's gray skyline gave way to rolling green fields, and dried wildflowers swayed in the breeze. This change was a nice relief for Pelin's nerves.

Their conversations shifted away from the two men and Shireen. With Erkin Ere, a Turkish pianist, playing smooth jazz on Spotify, their minds drifted back into memories. They reacted to the sights passing by. The music blended in with the changing scenery, creating a nice vibe that lifted their spirits after the call with Shireen. They were putting some distance between themselves and whoever was looking for them, finding a bit of relief from reality.

They laughed as they tried to pronounce the words and names on billboards—billboards were rare in Turkey.

Pelin reached over and placed her hand on Kemal's, giving him a small smile of reassurance. "We'll make it," she said softly. "Together."

* * *

Pelin scrolled through her phone for info about each historical monument and the unfamiliar town names they passed. Knowing Kemal loved trivia and history, she read aloud snippets about the towns and their attractions while he drove.

"Here's something," Pelin said, turning her phone toward him. "Washington, D.C. was laid out by a French architect who designed wide avenues to create sightlines to all the major monuments."

Kemal responded softly. "And here I thought the confusing street grid was just an accident."

She laughed. "Nope. It was supposed to be symbolic. The open spaces were for democracy, and grand views to inspire pride. Different from today."

Kemal nodded. "Makes sense. Power needs a good stage."

Pelin scrolled further, her smile fading a little. "It also says the city was built on a swamp. Literal, not just a political one."

She looked out at the big blue sky above them, which was a stark contrast to Manhattan's skyscrapers and cramped streets. Outside the city, there was space to breathe and think.

Looking down at her notebook, she began jotting down details of landscapes, emotions, and fleeting moments. One day she planned to write about this journey—the tension, the unknown, and how the road was leading her to meet a stranger who was waiting to save them.

Miles away from Delaware they finally saw the Welcome to Washington D.C. sign. Pelin sat up straighter as the tall Washington Monument came into view. The landscape was a big change from the busy streets of Brooklyn and Manhattan.

Kemal was blown away seeing the monuments and green spaces from the highway. "Look, there it is." Pelin's eyes lit up, her heart racing—not out of fear, but from seeing American history right in front of her. Her early American studies had taught her that the Washington Monument represented the nation's capital and honored its first president.

Pelin leaned over Kemal and snapped a photo. He couldn't slow down with all the cars speeding behind him, and she could hardly wait for him to get off the highway. She admired the city's simple yet classy designs, so different from New York's skyscrapers.

Kemal decided they'd find a place to crash for the night. "I've seen the monument in pictures and online so many times, but it's something else in person." His voice was calm, but another thought lingered: It doesn't compare to Istanbul.

Heavy traffic brought them to a stop. Sitting next to him, Pelin noticed a change in his expression; a frown crossed his face as he tapped his fingers on his knee. She could almost feel what he was thinking as he stared out the window, lost in thought.

"I'm sorry," Pelin said softly, her voice barely rising above the noise around them.

Kemal turned to her, surprised. "Sorry? For what?" he asked, his tone a mix of confusion and defensiveness.

Pelin could see how hard he was trying to hide his feelings, and she understood his struggle. She had seen that look before—the way his eyes seemed distant, lost somewhere far away.

Pelin hesitated, choosing her words carefully." I'm sorry for this. I hate that you had to leave your home and that you feel like you have to pretend you're okay."

He took a deep breath and let it out slowly. For a moment, he didn't say anything. She was right; he missed home more than he wanted to admit. No matter how hard he tried to push it aside, Istanbul was inside him—a city deeply rooted in his being, impossible to forget.

"Hey, Pelin, it's not your fault." He paused, his voice softening. "I'm really glad to be here. Seriously. Being with you and experiencing all of this is amazing. Look at that." He nodded toward the distant Lincoln Memorial. "I never thought I'd see this in person. But…" His words trailed off.

Not sure what else to say, he turned his head and stared out the window, trying to shake off memories of home.

Pelin reached out and touched his arm, wanting to comfort him.

"I just don't get why I keep feeling this way. I know what you're dealing with is way bigger than my feelings. I don't want to be selfish and add to your worries," Kemal said.

When the traffic cleared, Kemal drove a little further and pulled off the highway, stopping in front of a hotel. Pelin stepped out, looking at the dome of the Capitol building. She took a deep breath and took another look at the Capitol dome, it was overwhelming.

Pelin shielded her eyes from the bright sunset by putting her hand on her forehead. Kemal felt a bit better and put his arm around her shoulders, sharing the moment of seeing the Capitol for the first time together. Even though they weren't citizens and didn't have a green card, looking at the Capitol sparked a little hope inside them.

They'd come to America with no legal status or documents other than their visitor visas. Reuniting with her sister made Pelin want to stay longer. She hoped that she and Kemal could create a temporary life in this so-called land of opportunity.

As they walked toward the Capitol, they exchanged glances in silence. Police barricades blocked off parts of the walkways, keeping the public away from the building. These security measures were put in place after the building was damaged by insurrectionists during the chaos on January 6, 2021. Kemal wondered out loud, "How could something so reckless and chaotic happen in a country admired by millions around the world?"

After leaving the capital, they hopped on a shuttle to the Lincoln Memorial. It was a beautiful tribute to the 16th President of the U.S. Even though they weren't American citizens, they really respected the guy who freed the slaves. Being of African descent, they felt a strong connection to the history of slavery in America and the ongoing fight for justice and equality.

After checking into their hotel, they chilled on the patio with a cup of jasmine tea, watching the sun set behind the Capitol's dome, turning the sky into a beautiful mix of orange, gray, and blue.

Pelin was wiped out from all the walking and adventures of the day. After a shower, she quickly crashed. Kemal was happy to see her finally getting a full day without any chaos or worries.

He thought about how the road trip had been a great idea for both of them. Before going to bed, he checked out the route they'd take to North Carolina, wondering what was in store. Whatever it was, he remembered the smile on Pelin's face when she said, "We are in this together."

Before sunrise, Pelin and Kemal were back on the road, heading south with no clear idea of what awaited them. Their destination: Weavers Valley. According to the road atlas, it was a hidden jewel—though whether that meant charm, mystery, or something else entirely, they had yet to find out.

Kemal kept his eyes fixed on the twisting road, that winded deeper into the forest. He sensed Pelin was getting carsick--driving in mountains tended to have that effect. He told her, "We should make it there sometime around noon, providing the traffic remains light,"

Scooping a spoonful of blueberry yogurt she had picked up back at the hotel, she said, "You don't have to rush to get there. I'll be okay. We can still enjoy the sights along the way,"

Kemal felt good about how Pelin was handling her first road trip in America so far.

Halfway through their journey, Pelin opened her eyes wider as Kemal crossed into North Carolina from Virginia. "I need a brief break," said Kemal. He exited the highway onto the last rest stop a few miles before the Tennessee border.

"And I need a break from my thoughts," said Pelin, as they approached the rest area. As soon as Kemal stopped the car, they got out and a breathtaking view of a deep and dense valley below greeted them. Pelin stretched her arms skyward while Kemal bent over and touched his toes. They both experienced an instant relief of stress as they took in the beauty of their surroundings.

The endless stretch of forest and the clear blue sky captivated Pelin as she looked out at the Great Smoky Mountains. She recalled her studies from her days back in university about the east coast of America. "It's a beautiful sight, but these are hills, nothing compared to the Ararat mountains we have back in Turkey," Kemal told her.

"You've got to stop comparing America to Turkey, Kemal. It's impossible to do," she said.

"There's no other place for me to compare it to," Kemal said, as he observed a couple and their small black and white dog emerging from a nearby walking trail. Inspired by their presence, he suggested they take a walk themselves. He had been longing to reconnect with the countryside after a couple of years of city living.

Kemal secured their belongings in the car's trunk, and they set off on foot, walking down the thick wooden steps built into the steep slopes of the hill. As they descended, the trail transitioned into a smooth paved path. It led towards a signpost showing the direction of the Pigeon River. It was a quarter of a mile ahead. "Shall we go farther?" Kemal asked, with his curiosity growing.

As they continued, they came across hikers with backpacks and walking sticks. The sound of a dog barking in the distance added to the sounds of nature that they were hearing. The scent of damp leaves and decaying wood filled the air, a reminder that the forest changes with the seasons. Pelin removed her jacket, tying it around her waist as they moved from the shady spots to the sunny clearings, where tall dry stems of wildflowers stood bent over.

Stopping in his tracks, Kemal pointed out two deer grazing on the hillside and a massive flow of water cascading down a steep cliff. "It's called a waterfall," Pelin remarked with a smile that quickly faded. The closer to the waterfall they got, they could feel the strong vibrations of the rushing water beneath their feet. Despite Pelin's previous request not to compare, he couldn't help but reminisce about the natural beauty of his homeland.

Pelin froze in her tracks. Her senses were on high alert. She raised her index finger to her lips; and placed the other on Kemal's shoulder. "Quiet, she whispered, and without saying another word, she listened to the crinkling of leaves. "I think someone is coming up behind us." Pelin look left and right, as if she was searching for an escape route.

"Relax, Kemal told her, with a calm voice. "It's probably just a squirrel or a deer. Remember, we're in the middle of nowhere."

"No, Kemal," she whispered, "Animals do not talk. These are voices. I can hear them getting closer."

Pelin's hypervigilance persisted, causing her to lose interest in their surroundings and yearning to return to the safety of the car.

Kemal turned and looked behind him to see what it was that had gotten her all upset. "Seriously, Pelin? We're on a hiking trail. We are not the only ones out here, and no one is out here coming to get us. You see, it's only two joggers. Everywhere we go, we're going to run into people. What do you think are the odds of someone searching for us in this vast forest?"

Kemal's question reminded her of their surroundings and a life that she had better get used to. But while out in the forest, she remained unconvinced. She ran over and stood behind a large tree, just in case Kemal was mistaken about who was behind them.

As they approached a sign showing that Weavers Valley was five miles ahead on the trail, Pelin insisted they turn back and return to the car. "First, let's take a selfie with the waterfall as a backdrop," Kemal suggested, attempting to lighten the mood as they retraced their steps.

When they emerged from the forest and back to the car, a cargo truck driver with binoculars stood looking down at the valley below, his longish gray hair ruffled by the breeze. "Isn't it beautiful?" the trucker asked Kemal. Kemal glanced back at the peaceful scene, still thinking about the occasional walks he would take back in his homeland, wondering to himself if he would ever see it again. "It's nice to see," Kemal responded politely with a smile. He was reluctant to have a conversation with a stranger. Especially in a place that he and Pelin had not intended on coming to. They ended up there only because, during their phone conversation, Shireen persuaded Pelin to go ahead with the plan.

Once they reach Weavers Valley, Shireen had faith that they would be safe, thanks to her friend providing them a place to stay for a while.

The trucker, with the binoculars hanging around his neck, sat on the edge of a picnic table looking down at the valley below. "This is one of my favorite spots," he said. "No matter how many times I drive this stretch of highway, I make it a point to stop here. There's something about this place."

Kemal struggled to understand more than a few words the trucker said, because of the man's thick southern drawl. To make matters worse, the highway was nearby, with the noise of trucks honking and cars zooming by didn't help.

Pelin was no longer interested in what the trucker had to say, and she didn't feel comfortable standing there. One thing she thought about was all the unexplainable horror stories that she read in novels and newspapers about some truck drivers in America's south. She walked over and stood by the car door, making facial gestures towards Kemal, urging him to cut his conversation short.

"That was a first," Kemal said as he ducked his head to get back into the car. Pelin looked at him, questioning, "Why did you have a chat with that stranger in the middle of nowhere? He could have been one of those freaks that I read about. And from the way you were looking at him, I don't think you understood anything he said."

Kemal chuckled, knowing Pelin was right about him not understanding a single word that the grizzled trucker said.

Still smiling, he told Pelin he too had read somewhere that few truckers had been known to be serial killers.

"It's called southern hospitality; I supposed they used greeting strangers as a way of luring their victims in.

Much different from in large cities, where people looked right through each other," Kemal added. "Not so different from Turkey. Small-town people there are friendly too."

Pelin smiled. Kemal always found a way to make her feel at ease when she became worried. "I'll try to remember that. In fact, I'll make a note of it. Maybe I could use it in my writing one day."

"I guess we should try to fit in as long as we're here," Kemal said, reaching for his phone on the console. He noticed the missed call, showing country code 212. (Turkey) He inhaled, wondering who it could be.

"Excuse me, I need to hit the men's room before we go." He hurried to the men's room, phone in hand. Seeing the familiar code stirred something between hope and dread, and he got an uneasy feeling in his stomach. Out here, exposed and miles from nowhere, calling back felt risky. Whoever it was would have to wait until they were in a safe place off the road.

When he returned to the car, Pelin was on the phone, with the speaker turned on. "It's Shireen," she told Kemal as he sat and readjusted the car seat.

"I'm sorry to bother you," Shireen said, "But I believe the call I received from Kemal's boss was important."

Kemal's heart skipped a beat as he heard Shireen say it was his boss. So that's who the missed call was from, he was thinking.

"Kemal's editor requested Kemal get in contact with him. He says he has important information to share with both of you," Shireen told her sister. His boss demanding to speak with him, and citing a crucial matter that couldn't wait? That left Kemal reeling with a mixture of anticipation and dread, as he thought about what could be so important that his boss called Shireen.

"I think what he has to say is serious," said Shireen. After Kemal's boss discovered that Kemal's number had changed, he looked up Kemal's emergency contacts and found Shireen's number. He pleaded with her for Kemal's new number. He needed to talk to him today and the matter couldn't wait.

Shireen continued, "Kemal's boss had information about someone looking for the two of you and wanted to warn you."

Holding the phone tightly in her hand, Pelin turned with a deep expression on her face. "She says it's serious. Did you see a number on your phone? That was from your boss, the bureau chief of the Istanbul *Times*," she told Kemal.

With his shoulders slumped, Kemal took a deep breath, his mind racing with possibilities. "Okay, I'm listening; let me have it. What's going on?"

Shireen recounted every detail of her conversation. "Whoever contacted the bureau chief already knew that the two of you were in America and were driving south. Supposedly, there are Turkish agents in New York who looked over your travel documents and found some kind of discrepancy. For those reasons, the man told Kemal's boss that Pelin and Kemal needed to be contacted.

Kemal placed both hands on the steering wheel. "Red flag or not," he said in a firm voice. "I'm not going anywhere near the Turkish embassy. That would be walking straight into their hands."

Pelin sat in the passenger seat with her arms crossed and looking out of the window. "This is so screwed up. We came here to get away. To see America and to get a break from all the chaos. Now there are people back in Istanbul and New York harassing my sister and your boss," said Pelin.

Kemal shook his head and squeezed Pelin's hand in reassurance. "You're right, we took this road trip to get away from our problems. Let's take it one step at a time. First, let's discover Weavers Valley and introduce ourselves to Shireen's friend the mayor."

Shireen had mentioned her friend from college, the mayor of a small town, once or twice before. But what Pelin mostly recalled was the story she told about there being only one family of color living in that little town. And the two teenage brothers, one named Luis, the other Diego. They both worked in a small café there and lived with their mom. Otherwise, the town was lily-white. That worried her.

"It should be interesting," Kemal said.

With that understanding between the two of them, Kemal turned, pushed the ignition button, and started the car. They took the side road, ready to face whatever challenges lay ahead in this unfamiliar place, nestled at the border of North Carolina and Tennessee.

— **32** —

Just before they reached Weavers Valley, Kemal noticed flashing lights in the rearview mirror. A local police cruiser was behind them. The siren was loud and signaling for him to stop. Kemal eased the car to the shoulder. A burly officer approached; his eyes were hidden behind sunglasses. The New York plates caught his attention instantly, and he became suspicious. In a town like this, outsiders from the city were rarely welcomed.

"Mind telling me what brings you folks down here?" the officer asked.

Kemal struggled to get his words out. His fingers trembled as he handed over his international driver's license. Images popped up in his head. He thought about American TV news, the numerous times he saw men of color pulled from cars, and pressed down to the asphalt, sometimes never getting up again. He forced himself to breathe, and to be polite.

The officer ordered both he and Pelin out. Minutes seemed like hours as he and his partner tore through the car, looking through bags and compartments, invading their privacy. Pelin stood stiffly nearby, with her arms crossed tightly, while Kemal could barely keep his legs steady.

At last, the search came up empty. The officer gave a tight nod, but no apology before saying, "You're free to go."

Kemal slid back into the driver's seat, still shaking from what just happened. They drove off in silence, but he kept looking in the rearview mirror long after the police cruiser disappeared.

Kemal drove past the big faded blue sign welcoming them to Weavers Valley, North Carolina. Cruising down the main street, he felt a mix of unease and curiosity. He couldn't help but chuckle when he saw the yellow sun painted on the sign, which boasted a population of 563. That was a stark contrast to the bustling cities they had just left behind. "Looks like there are fewer folks here than in Shireen's New York apartment building."

Pelin didn't find the comparison funny at all and was nervous about how they might be received. As they drove deeper into the sleepy town, she took in the sights. A few people walked down the narrow street, that were lined with colorful fall flower baskets hanging from lampposts. The houses were a mix of grand Southern mansions and some with peeling paint and sagging porches. Everything she saw unsettled her.

"It'll be different, Pelin. But different can be good too." Even as he said it, Kemal's voice revealed some uncertainty. Pelin sat up straight and squeezed her knees together. "What if we made a mistake?" Weavers Valley didn't look like what she had expected. She wondered why her sister would recommend a place like this.

Her anxiety grew when Kemal parked in front of a barbershop, its candy-striped pole a throwback to another era in America. The moment he stepped out of the car, he felt out of place. His eyes locked onto two men sitting on a nearby bench, smoking. They looked as foreign to him as he and Pelin must have looked to them. One man wore a John Deere cap, while the other sported a bold red "Make America Great Again" hat. Kemal felt a prickle of unease crawl up his spine, knowing what that red hat stood for. When the men exchanged glances with him and Pelin, she felt her stomach tighten.

"We'll take it step by step," Kemal muttered under his breath, more to himself than to her.

They walked up to a café with a bright blue awning over a large glass window, where the name Weavers Valley Café was etched. The name was simple, but Pelin struggled to pronounce it; her "R" rolled in a way that revealed her Istanbul roots. She looked around for a menu but didn't see one posted. Kemal kept glancing over his shoulder, worried about the two men who were watching them.

Pelin hesitated, her voice barely above a whisper when she suggested, "Let's see what this place has." She stepped aside, wanting Kemal to take the lead.

"Are you sure?" he asked.

Pelin smiled and tucked a few loose strands of hair under her hijab. "I've been feeling uncomfortable a lot lately, and it doesn't change anything," she replied, a bit sharply.

Kemal pushed the glass door open. As soon as they walked in, the noise and chatter surrounded them. All eyes turned to them, except for one guy with his face buried in the Wall Street Journal. Feeling uncomfortable, Pelin and Kemal stood awkwardly near the entrance. A young server with a blond ponytail approached them. "Y'all aren't from around here, are you?" she asked, her voice thick with a Southern drawl. She asked a few questions as she led them to a dark booth near the restrooms, which made Pelin even more uneasy. She looked at Kemal, and he knew what was coming.

"Excuse me," Pelin said in her best English, "I'd rather sit at one of those tables instead?" She pointed to three empty tables catching bits of sunshine. "I don't want to sit so close to the restrooms."

The server wiped a drop of sweat from her brow with the cloth from her apron. Her patience was wearing thin. Pelin's refusal to take the booth didn't sit well with her. "We reserve those tables in the front for our regular customers. If you don't mind waiting a few more minutes, I can see what else is available."

Putting them by the restroom felt like a deliberate way to keep them separate from everyone else. With no other restaurants in town, they had no choice. Pelin looked directly into the waitress's eyes. "That's fine; we'll leave." Her voice was calm, but her eyes were steady. Kemal placed a hand on Pelin's arm, knowing she wouldn't let anyone treat her differently.

As they turned to leave, they could feel all eyes still on them. Then someone muttered the word "Foreigners."

The café went quiet, quieter than normal. The guy with the newspaper lowered it to check out the silence. He noticed Pelin and Kemal walking away from the server toward the door. From their looks, he figured they were Shireen's family. Besides, who else could they be? Shireen had given him a perfect description of them.

"Hey, excuse me, wait!" The mayor stood up and called out. "Please, before you go, there's plenty of room at my table," he said. Pelin figured it was Shireen's friend calling them. Shireen had given an accurate description of him too. She and Kemal felt relieved to see someone show a bit of kindness and gladly accepted his invitation.

"You must be Mrs. Pelin Korkmaz, and you must be Mr. Kemal Korkmaz." Pelin smiled with relief after the treatment they had just received. "Yes, Shireen is my sister."

"I'm Johnny, Johnny Stewart, and I've been expecting you." Johnny pulled a chair out for Pelin and waved for Kemal to sit at another one. He started the conversation by apologizing for the seating arrangement and continued welcoming them to Weavers Valley.

"So, you're in charge of this town?" Pelin wasn't sure if that was the right way to ask, nor how to address someone of his position.

"Oh no, please call me Johnny. It's a small town, so the job isn't too tough." The mayor entertained them with stories about Weavers Valley, its history, the people, and how he became mayor. He told them he'd "sort of inherited" the job from a childhood mentor; Johnny had grown up in Weavers Valley.

Settled at the table with Mayor Stewart, Kemal and Pelin felt their worries ease. They tried to ignore the curious glances and focused instead on the mayor's stories and the menu. Once the waitress saw that the mayor had invited Pelin and Kemal to sit at his table, her whole demeanor changed. She stopped wiping tables and hurried over to where they sat. "Sorry, we get pretty busy around here on the weekends," she said, "especially during the cooler seasons," trying to make conversation.

It wasn't every day that strangers came into the café, at least not ones who looked like Pelin and Kemal, especially not dressed in stylish clothes and gold jewelry.

Not catching everything that was said, Pelin nodded as if she understood. The waitress did her best to make up for her poor hospitality earlier. She apologized to them, especially to the mayor, because she had a crush on him since she learned he was single.

The waitress's thick Southern drawl and Pelin's accented English tangled together as Pelin tried to order something as simple as coffee and pastries. It felt strange for Pelin. She had spoken to English-speaking audiences in various countries, and they seemed to understand her just fine.

The whispers grew louder when other customers saw their mayor inviting the two foreigners to sit with him, something he rarely did for anyone unless it was for business.

Kemal kept up the act, pretending everything was cool—until he glanced out the window. He saw the same two men he had noticed when they first arrived. The men were focused on the rental car. Kemal couldn't hear what they were saying; he just saw one of them pointing at the orange New York license plates. Their fascination with the car was obvious. The other guy was bold enough to peek through the window and muttered something to his buddy before walking inside the café.

Finally, Pelin and Kemal settled into their chairs at the table with Johnny. Still, Pelin kept looking around the diner, trying to get a good mental picture of the place. She felt uneasy and curious about her surroundings and the people staring at them.

Pelin saw the look on Kemal's face. He didn't have to say anything; she already knew what he was thinking. She reached under the table and patted his knee. "Calm down," she told him. "We could get similar treatment in restaurants in Istanbul, London, or New York, given the rise of racism and nationalism everywhere."

She trusted Shireen's judgment in recommending Weavers Valley. Shireen had said it was a safe place, a spot she had visited twice since being in the U.S.

"Excuse me, could you speak a little slower?" Pelin asked, her voice carrying to those nearby. "Oh no, you didn't," whispered Kemal. He dropped his head, not surprised by his wife's actions. The waitress struggled to understand Pelin too. They spent a few moments going back and forth as Pelin tried to explain that she just wanted coffee and a pastry. She was unable to make sense of anything else on the menu.

"People here are not used to a lot of visitors," Johnny said, stirring his coffee absentmindedly. "Most outsiders only stop at the rest stop on the interstate and keep moving on." He gave Pelin and Kemal a pointed look, watching their reactions. "But don't let that scare you off. Weavers Valley isn't a bad place it just takes time for folks around here to warm up."

Kemal nodded, but his eyes kept flickering toward the window. The man in the red hat had stepped inside. He didn't approach their table, but he lingered near the counter, pretending to browse the selection of pies in the glass display. His glances were deliberate, he stood up straight. He wasn't just curious—he was watching them.

Pelin pretended not to notice, but she felt the tension in Kemal's arm as she rested her hand on his forearm. "So, Johnny," she said, keeping her tone light, "Shireen said you and she go way back?"

Johnny chuckled. "We sure do. That sister of yours has a way of getting under people's skin and making them like it." Johnny talked about meeting Shireen when they both were attending Columbia College in New York, before he came back home to run his family's business . . . and eventually get elected mayor. Johnny mentioned that Shireen had spent some time in Weavers Valley and had helped Johnny set up a library for the town.

"She's done a lot of good around here. That's why when she told me you two were coming, I figured I'd make sure you got a proper welcome."

Kemal leaned forward. "Proper welcome?" His voice was even, but Pelin could hear the doubt laced through it.

Johnny sighed, rubbing the back of his neck. "Let's just say, not everyone sees it that way." His looked briefly toward the man at the counter, who was now engaged in a low conversation with the waitress. She nodded once, then disappeared into the kitchen. "But like I said, give it time."

The bell over the door jingled as another customer walked in. Kemal and Pelin turned instinctively, their muscles tightening. It was the other man—the one in the John Deere cap. He didn't even try to hide the way he looked at them. He walked past their table, slow and deliberate, and took a seat nearby.

— 33 —

Five months had slipped by since Pelin and Kemal had sought refuge in Weavers Valley, living in a small cabin that had once belonged to the mayor's father. They were waiting for the turmoil in New York to cool down. The cozy cabin offered a sense of security amid the uncertainty that had become their constant concern.

The townspeople's reactions to their presence were mixed. Some welcomed them with caution and kindness, offering warm smiles and neighborly gestures. Others kept a noticeable distance, their reservations evident in sneaky looks and hushed conversations. The chief of police maintained a cool demeanor, keeping a constant watch on them and ordering his three other officers to do the same.

Tension hung heavily in the air. Whispers of discontent seemed to echo through the quiet streets. Rumors spread through every alley and corner, casting shadows of doubt and unease over the town. Despite the tense atmosphere, Pelin and Kemal found solace in the simplicity of their new surroundings, hoping that in time the townspeople would come to accept their presence.

The chief claimed to have spotted Pelin's name on an international wanted list, accusing her of treason by the Turkish government. After contacting the SBI and FBI, he learned that Pelin and Kemal had been granted green cards and were in the U.S. legally. To calm the chief's worries, they informed him that they had been tracking Pelin and Kemal since their arrival in America. However, due to the chief's dislike of immigrants, whether legal or illegal, he kept this information to himself and started a rumor that spread like wildfire.

While at the diner with a group of locals, the chief leaned back in his chair and lowered his voice, just loud enough for those at nearby tables to hear. "You didn't hear this from me," he said with a sly grin, "but those two foreigners have a history back in their country. Word is, they're running from the law. Those two Muslims are terrorists."

The chief walked out of the diner, satisfied with the storm he had unleashed. By the time the sun set, the rumors had reached every corner of town. The story grew legs, sprouting new details with each retelling. The mayor knew the truth and regretted the damage caused by these lies. To calm the citizens' nerves, he called a town hall meeting and read a copy of the unclassified email that the chief had received from the FBI. Before the meeting, he warned Pelin about the spreading rumors and advised her to simply ignore them. None of the rumors had reached her or Kemal; they kept to themselves and tried to live a peaceful isolated life in Weavers Valley.

Being isolated from the community and not receiving harassment from the Turkish authorities was a welcome change. During their time there, Pelin completed her latest project and sent copies to both her editor and agent. In her work, she maintained her campaign criticizing the authoritarian government; this even gained momentum as she wrote.

Pelin wanted the world to hear her truth and expose the injustices of her government. Her goal was to reveal their true nature. She became bolder in her criticisms of the strict regime, writing with urgency. Her words caught the attention of people in far-off places, as well as some within the government.

She accused her government of targeting those with differing opinions. The regime was dismantling everything that once gave people hope. Free speech was becoming a relic of the past, replaced by fear and whispers. Social welfare programs and jobs programs—lifelines for the vulnerable—were being gutted. This was disguised as "reform."

"This isn't reform," Pelin wrote in one of her essays. "It's a calculated power grab meant to silence opposition and reshape our future into something unrecognizable."

When Pelin took breaks from her work, she focused on her surroundings. She loved the quiet space along the Pigeon River where it flows into the Broad River before entering Tennessee. She and Kemal often spent their free time walking along the banks, enjoying the sights and sounds of nature.

Sometimes, while strolling along the river, they would receive unfriendly stares from people they passed. However, this form of harassment was much less than what they had experienced in the past, so they didn't let it bother them.

Kemal was happy that Pelin had returned to her true self and adjusted to her secluded new life. He still worried about her safety, especially as she began writing more openly to expose her government. He too had concerns about what was happening to his country. And he wasn't completely silent about these concerns. He was just much more subdued than Pelin was. She confronted the system defiantly.

Kemal took a more cautious approach. Sometimes he used the pen name 'Omer Kaya' when publishing critiques of his government. This pseudonym allowed him to express himself freely without the fear of retribution. Maintaining his anonymity allowed a quieter form of rebellion. His layers of stories, opinions, and insights had been the heartbeat of the newspaper for over a decade. Though no one knew his face, the power of his words reached far beyond what he had ever imagined.

Pelin missed her home but accepted her life as it was. She immersed herself in her work, stepping away only to watch the river rush past their cabin. Its steady roar reminded her of the Bosporus and the bustling life she had left behind in Istanbul. These were things she had never noticed until she arrived in the small town of Weavers Valley. The ordinary experiences she once took for granted—cafés, crowded streets, and the hum of city life—were now painful memories. She often wondered what would have become of her had she stayed in Istanbul.

As she stared out the cabin window, she contemplated whether this was what exile felt like. Pelin faced the reality that returning home was not possible, at least not anytime soon. However, she still had Kemal. On Fridays, their day of prayer, they spent the entire day together, either relaxing or taking walks by the river.

In contrast to Pelin, Kemal missed everything about their home. He struggled more to adapt to the mountain town and his new reality. His daily prayers gave him hope that one day things would change, and they could return to Istanbul. He used to love going out to teahouses with friends and other journalists. In this mountain town, he felt he had nothing in common with anyone.

The mayor invited Pelin and Kemal to his home for tea one Sunday around noon. As they sat in the mayor's living room, he poured a second round of tea. That's when Pelin surprised both Kemal and the mayor with a question. "That vacant property across from the cabin," she asked with a spark in her eye, "Who owns it?"

Her question was met with a moment of silence. Because of the question, the mayor could sense that tension was growing between Pelin and Kemal and hesitated before answering.

"It's a beautiful spot, don't you think, Kemal?" she added, her excitement evident in a way he hadn't seen in a while. Pelin had been gazing out the window for days at the vacant property, imagining herself and Kemal as its owners.

"Oh yes, that place once belonged to two men who decided to move out west to San Francisco. It's been vacant ever since," the mayor replied.

Kemal found himself at a loss for words, distracted by Pelin's question. "Pelin, this isn't the right time to consider buying property, especially with the way things are going for us," he said, hoping she would take the hint and refrain from asking more questions about the property. He didn't like the idea of discussing business matters in the presence of a stranger.

Pelin was not concerned about privacy; her focus was solely on the property. There was no one else in town she could ask about it. She envisioned the property as the perfect place for her and Kemal to live until their lives returned to normal. With her head hung low, disappointment washed over her at Kemal's reaction. It seemed he did not share her interest in settling down. "Isn't this why we came to America? To rekindle our lives?" she asked.

The mayor excused himself to take a phone call. Kemal sat on the edge of his chair, looking at Pelin. "This isn't the time to buy property, given our circumstances," he said, while concealing his true feelings. He held his frustration in until they returned to the cabin.

The walk back to the cabin was almost silent and filled with tension. Once inside, Kemal opened up. "How could you bring that up in front of a stranger?" he demanded, pacing the room. He struggled to keep calm. "Pelin, you know I want what's best for us, but how can we commit to a property when our future is so uncertain? Our safety and our very lives are at stake here."

Pelin met his anger head-on. "And how long are we supposed to keep running? We have been on the run for so long, always looking over our shoulders. At some point, we must stop. This place could be a temporary refuge for us."

From the look in her eyes, he could see she was serious. The willpower she possessed was the same determination that had convinced him to follow her into exile.

The clock interrupted them, chiming twelve times to signal that midnight had arrived, yet they were still discussing the property. They both recognized their need for a safe haven. Kemal changed his tone, taking a moment to reflect.

"Alright," he grumbled. He was tired from the long day and wanted to end the discussion and get some rest.

"Let's at least agree to look at the property; seeing it won't hurt," Pelin said. "Once we see it, we can weigh our options."

She smiled as Kemal stepped into the shower. "Thank you, Kemal. Whatever decision we make, we will make it together and cautiously."

As he stepped into the shower, the tension he had built up washed away down the drain.

* * *

Pelin could hardly wait for sunrise to call the real estate agent in Maggie Valley and arrange a showing. She was excited about the prospect of their own home, despite its isolated location. Sitting on the edge of the bed, she thought about the challenges they might face in a small town, even if their stay was intended to be temporary. Acknowledging that they were the only foreigners in Weavers Valley, they realized many residents would be suspicious of who they were and why they were there.

Despite the challenges they faced, the opportunity to purchase this place was too good for Pelin to pass up. She believed the seclusion of the property would provide the privacy and security she needed. It would not only be a home but also a place where she could write, and Kemal could continue his work with the newspaper from afar. This was a chance for both of them to return to a normal life.

Kemal couldn't stop thinking about what it would be like to live in a small town like Weavers Valley for a long time. He knew that many residents did not want him there, and he didn't particularly want to be there either. He longed to spend his life among people who understood him and shared his worldview. In a place like Weavers Valley, with so few people and so many barriers, he realized that this was unlikely.

He wasn't sure if buying a house there was the right decision. Yet, for Pelin's sake, he had gone along with it. As he looked out at his surroundings, he dreaded going to bed and waking up, day after day, in a place where everyone was suspicious of himself and Pelin.

Standing on the wraparound porch, Pelin felt a sense of peace wash over her. It was official: the large two-story white brick house, surrounded by a beautiful garden of native wildflowers, now belonged to her and Kemal.

Just across the street, amidst the tall trees, flowed the winding Pigeon River. Pelin envisioned their new home as a sanctuary where she could move forward and leave the chaos of the outside world behind. She settled into the rocking chair and whispered to herself, "Finally, this is it. This is a fresh start."

This was the same property she had admired from the cabin's window since the day she and Kemal moved in. Now it was theirs—a symbol of the new beginning they had longed for, a crucial first step toward restoring a sense of normalcy after enduring several emotional storms.

Kemal sat beside her, gazing over the property with a blend of happiness and concern. He couldn't shake the feeling of apprehension about their impulsive decision to buy the house. Not wanting to dampen Pelin's joy, he kept his worries to himself, but inside, he feared they had made a hasty and irreversible choice.

Sensing Kemal's unease, Pelin reached over and squeezed his hand, a silent gesture of reassurance that they would be okay.

As they sat on the porch, enjoying their newly purchased home, they were unaware that their actions had sparked a firestorm of suspicion. The news unsettled some townsfolk, and within hours, despite the cold wind, dozens gathered outside city hall to protest Pelin and Kemal's presence in Weavers Valley. The uproar intensified upon learning that the couple had purchased the large house and the 15 acres of forest on the edge of town.

The property closing took place behind closed doors at city hall, as there were no banks in Weavers Valley. A real estate attorney had driven over from Maggie Valley with a briefcase full of documents to finalize the deal. The real estate agency and the bank involved had agreed to accept full payment and had no issue with the location of the closing. However, the crowd outside city hall was outraged by the lack of transparency; no private business deal had ever been conducted behind closed doors there before.

The crowd shouted and waved signs opposing the sale. Simultaneously, a petition was being drafted, demanding that the chief of police arrest Pelin and Kemal and hand them over to the FBI.

The mayor saw no reason for legal action against the Korkmaz. His refusal to intervene led some to accuse him of being complicit, suggesting he was being paid to ignore the situation. The disapproval of the mayor's involvement in a private business deal had some calling for his resignation.

A sudden hush fell over the crowd when Pelin, Kemal, and Mayor Stewart emerged from behind closed doors, the sale complete. All eyes were on them. Pelin carried a thick manila envelope stuffed with papers under her arm. One woman, dressed in tight jeans and cowboy boots, approached the police chief overseeing the crowd.

"You can't let them get away with this!" she shouted. "We don't want terrorists living here!"

Another protester near the chief yelled, "Are you really going to let this happen?"

As Pelin walked arm in arm with Kemal and the mayor across the street, she noticed the hostile stares directed at her. She was not surprised by the woman's outburst; she had encountered worse since fleeing her homeland. Forcing a smile, she ignored the jeers and insults, focusing instead on getting away from the crowd.

Kemal did the same, glancing around anxiously, hoping no one would attempt any physical harm.

The real estate agent ran behind them seeking one final signature that needed to remain in town hall. The agent smiled as the last document was signed.

"Congratulations," she said, relieved to see them as the new owners.

"The property is officially yours." Pelin forced a polite smile and gathered her folder, feeling the weight of more than just paperwork settled onto her shoulders.

Kemal brushed his hand lightly against hers, assuring her she'd be okay. As they walked across the street the mood shifted sharply.

A small crowd had gathered, signs raised, faces grim. "Go back where you came from!" someone yelled.

Others muttered, shouted, hurled accusations. Ugly words that Pelin had never heard before nor did she understand. She tightened her grip on the folder. Her heart was hammering in her chest. Kemal kept his arm around her, guiding her steadily toward their car.

"Don't look at them," he murmured. "Just keep walking."

The quiet streets of Weavers Valley were now thick with tension. "Can you believe the mayor allowed his office to be used to plan a terrorist attack against us?" a man told the crowd.

"Lord, they're going to kill us all," a woman overheard him tell her friend, who stood beside her in protest.

"And the mayor is helping them do it," the friend replied.

A middle-aged woman stepped up to the police chief and bluntly urged, "Arrest them! Your job as police chief is to keep us safe!" She believed the story that Pelin and Kemal were terrorists. Like the others, she was upset that they owned the largest house and tract of land in the valley.

"We don't want any terrorists living in our town or our country," another woman cried out, catching Pelin's and the mayor's attention.

Pelin smiled, ignoring the shouts directed at her. Kemal smiled too, but he kept scanning the area.

Pelin suggested to Kemal and the mayor that they go into the diner to celebrate their new homeownership with a cup of tea and to escape the hostility outside.

Inside the diner, the atmosphere was little different from outside. While conversations were quieter, they were far from silent. The mayor sat at his regular table with Pelin and Kemal, having tea. He tuned out the chatter until someone muttered, "Foreigners don't belong here. Eventually, they'll try to take over our town."

He had heard enough and felt torn between his duty to serve the citizens of Weavers Valley and his empathy for Pelin and Kemal. His role now was to bridge the gap between them and the townsfolk. The mayor walked to the center of the diner and spoke up. "This is nonsense," he declared in a tone he had never used before.

The diner fell silent; everyone listened. "Weavers Valley has always prided itself on being a welcoming place," the mayor told those present, looking directly at the chief of police as he spoke. "If we don't open up to the outside world, we will die in poverty. We need people like the Korkmaz who want to live here and invest in our community."

Mayor Stewart reminded the property owners in Weavers Valley that they had all gone through the same process of closing.

"It doesn't matter where your closing was held; it's official county and town business. All your tax and property documents are filed across the street in the town hall. Throughout this country, closings are held in town halls and city offices every business day."

The crowd was stunned by the mayor's words, with some nodding in agreement. "I suggest you end your protest, accept what has happened, and go home."

Most of those inside the diner heeded the mayor's advice and left. As his words reached those outside, some protesters began to disperse as well.

The mayor's job was now to bridge the gap between Pelin and Kemal and the townsfolk.

Pelin looked around at the customers whose eyes were fixed on her, and she remained steady. She had faced worse in the past two years—being forced to leave her homeland, spending nights on the run—but she never expected to encounter such hostility in the quiet hills of North Carolina.

"I don't believe we can trust our mayor anymore," Kemal overheard an outspoken woman at the table behind him say to the two men with her. "He's allowed terrorists to buy that spot at the end of town." She wondered out loud if the mayor had lost his mind.

Pelin tried to ignore the hostile stares that she and Kemal were getting. She was hoping that the citizens of the town would see them for who they truly were. Pelin could not understand how anyone could judge them without even speaking one word to them. That welcoming that she was hoping for now seemed impossible. She heard hate.

Kemal's jaw tightened as he heard some nearby whispered accusations. His shoulders rigid, the muscles in his neck were filled with tension. Though he maintained a calm exterior, his eyes continuously darted to the door, mapping escape routes—a habit he'd developed since fleeing Istanbul. Under the table, his right foot tapped an anxious rhythm against the wood floor.

The mayor's unexpected defense had momentarily stunned the room into silence, but as some patrons walked out and the room it became less noisy, still the atmosphere remained charged with a lot of suspicion that lingered in the air like the smell of burnt coffee.

Outside, the late afternoon sun cast long shadows across Main Street as protesters dispersed in small clusters, their signs lowered but their voices still carrying through the thin glass of the diner windows.

Pelin caught the eye of an elderly woman at the counter, who offered a hesitant nod—it was the first gesture of real acceptance from a town resident that they'd received since arriving in Weavers Valley. The simple acknowledgment sent an unexpected wave of emotion through her chest, a tightness that threatened tears she refused to shed in public.

Despite everything, a small flame of hope flickered within her. This place, unwelcoming as it might be, was still somewhere they could call home, even if temporarily. Perhaps, with time, they could transform it into a space that truly felt like home.

The bell above the diner door jingled as three men entered, their heavy boots scraping against the floor. A hush fell over those inside. The tallest of the three, wearing a worn leather jacket and a dark expression etched into his weathered face, looked directly at Kemal.

"You folks picked the wrong town," he said, his voice deliberately could be heard across the diner. "Weavers Valley ain't for everybody."

Kemal's hand found Pelin's under the table, squeezing it tightly. The mayor stood up, placing himself between their table and the newcomers.

"That's enough, Frank," the mayor said firmly. "They've purchased property legally, just like your father did forty years ago."

Frank's nostrils flared. "My father was born in this country. These people—"

"These people," Pelin interrupted, rising slowly to her feet, "have names. I am Pelin. This is my husband, Kemal." Her voice remained steady despite the trembling in her knees. "We were journalists in Istanbul. We reported on corruption, and it became unsafe for us to stay."

Silence fell inside the diner, broken only by the ticking of the wall clock and the soft hiss of the coffee machine.

"We don't want trouble," Kemal added, standing beside his wife. "We just want peace."

The mayor exhaled slowly. "Baby steps," he whispered to Kemal and Pelin. "This town changes slowly, but it does change."

—35—

Days after Pelin and Kemal settled into their home, a storm was brewing, down at city hall. Citizens of Weavers Valley were calling for a town hall meeting. The subject? Whether the chief of police should step in, as many in the town expressed bitter disappointment in the mayor, the state, and the federal government for what they called a failure to act.

They wanted Pelin and Kemal kicked out of their quiet town, arrested and deported

Like all residents, Pelin and Kemal received a flyer in their mailbox. It was an invitation informing them of the community forum. They knew exactly what it was about.

The committee behind the meeting had one goal; measure public sentiment about "foreigners" and use that as justification to expel them. The petition was blunt. The flyer was worse. Mayor Stewart showed up knowing the night would go badly for him. He expected harsh words, but he didn't expect a riot.

He stood at the crossroads of tradition and change, caught between the familiar flow of a sleepy valley town and the unsettling winds of transformation blowing in from beyond the mountains.

Since Pelin and Kemal's arrival, whispers had grown into accusations. There were claims that the mayor was supporting terrorism simply by supporting Muslims. Once again, he found himself balancing on a tightrope stretched between progress and prejudice.

Before the gavel could drop, a woman stood and shouted directly in his face.

"We don't want terrorists living here!"

Disappointed but not surprised, Mayor Stewart sat down in his chair, as he alone was up against a town in turmoil. He had hoped to welcome people from across the country and the world. But convincing Weavers Valley that diversity wasn't a threat but an opportunity? That was proving to be a tougher sell than he ever imagined.

"They're not the kind of people we want here!" the woman shouted again with her voice in a high piercing tone. "That Muslim lady says she's a writer. Well, we don't want her or her books neither."

The woman was one of many who read nothing beyond the church bulletin and the diner's gossip bulletin. She held on to the idea that America and Weavers Valley were a Christian nation. Most of the room nodded in agreement. Only the mayor and one or two others held back.

Then, from the back of the room came a worn and weathered voice "Now, just hold on a minute here," said Calvin Reynolds.

Heads turned. Everyone in town knew Calvin. At ninety-seven, he was the oldest living resident, a fixture in the community. He stood with the aid of a cane carved decades ago by his own hands. His frame stooped. His voice trembled—not just with age, but with the conviction of a man who'd lived long enough to know when something wasn't right.

"These folks haven't done a thing to deserve this," he said, with his eyes scanning the room. "They've been here nearly a year, and we don't even know them yet." His words hung in the air, and they were impossible to ignore.

"That's the point!" the woman snapped, her voice sharp in contrast. "We don't know them, and we don't want to!"

The mayor yelled "Silence, silence." He was desperate to restore order. He urged the crowd to avoid inflammatory language, and to give Pelin and Kemal a fair chance. He challenged them to set aside their fear, to recognize the misinformation feeding their hatred.

Back at home, Pelin sat on her porch in a wooden rocking chair, looking over the land she and Kemal had bought. She didn't allow the distant noise of the shouting from the square to bother her. She didn't need to hear the details of what they were saying. She already knew.

She had learned a long time ago not to flinch at noise. "Let them fight among themselves," she said to Kemal. "In time, they'll get to know us. Their fears will fade."

She had lived through enough pain and prejudice to know that people often fear what they refuse to understand. The recent publication of her novel had only sharpened the divide between admiration and resentment. But Pelin refused to be defined by ignorance.

She was more than their fears. More than their assumptions. She was a writer. A fighter. A dreamer. She would not be judged by the color of her skin, her faith, or the labels others attempted to put on her.

She remembered the quiet meeting she'd had with Mayor Stewart. They talked about investing in Weavers Valley. A coffee shop for Kemal. A bookstore for her. She hadn't told Kemal. He believed in traditional roles, that a man should lead, that doing outside business was not for women, especially not without a husband's approval. He still hadn't come to terms with her meeting with Emir.

From inside, Kemal peeked through the curtains. He heard the shouting all the way from town square and as it got louder, he burst out the door to where Pelin sat, "They're probably calling us terrorists!" he yelled, frustrated." And I bet they think we're here to take their jobs or blow up the town!"

"Let them rant, Kemal," Pelin said calmly." We won't stoop to their level."

But even as she said it, a bit of anxiety got caught up in her chest. She hoped Mayor Stewart would hold his ground and calm the town before things spiraled.

Back at City Hall, the mayor stood before a crowd that had stopped listening. Every time he opened his mouth; he was shouted down. He wiped his forehead with a handkerchief and waved it like a white flag, though he hadn't given up the fight.

"We don't want any Muslims in our town!" a burly man bellowed. "They're terrorists!"

The mayor's career was on the line. Still, he stood tall.

"Our newest residents are quiet people who ask for nothing more than peace," he said.

"I challenge each of you to step out from the shadows of fear. Get to know them."

He pointed down the road toward Pelin and Kemal's house.

"Read her writings. Talk to them. You might find something you didn't expect."

For a moment, the crowd fell silent.

"You expect us to welcome them?" the angry woman said, folding her arms. "With everything going on in the world? We're supposed to pretend they're just like us?"

"Have they given you any reason to believe they're not?" Calvin Reynolds asked again, stepping forward. "You're afraid of a story you made up in your head. That story is not the truth."

"You're damn right I'm afraid! And you should be too!"

Mayor Stewart's voice cut through the noise. "Fear is not an excuse for cruelty."

Back on her porch, Pelin's hands gripped the arms of her chair. Her heart pounded, as she tried to remain calm. She reminded herself that she'd survived worse than this.

Kemal paced behind her, restless. "We can't just sit here," he said.

Pelin turned to him, steady and still. "If we leave now, we prove them right."

"And if we stay?" said Kemal.

She took a deep breath and held it for a few moments. "Then we prove them wrong."

Back at City Hall, the mayor watched the crowd. Some faces still burned with anger, but others were shifting around looking confused. They seemed to be unsure.

To the mayor, uncertainty was better than hatred. It meant there was still hope.

Maybe, just maybe, a way forward existed.

—36—

The town hall meeting was one for the history books. Never had there been a meeting, assembly, or congregation in Weavers Valley that generated such a storm of heated arguments. When the dust settled, John Stewart remained the mayor, and Pelin and Kemal were still living at the property on the end of Main Street.

Although calm had seemingly returned, tension simmered beneath the surface. Mayor Stewart's handling of the Pelin and Kemal affair left his opponents seething. They were more determined than ever to see that they got their way. They saw the mayor's defense of the newcomers as the final straw, fueling their resolve to see him removed from office.

His plea urging the townsfolk to welcome the Korkmaz as neighbors seemed to have fallen on deaf ears. It did nothing to quell the suspicion of those opposed to Pelin and Kemal living there.

Whether for or against them, nearly everyone in Weavers Valley had an opinion about the two foreigners residing in the most expensive house southwest of Asheville. The farmers, who worked hard every day to earn a living, were astonished that someone who simply wrote newspaper articles and books could afford to purchase that much property.

Due to the high price the owners had initially asked, the house sat vacant for years, accumulating some decay around the exterior. However, after extensive renovations—including fresh paint, new windows, and beautiful gardens—the place looked stunning. With people walking by and stopping to look, Pelin felt as if their home was under constant surveillance. Each time she glanced out the window, someone stood outside the front gate, staring at the house.

Pelin often watched the neighborhood kids ride by on their bikes. Initially, they zoomed past as if afraid of the people who lived there. Over time, some kids gathered the courage to stop. From behind the curtains, Pelin could see the curiosity on their faces as they stared at the house like it was a puzzle. She imagined their parents had warned them, saying things like "Muslims are not like us," and advising them to stay away.

It was during the late-night hours that she felt uneasy. That was when she would hear voices coming from the direction of the front gate. Once, she woke in the early hours of the morning and looked out to see a man standing there. She became worried when she noticed him looking through binoculars at the house.

Kemal tried not to worry, but he was troubled by the same faces reappearing day after day. After everything he and Pelin had been through in the last couple of years, he decided to call Mayor Stewart.

He wanted to voice his concerns about the people gathering outside the gate of his home. The mayor reassured him that the group of onlookers was simply curious. Although sometimes noisy, they meant no harm. They were just stopping to look after years of passing by while the home remained vacant, especially now that it had been transformed into a beautiful residence.

"I think it's normal for those passing by to stop and look," said the mayor. Although he understood Kemal had reason to be concerned, he tried to convince him not to worry.

"Okay, if you say so, but I'm just not used to people hanging around my home. This is our home, not a zoo," Kemal added.

Kemal ended the call and decided to go for a walk before it got too late.

In the end, the mayor said he would ask the police chief to keep an eye out for any irregular or unlawful activity that might occur.

Still, the mayor's response did little to calm the unease Kemal felt about the people lingering outside his gate.

Later that evening, as the sun settled behind the mountains, casting shades of purple and orange over the western sky of Weavers Valley, Pelin stood by the bay window once again. Looking out the window had become routine for her. It was her way of reassuring herself that everything was normal.

With the temperature dropping, the crowd of onlookers had dwindled. She hoped it was because the people of Weavers Valley had seen enough and were getting used to her and Kemal living there.

Pelin took one last look out the window, and out of the corner of her eye, she spotted a man at the gate. He wore a long black trench coat and a dark knitted ski cap, seemingly fumbling with something in his backpack. He pulled out a pair of binoculars, raised them to his eyes, and looked toward the house.

Pelin staggered backward and pressed herself against the wall, easing behind the curtain to avoid being seen. It was particularly unsettling because she was home alone. Seeing someone outside the gate with binoculars trained in her direction was frightening. Unable to identify the person, she quickly drew the curtains shut.

Her first instinct was to call Kemal, but after several attempts, the call went to his voicemail, leaving her a nervous wreck. Pelin moved through the first floor, locking the doors and windows and double-checking each latch.

As the hours passed, Pelin kept glancing at her phone, hoping for a response to her calls or texts. She grew increasingly worried; by this time, Kemal had always returned from his evening walk.

With no choice but to sit and wait for his return, she picked up a magazine from the coffee table, hoping it would distract her from Kemal's absence. He sometimes took a longer route home, stopping to rest now and then, but he always made it back before this.

Though Pelin tried to read the magazine, her fingertips trembled each time she turned a page. Tears welled in her eyes, and the article did little to calm her nerves. Every rustle of leaves outside made her pray it was Kemal walking through the gate. Again, she looked at her phone, but there was still no response.

A tweak of nausea formed in her stomach, and tension built inside her. She kept telling herself that Kemal was simply sitting on a bench, watching the sunset as he usually did, but she couldn't understand why he wasn't answering his phone.

Finally, the sun sank below the horizon. Unable to sit still, Pelin made herself a cup of tea, still trying to calm her nerves. The tea kettle's soft whistle and the steam billowing from the pot provided a temporary relief from the silence. But when she glanced at the kitchen wall clock, her anxiety intensified. Where is Kemal? The question circled her mind like a trapped bird.

As she poured the steaming water over the chamomile tea leaves, the aroma that filled the kitchen offered respite from her worries. With the warm cup of tea in her hands, she returned to the living room window, hoping for any sign of Kemal. There was none. She noticed that the man who had sent shivers down her spine earlier had left. Unable to endure the wait any longer, she wrapped herself in a thick blanket and stepped out onto the porch.

From the porch she called out Kemal's name several times, but there was no answer. Her worry was compounded by a simmering anger that he was not answering his phone.

Pelin felt she had run out of options. The only sound, apart from the noisy refrigerator, was her heartbeat. Her frayed nerves and desperation drove her to pick up her phone and call the only person Kemal occasionally talked to: Mayor Stewart.

As soon as the mayor answered, Pelin launched into a frantic conversation without greeting him or introducing herself. From the tone of her voice, the mayor sensed that something was wrong. He also noted that Pelin had never called him before.

"It's Kemal! He hasn't returned home, and he's not answering his phone!" The mayor could hear her sobs and almost feel her frustration through the line. "Tell me, how long has he been gone?" he asked.

"For hours!" Pelin shouted. Immediately, she felt ashamed; her voice was choking with tears. "I'm so sorry, but I didn't know who else to call."

"It's alright, Pelin," he said, doing his best to remain calm. "I'll call the police chief right away and ask him to have the officer patrolling the town look for him."

He promised to stay on top of the matter until he received word that Kemal had returned home safely. However, his words offered little comfort to the growing pain in Pelin's heart.

Pelin clutched her phone tightly after ending the call with Mayor Stewart. His reassurances made little difference. She stood motionless in the living room. The warm tea in her cup had gone cold. The silence in the house was almost unbearable, and each creak of the old wooden floors drove her crazy.

She looked out the window one last time. The porch light flickered, casting shadows across the empty front yard. Just as she turned away, something caught her eye: a dark shape at the edge of the gate. Her pulse quickened as she peered closer, her heart racing.

The figure remained still, motionless and staring, but it wasn't Kemal. Her stomach churned as the man raised his hand and pointed directly at her.

Pelin's scream caught in her throat as she stumbled backward, fumbling for her phone. Before she could call the mayor back, the porch light flickered once, twice, and then went out.

A cold sweat broke across her skin. Her instincts screamed at her to run, to hide, but she was frozen. The seconds stretched into eternity as she debated her next move. Her first thought was to grab a knife from the kitchen, but would that even matter if whoever was outside decided to come in?

Her fingers fumbled across her phone screen as she tried to redial the mayor. Her heart pounded so loudly that she barely heard the dial tone.

"Come on, pick up," she whispered, her voice barely audible.

Then, the figure moved.

Pelin's pulse spiked as she watched him step away from the gate, disappearing into the darkness beyond the property line. Had he left? Was he coming around to the back? Her mind raced with possibilities, each worse than the last.

Just then, a noise broke the silence: a soft but deliberate knock at the front door.

Pelin gasped, nearly dropping her phone. Her whole body stiffened as she turned toward the door, barely daring to breathe. Whoever was out there wasn't trying to break in—not yet. They wanted her to answer.

The knock came again, louder this time.

Her thumb hovered over the emergency dial button. She should call the police. She should scream. But her voice was stuck in her throat, trapped beneath the weight of fear. Then, just as suddenly as it had begun, the knocking stopped. Silence swept through the house once more. Pelin's breath was shallow, her body stiffen as she strained to listen. Nothing. Minutes passed—maybe more. Then, footsteps. Not at the door. Not at the gate. But somewhere behind the house.

A chill slithered down Pelin's spine. Finally, the phone in her hand buzzed. She nearly jumped out of her skin before glancing down and seeing it was Mayor Stewart. She answered immediately, whispering frantically, "Someone is outside my house!"

"Stay inside. Lock the doors. I'm on my way."

But before Pelin could respond, something slammed against the back door.

She screamed.

Kemal had just watched the end of one of the most astonishing sunsets he had ever seen, a view unlike any he'd encountered in his travels. The sky was painted with fiery oranges and purples that bled across the horizon. As the sun dipped behind the mountains, Kemal rose from the bench, still focused on the harmony of colors in the western sky. He had taken only a few steps when a voice from behind startled him.

"Turn around and put your hands up over your head!" the stranger yelled.

The command was delivered with a distinct Southern twang that Kemal could not understand. He was confused and had no idea why the man was yelling at him. He turned around, his hands buried in the pockets of his dark hoodie. He saw a familiar face—one of the first he had encountered upon arriving in Weavers Valley.

The man was holding a handgun, pointed directly at Kemal. "You should've left this town when you had the chance. Now it's too late!" the man yelled.

Meanwhile, Mayor Stewart reached Pelin. He sat trying to calm her nerves, by reassuring her that everything will work out.

Moments later he heard loud noise coming from the town's square. He walked out on the porch and saw from a distance that the loyal patrons and other customers had rushed outside. They were climbing into their pickup trucks and jeeps to follow the wail of sirens leaving the fire and police station.

While Mayor Stewart was standing and looking out the window, his phone buzzed. It was a call from the chief of police. "There has been a shooting on the trail, and Kemal was involved."

Mayor Stewart's heart sank at the news. The details were scarce. Without hesitation, Stewart turned and looked at Pelin standing by the other window. Her hands still wrapped around a cold cup of tea. She noticed the confused look on his face, as he gestured for her to grab her coat.

"Pelin, come with me. We have little time."

"It's Kemal, isn't it? He's in trouble," she said.

She reached for her purse.

"Don't worry about your appearance. We have to go." With a voice just above a whisper, she asked, "What happened?"

The mayor struggled to find the right words. With dread and regret, he broke the news that Kemal had been shot, and they were airlifting him to Haywood Medical Center in Asheville. The drive to the hospital was tense and silent, except for the occasional instructions bellowing from his GPS.

As soon as they entered the building, they rushed down the ER hallway. Pelin took deep breaths to calm herself. Before reaching the room, a team of doctors met them outside the door with somber faces. "We did everything we could, but…" Their words were heavy and incomplete, confirming what Pelin had been fearing during the ride.

Her knees buckled, and she collapsed into Mayor Stewart's arms. Throughout the ER, her screams echoed. Gently, the mayor lowered her into a wheelchair provided by a quick-thinking doctor. When she came to, she found herself in a family lounge. The walls felt as if they were closing in, and she was drowning in grief.

The mayor explained what had happened as best he could. Despite her overwhelming sorrow, Pelin requested to be taken to the room where Kemal lay. She needed to see him one last time. Tears streamed down her cheeks, and her intense pain was evident.

Despite the people surrounding her, she felt an overwhelming sense of isolation.

An evangelical chaplain entered the room and sensed her distress. He knelt before her, showing his respect. He extended his hand toward hers and spoke with a deep Southern drawl, soft yet annoying. "Now is the time to pray," said the chaplain.

Out of instinct, Pelin snatched her hand back, crossing her arms tightly against her chest. She made direct eye contact with the chaplain and said, "I'd rather not. My prayers are always private, between me and my God."

Her actions puzzled the chaplain. He stood but kept his eyes on her, taking a few steps backward. Without saying another word, he turned and left the room. The room was silent until the door clicked shut. That was when Pelin thought of Shireen.

Pelin's hands shook as she frantically patted the pockets of her coat, beginning to gasp in panic. "My phone… where's my phone?" Her voice was weak and filled with disbelief. The grief was too heavy to bear alone; she needed to hear Shireen's voice, to feel her sister's presence amid the chaos.

Kemal was gone, shot and killed in this Southern Mountain town. The words echoed in her head—relentless, unbearable. She had to share this pain before it consumed her whole. The mayor, who'd stayed with her, handed her the phone; she had left it on the seat in his pickup.

As she prepared to call Shireen, she noticed a message from Kemal's phone. She played the message, but it wasn't Kemal. Instead, a man spoke with a crackling voice and a thick Southern twang coming through the speaker. "You think this is over, but it ain't," the caller said.

Pelin froze. She said nothing, allowing the message to continue playing. "He's gone, but that's just the beginning. You are next on the list."

She gripped her phone as she had the night she received a threatening call two years earlier in Istanbul. Panic surged within her, and she stood abruptly. The chair scraped against the tile floor, making a loud sound. Mayor Stewart rushed back into the room, alarmed. "What is it?" he asked sharply.

Pelin struggled to form her words. "Someone… they just text. They said this isn't over." Fear welled up inside her.

"Let me see your phone," Mayor Stewart said, this time speaking as an investigating official. He knew the message needed to be preserved as evidence for the investigation into Kemal's murder.

Pelin thrust the phone into his hands, her hands trembling. She sat back down and wiped away the tears from her cheeks.

Handing her back her phone, the mayor said, "Whatever you do, don't erase that message."

Her voice trembled as she tapped her sister's number into the phone. Each button press felt heavier than the last. Pelin cleared her throat and waited for the only person in the world with whom she could share her grief to answer.

"Pelin," Shireen said, recognizing her name lighting up on her phone.

"Shireen, it's me."

Shireen knew something terrible had happened.

There was a moment of silence shared between them. Shireen braced herself as Pelin tried to find her voice. The words Shireen anticipated were almost unnecessary; she could sense what her sister was about to say.

"It's Kemal," Pelin told her sister, explaining as best she could that someone had shot and killed him. Shireen promised to catch the next flight to Asheville. Despite her emotions, she quickly packed a few things and called a taxi.

As soon as the phone call ended, Pelin realized she needed to make another call. She had to call Tarek. She regretted having to inform him of the sad news about his brother. Again, she braced herself to share the tragic news.

"I'm not sure how long it will take, but I will be there as soon as I can get an emergency B-2 visa to travel to the States," Tarek told

Pelin, his voice breaking as the reality set in. "I'm familiar with the process because a dear friend had a similar situation."

Not only had Tarek lost a brother, but he had also lost his best friend, a victim of America's ongoing gun violence.

As soon as Pelin ended the call with Tarek, the mayor said to her, "Maybe you should go away for a while. It's not safe here for you right now."

"Go? Where would I go?" she asked, raising her voice.

"Some place safe, until we know more about what's going on. Maybe back to New York."

"NO! I will not leave Kemal's body in the hands of strangers," Pelin said, glancing back toward his body covered with a white sheet.

"Besides, my sister and Kemal's brother are on their way here," she told the mayor as she wiped away one last tear from her cheek.

"I will stay here until I find out who took Kemal's life and why."

Mayor Stewart exhaled, rubbing his hands over his tired face. He knew Pelin wouldn't be easily persuaded to leave, but every instinct told him that staying in Weavers Valley could get her killed.

"Pelin," he said carefully but urgently, "I understand why you want to stay. I do. But listen to me—whoever did this is still out there. That message you got. That wasn't just a warning. It was a promise."

Pelin pressed her lips together tightly. The fire in her eyes was stronger than her grief. "Then let them come. I'm not running."

The mayor sighed. "You don't understand. This isn't Istanbul, or London, or New York. This is a place where folks handle things their own way, and right now, some of them think they already have."

Before Pelin could respond, the door to the waiting room swung open. A police officer entered, his uniform damp from the cold mountain air outside. The police chief stood beside him, his expression grave.

"Pelin Korkmaz?" the chief asked, looking for confirmation.

"Yes." Her voice was hoarse.

"I need to ask you a few questions."

Mayor Stewart stepped forward. "Chief, can this wait? She just lost her husband."

—38—

The midday clouds cast a dark shadow over Weavers Valley, creating an atmosphere of mourning and disarray in the wake of Kemal's murder. This tragedy marked the first murder in the town in a century, leaving citizens divided in their reactions. Some believed that God had brought this catastrophe upon the community, opposing the presence of Pelin and Kemal. Others expressed sympathy for the loss, arguing it was absurd to think God would permit such violence against humanity.

"It was pure evil," declared Calvin Reynolds from the diner's counter, his voice quivering with conviction. The murmurs around him fell silent as his words resonated in the small community. However, it remained too soon to determine the exact cause of Kemal's death or who was responsible. The town buzzed with speculation, with each person offering their own theories, fueled by fear and uncertainty. "Speaking first and thinking second has always been a problem for some folks around here," Calvin told those who were gathered in the crowd, eager to learn who had fired the fatal shot.

He looked around the room, spotting those who nodded in agreement. Their faces seemed to be full of worry. Mayor Stewart refrained from engaging in the gossip swirling in the diner; he had other priorities. He felt Pelin needed support and was determined to be there for her. That's why he had volunteered to meet Shireen at the airport and drive her to Weavers Valley.

He'd driven to Asheville to meet her. "Shireen," he called out over the noise in the busy terminal as he spotted her coming through the arrival gate. He waved his hand, trying to catch her attention in the sea of travelers.

She set her bags down and hurried past the security line when she saw Johnny waving and calling her name. She wrapped her arms around him, sinking into the warmth of his embrace, which felt comforting after her long and bumpy flight down the East Coast. "Johnny, thank you for being there for Pelin," Shireen said, her voice trembling. He held her tight for a moment, unsure of what to say. "It's the least I can do," he replied, his mind focused on the task ahead: comforting Pelin and managing the town's affairs.

"How is she holding up?" Shireen asked quietly as they walked toward the terminal exit. It was difficult hearing her over the airport's noise. "She's been through a lot," he replied, his face grave.

He looked into Shireen's red eyes as she told him, "She's strong, but this has taken a toll on her."

The drive back to Weavers Valley was mostly silent, both lost in their thoughts as the weight of Kemal being killed bore down on them. The mayor parked the car in the driveway and watched as Shireen rushed up the walkway to be with her grieving sister. The porch, usually the most inviting part of the home, now felt like a place where sorrow had taken up a permanent residence. Pelin stood there with red-rimmed eyes, swollen from hours of crying. Without a word, they fell into each other's arms, their embrace a silent testament to their shared grief.

Mayor Stewart remained by his car, hands in his pockets, allowing the sisters a moment of privacy. He could almost feel their sorrow; the cool breeze did little to ease the heaviness in his heart. Finally, Shireen whispered "sorry" in Pelin's ear, tears streaming down her cheeks. "I got here as fast as I could." Pelin nodded, unable to speak through her sobs, grateful for her sister's comfort and their reunion, even under such tragic circumstances.

With a pained expression and cloudy eyes, Pelin found her voice. "He's really gone, Shireen. Kemal is gone." Her words hung heavily in the air, a stark reminder of their profound loss. Shireen patted her sister's back, offering what little solace she could. Not knowing where to look or what to say, she told Pelin, "I am here for you. I know how much you loved him."

Watching the two sisters was one of the hardest things Mayor Stewart had faced since becoming mayor. He hoped that in time, this family's pain would ease and that Pelin having her sister by her side would help her heal. Given the reason for Shireen's visit, it felt inappropriate to admire the beauty of Pelin's home. Instead, Shireen turned and waved for the mayor to join them. He walked slowly; his footsteps were heavy, with Kemal on his mind.

With a sad smile, Shireen thanked the mayor again for being there. Holding her sister's hand, Pelin opened the door for him to enter. "I really should be going; there are matters I need to attend to at the town hall." Before leaving, Mayor Stewart embraced each sister separately. "Thank you again," Pelin said. She was grateful for all he had done, and all he'd tried to do.

Shireen sank onto the sofa and exhaled deeply. She was exhausted from her travels and full of concern for her sister. Pelin sat across from her and suddenly realized she was in Kemal's favorite recliner. Sitting there felt comforting, almost like he was still present. She began to share with Shireen some details about that terrible day when Kemal was killed. Pelin recounted the crowds that had gathered outside the gate and the one individual who stood out with binoculars.

She smiled at Shireen. "It doesn't matter how tragic Kemal's death was; I believe he died peacefully in the end. I bet he experienced something spectacular in his final moments."

Shireen was confused, struggling to understand what exactly Pelin meant. She did not understand how Kemal could have died peacefully after being shot and lying on the ground bleeding to death from two severe gunshot wounds.

Pelin explained, "Kemal lived in harmony with nature, and being outdoors was spiritual for him." He usually returned home after his walks, sharing stories of something beautiful or different he had encountered. It seemed he always found something that connected him to the spiritual world. "Kemal's life ended just as he was starting to adjust to being here in Weavers Valley," Pelin described how supportive he had been. "He put his life on hold so I could continue my own."

Just as she was about to share more, Pelin noticed a car driving up to the end of the driveway and coming to a stop. She saw a man step out with two suitcases and ring the buzzer on the gate. "Pelin, it's me, Tarek," he said through the speaker.

He had traveled all the way from London to be with his sister-in-law during this difficult time. He was filled with a mix of anger and grief. Pelin pushed the buzzer, allowing Tarek to enter. She and Shireen stood on the porch as he hurried up to greet them.

They both thought that Tarek's journey from London must have been gloomy one. That much was true. Tarek spent the entire flight thinking about the Kemal's death.

Pelin and Shireen watched from the porch. Their own sorrow momentarily overshadowed by Tarek's pain. As he got closer, his face formed a heart-wrenching portrait of grief. His eyes were rimmed red, full of tears he refused to let fall. The dark rings beneath his eyes revealed his sleepless nights and endless hours of torment as he grappled with the reality of his brother's untimely death.

"Tarek, I am so sorry." Without saying it, Pelin sensed that Tarek might blame her for Kemal's death. Tarek stepped back and looked her in her eyes. "Tell me… tell me what happened. It's important that I know what happened to my brother."

Shireen placed her hand on Tarek's shoulder to comfort him. A few people walked by outside the gate. "Let's go inside where we can talk," she suggested. She offered Tarek a seat on the sofa, but he chose to stand after sitting for eight hours on the plane.

"Kemal came here to keep you safe. It was his way of supporting your campaign against book banning and all the other nonsense that the government was doing to suppress its citizens. Now he is gone," Tarek said, his voice heavy with emotion. "Killed in a place where he was supposed to be safe." He was not blaming Pelin for Kemal's untimely death, but his words affected her. She lowered her head, allowing a few tears to run down her face. Shireen handed her sister a couple of Kleenexes.

Feeling somewhat responsible, Pelin struggled to meet Tarek's gaze. "I don't know what happened, Tarek. The mayor said the chief and a few borrowed investigators from Maggie Valley had opened an investigation."

Tarek listened, but Pelin's mention of an investigation did little to ease his pain. A short while later, he took a seat on the sofa and calmly told Pelin and Shireen, "The more I think about it, I have to ask myself, how could my brother be happy in a place like this? A country where people carry guns and kill each other like it's nothing? This country is in a crisis right now, worse than our own."

Shireen placed her hand on Tarek's shoulder. "Tarek, we're all grieving. Being angry or saying hurtful things won't bring Kemal back." Tarek slumped deeper into the sofa, shoulders drooping. "You're right, Shireen. It's just so hard to believe he's gone. My brother... my only brother," he muttered between sobs. Pelin reached out and took Tarek's hand in hers. "Tarek, Kemal loved you. He talked about you all the time. He was so proud of you."

Tarek's eyes filled with tears as he took a deep breath to regain control. "I loved him too. And I want to know what happened to him. I want to know who did this and why. That's all."

Shireen nodded. "We all do, Tarek. And we'll find out, together. But right now, we need to be here for each other. Kemal would have wanted it this way."

Tarek looked at Pelin and Shireen, seeing the pain and grief on their faces. He knew they were right; they needed to support each other through this difficult time. Yet his anger simmered beneath the surface, waiting for the right moment to erupt. He silently vowed to himself that he would not rest until he uncovered the truth behind Kemal's death, no matter the cost.

$$—39—$$

Pelin was emotionally exhausted and had lost ten pounds since Kemal was murdered. She felt as if her body was sinking into the ground. She was doing her best to stay strong, but Kemal's death had taken a toll on her, both physically and mentally. Now that he was gone, she found herself in a world that seemed to grow darker by the moment.

Her fight for justice had cost them more than either of them could have ever imagined. Now, she faced a future where his presence was reduced to memories, a world where his voice no longer filled the quiet spaces of their home. And yet, she knew she couldn't afford to fall apart. Not now. The battle wasn't over.

As the world continued to turn and her heart continued to ache, it was a grim reminder that life goes on regardless of her own circumstances. Being without Kemal, her days felt empty, as if everything she had worked for was about to unravel. However, she knew she had to find the strength to keep going.

In the stillness of the night, Pelin whispered a prayer. She prayed that Kemal had found peace. She prayed for strength to face another day in a town that had turned its back on him. She prayed for her own strength to move forward without the love she had lost and the future that had been stolen from her. She was alone now in a town that did not or would not try to understand her.

As she prayed, she could almost feel Kemal's presence, his spirit reaching out to comfort her. It was as if she could even hear him saying, "Life seems unbearable now. But God will give you strength. You are at a low point, but you are not one who quits. Keep going."

Tears welled in her eyes. He had always believed in resilience. She had to believe in it too, though the world outside was cruel. Pelin knew the difficulty of her road. She would face challenges and obstacles that she would struggle to overcome. How would people perceive her in the world now?

She had long avoided social media, but even without looking at it, she knew what people were saying. She was being painted as the villain. A Muslim woman leading her husband to his death. A foreigner stirring trouble in a place she didn't belong.

It was almost midnight, and she knew she needed to get some rest. The next day would be challenging, requiring her to make another trip to Maggie Valley to review and sign Kemal's death certificate and arrange for his cremation.

She thought nothing else could hurt her. But then the letter arrived, with the envelope bearing the return address of the only church in Weavers Valley; her heart sank. She hesitated before opening it, her fingers trembling as she unfolded the crisp paper. The words written in the letter cut deep:

"We will not permit a Muslim service to be conducted within our sacred walls, nor will a Muslim memorial be welcomed in our town."

She read it again, and then again, her stomach twisting tighter each time. Each word struck a nerve, highlighting their cold prejudices against Muslims. She felt a wave of despair wash over her, the sting of rejection burning in her chest. The letter, signed by two of the church's elder members, was a stark reminder of the divisions that still ran deep, even in this quiet corner of the world. She clutched the paper, her knuckles white, as tears welled in her eyes. Their words indeed upset her, but she refused to let them break her spirit.

Maggie Valley echoed the same sentiment; no one was willing to hold a memorial for a Muslim. The news was not surprising to

Pelin, and she refused to let it bother her. Out of sympathy, Mayor Stewart had reached out to friends in Asheville. They were more open-minded and agreed to allow Pelin to hold a memorial service in one of their special event centers, if she so desired.

Despite the kind offer, Pelin had no plans for a memorial service. "Thank you, Mayor. It means a lot."

Asheville's kindness was a stark contrast to the coldness of Weavers Valley. It showed Pelin that even amid prejudice, support existed.

She and Kemal had made a promise to each other before leaving their homeland. If one of them were to die, the survivor would ensure that their ashes were returned to Istanbul and scattered into the Bosporus, without a memorial service. They both promised to uphold their agreement.

"I understand it is your desire to uphold your end of the agreement. But Pelin, there is no way you can carry Kemal's ashes back to Istanbul," said Tarek. He knew that authorities would arrest her immediately upon her return. She would likely face harsh consequences for protesting against the government.

Tarek took a deep breath. "I'll do it. I'll be the one to honor both your wishes. I'll take Kemal's ashes back to Istanbul and scatter them into the Bosporus."

Pelin placed her hand on Tarek's shoulder. "Tarek, I'm so sorry you have to go through this. It's a heavy task, and it shouldn't fall on you alone."

She knew how difficult this task would be for Tarek. And he knew how important it was to her, and other family members, that his brother's last wish be honored. It was something he would do, no matter how painful.

Along with all her worries, this was to be her first night sleeping in her own bed, alone. The first two nights after Kemal's death, she had slept in the guest bedroom. The thought of lying down without him was almost unbearable. But as soon as she climbed into bed, she reached for Kemal's pillow. When she squeezed it to her chest, all the tension left her body. Only thoughts of the good times they had shared entered her mind. She remembered the stories he would tell her almost nightly, while lying beside her until she drifted off to sleep. Each memory was a soothing comfort to her aching heart.

Pelin didn't feel alone, and she didn't feel the emptiness in the room. As she held the pillow, she fell asleep with a smile on her face.

In contrast, Tarek lay in the guest bedroom, thinking about how he would never see or speak with his brother again. The tears he had been holding back finally broke in the night's darkness. His grief was too much to bear. At one point, he felt as if he were suffocating, and at other moments, he felt the walls closing in around him. This was a night like he had never experienced before, even compared to the night he learned their father had died. He lay in the guest room and cried silently, his tears soaking the pillow.

He kept thinking about how his other family members must be feeling. Neither he nor they understood why Kemal would leave his home and his passion for his work. Why would he follow Pelin into exile, someone he had only been married to for a short while?

Some of his family members saw Pelin speaking out against the government as a mistake. To them, she was nothing but a trouble-maker who led their beloved Kemal down a path of danger, and ultimately to his death.

Tarek himself had been against their decision to leave for America. He remembered his reaction when they told him of their plans to leave the UK. Kemal's voice still rang in his ears when he said, "We're leaving for America." Kemal spoke with uncertainty when he broke the news to Tarek.

Tarek remembered how worried he became after Kemal shared the news. He recalled telling Kemal that it wasn't a good idea. "You shouldn't go. America isn't safe for those who look like us." But Kemal had made his decision, and nothing Tarek could do or say would change it. He never thought when Kemal said goodbye at the airport that it would be the last goodbye.

—40—

Pelin stood beside the airport's large glass wall, her palm pressed firmly against its cold surface as if she could reach through to the other side. Shireen and Mayor Stewart waited quietly nearby, offering silent and comforting support.

This was Pelin's final farewell to the love of her life. Tarek turned back once more, gently lifting the carefully wrapped urn in a final gesture of goodbye. Despite her heartbreak, Pelin felt solace in knowing Tarek was honoring his promise, to lay Kemal's ashes to rest in the gentle waters of the Bosporus Strait. That's where Kemal's spirit would await Pelin's own return someday.

After the somber drive from the airport, Pelin suggested stopping by the diner. She dreaded returning to the home that now felt empty without Kemal, but she was also curious. She wondered how the town would perceive her now that she was a widow.

Mayor Stewart expressed his hesitation immediately. "Are you sure about this? The diner can get rowdy around this time, of day." He warned her gently by recalling the insensitive remarks he'd overheard since Kemal's death. He feared Pelin facing such hostility so soon after her loss wouldn't be good for her.

But Shireen, intrigued by Pelin's stories of Weavers Valley, smiled confidently. "Don't worry. Sis and I can handle ourselves."

Without hesitation, the sisters entered the diner alongside the mayor, both dressed impeccably in traditional Arabic attire, their elegant hijabs drawing immediate attention. Conversations ceased abruptly, replaced by tense silence. Eyes tracked them closely as they took their seats at the mayor's usual reserved table.

Pelin felt the burning stares from nearby tables, particularly from a group of old-timers, whose murmured disapproval hung heavily in the air. An older man muttered loudly enough for them to hear, "Can't figure out what's gotten into our mayor lately."

Whispers escalated, stoking paranoia about more Muslims arriving to avenge Kemal's death. Although Pelin couldn't discern the exact words, their hostility was unmistakable. She held their gazes defiantly, refusing to show fear.

Mayor Stewart, troubled by the escalating tension, stirred his tea nervously. He glanced repeatedly toward the exit, ready to leave. Relief flooded his face when the waitress finally approached with the bill, but Pelin insisted on paying. She reached for the check, then froze as her eyes caught a hastily scribbled note attached to it:

"Isn't your business here done? Your husband is dead. It's best you leave. You've caused enough trouble."

Pelin's heartbeat quickened, anger boiling beneath her composed exterior. Instead of reacting visibly, she calmly pressed a generous twenty-dollar tip into the busboy's hand, ensuring everyone noticed.

The mayor's face frown with concern. He reached out cautiously. "May I see the note?"

Not knowing what to say, Pelin handed it over, and she continued to watch the nervous young busboy hurrying away. Moments later, the busboy returned discreetly, slipping another folded note into her hand. Shireen and the mayor exchanged anxious glances.

"What's going on?" Shireen whispered.

Without hesitation, Pelin grasped the busboy's wrist firmly. The diner went utterly silent as everyone watched with amazement.

"Who's behind these notes?" Pelin asked, in a calm but firm voice. "Tell me now."

The young man was nervous and looked around anxiously. "I'm off at seven," he whispered urgently, pulling his wrist free. "Meet me outside your gate, not here."

Mayor Stewart shook his head, confused. "I don't understand."

"Yes, at seven," Pelin confirmed firmly, her voice determined despite the turmoil inside.

"Pelin, this could be dangerous," Shireen warned softly, her eyes were filled with concern. "What if it's a trap?"

"Then it's a risk I must take," Pelin replied determined. "I need answers. They won't scare me away."

Mayor Stewart sighed. He was deeply troubled. "You shouldn't face this alone."

"I'm not alone," Pelin answered, looking at both him and Shireen. "I have you two with me."

Evening fell heavily as they returned home. The trio waited anxiously, lights dimmed, eyes fixed upon the gate from the shadowed living room. Shireen paced restlessly while Pelin sat nervously by the window. The clock struck eight, an hour beyond their agreed time. Pelin's anxiety deepened.

"Maybe he changed his mind," Shireen finally whispered, settling into the chair beside Pelin.

"Or someone stopped him," Mayor Stewart suggested as he stared out into the growing darkness.

As tension thickened, Pelin's eyes caught a shadow moving out by the gate. Before she could voice her suspicion, the buzzer at the gate rang sharply three times.

Shireen gasped, grabbing Mayor Stewart's arm instinctively.

"That's him," Pelin whispered firmly, heart pounding. "It has to be."

Pelin placed her hand on the door to walk outside.

"What do you think you're doing?" Shireen asked.

"I'm going out to meet with the waiter."

"Pelin, no. You can't go out there in the dark to meet him; we don't know what he might be up to," Shireen said, the mayor standing behind her murmuring agreement.

Mayor Stewart feared the waiter was leading Pelin into a trap, and the threatening notes Pelin had been receiving seemed to originate from someone inside the diner. Ever since the first note was passed, Stewart had kept a close eye on the waiter, but the identity of the person behind the threats remained a mystery. "One thing's certain, Pelin," the mayor said firmly. "The waiter didn't write those notes himself."

"You can watch me from the window," Pelin told Shireen and the mayor. "But you both wait here inside. I don't want to chase him off," she added as she grabbed her jacket and walked towards the gate.

"You made it," Pelin said, smiling but also nervous, trying her best not to make the waiter feel uncomfortable.

"Sorry I'm a little late; I had some extra cleaning before ending my shift. I also stopped by home and gave my mom the money you gave me for safekeeping."

"I'm sorry. My name is Pelin. What's yours?" she asked.

"I'm Luis, and I already know your name. I think everybody in town knows your name," Luis replied with a smile.

Unsure if he was alone, Pelin asked him to come inside, for her safety.

Shireen and the mayor had already gone to the kitchen, sitting at the counter within earshot but out of sight, giving Pelin and Luis a little privacy. Mayor Stewart continued to feel uncomfortable about Pelin meeting with Luis.

Pelin offered Luis a seat on the sofa. "Would you like something to drink?" she asked.

"No, thank you. I had plenty back at the diner." Before taking his seat, Luis looked around the room, checking to ensure they were alone. "You have a nice house," he said, pulling his hood down from his head.

"Thank you; I appreciate you coming," Pelin replied.

"You talk different, just like everybody in the diner says you do." This was Luis's first time speaking with someone who was Turkish.

Pelin looked at him with a warm smile, trying to make him feel comfortable.

"I suppose you want to know what happened that night."

"Yes, I need to know," Pelin responded.

Luis took a deep breath before telling his story. He began speaking slowly. "This is what I saw. I had just left work and was riding my bike down the trail. I heard voices ahead of me, just a few feet off the main trail. The voices were coming from the path leading into the forest."

Pelin moved closer to Luis, eager to hear his every word. "Go on, Luis. You are safe here."

Luis peeked around the corner toward the kitchen, where he heard movement. "It's my sister. She's in the kitchen, but it's okay. She's on our side."

"I was there that night," he said, his voice shaking. "I ran behind a tree after stopping my bike. I could see everything from there. When I saw a man with a gun, I knew there was going to be trouble."

Luis paused and took a moment to catch his breath. "I don't believe either the man wearing the green cap or Mr. Kemal saw me." He would witness a murder while hiding behind that tree. "I peeked and saw Mr. Duncan. Yes, that's the man's name. Mr. Duncan: I know for sure it was him because he always wears that old green John Deere cap. He was shouting and calling Mr. Kemal racist names, telling him he didn't belong here." Luis paused, looking around again, fearing he had said too much. He wasn't sure if he should stay or leave.

He wiped a tear from his eye with the sleeve of his hoodie. "It's okay, Luis; take a moment," Pelin said.

Mayor Stewart looked at Shireen and lifted a finger to his lips, wanting her to be as quiet as a mouse.

"Your husband acted as if he didn't understand. Then Mr. Duncan yelled at your husband again, asking him to stop and turn around with his hands up. But Mr. Kemal kept walking and placed his hand over his heart."

Luis took another deep breath as he continued his story. "I was so scared. I was just frozen. I couldn't move. I just took out my phone and started filming the whole thing."

"I'll show you the video. Here's Mr. Duncan yelling for Mr. Kemal to put his hands up. This is when Mr. Kemal turns around to face him." Luis pointed with his index finger as he described the events in the video. "Watch as that mean old man shoots your husband. He shoots him twice."

"You see it; it's right there." Luis pointed to himself, easing from behind the tree. Mr. Duncan looked around to see if anyone was nearby, then began walking at a fast pace, leaving Kemal lying in a pool of blood. Mr. Duncan took one more look, then walked back onto the path, back to the trail, and up the hill toward the rest stop near the Interstate.

Tears welled in Pelin's eyes, but she held them back, not wanting to cry in front of Luis. Instead, she reached for his hand. "You're so brave for coming here and sharing what you saw with me."

Stewart turned pale; he didn't know how to respond. "Yes, it's true that Mr. Duncan wears a green John Deere cap," the mayor whispered to Shireen, as if she knew who Mr. Duncan was. "The man who wore the green cap was mayor of this town for 12 years." Shocked, in disbelief, Stewart recalled how he once looked up to Mr. Duncan. He had wanted to follow Duncan's footsteps and become mayor himself. How could he do something like this?

As soon as she heard Luis say goodbye and the door close, Shireen rushed to her sister, leaving Stewart alone in the kitchen, trying to digest what he had just heard. Pelin was standing near the door. "Can you believe anyone could be so evil?" she asked her sister. What Pelin had just learned from Luis was, for her, the most difficult thing she had ever had to listen too.

Pelin sat with her arms wrapped around herself. Stewart stood still, fingers pressed against his lips, staring at the empty chair where Luis had sat moments before.

Finally, he turned to Shireen. "Where's my phone?" She pointed to the kitchen counter, still watching him with wary eyes. He picked it up, and scrolling for a number. Once he found it, he tapped it in and brought the phone to his ear.

"Who are you calling?" Shireen asked, sounding very curious.

He looked at her. "The State Bureau of Investigation."

Pelin sat up straighter. "Not the local police?"

"I can't," he said. "The police chief answers to the town council. And half of them owe Duncan favors or still think of him as the good old boy. No, this can't stay in town."

After a few rings a calm voice answered. "State Bureau. What's the nature of your emergency?"

Stewart spoke clearly. "This is Mayor John Stewart of Weavers Valley. I have a witness to a murder. A young man. He has video evidence. The suspect is a former elected official. Armed and Dangerous. And he is still walking free."

A pause.

"We'll need that video, sir," the agent replied. "Can you ensure the witness is safe?"

Stewart swallowed hard. "Not for long. That's why I'm calling you."

"I'll dispatch a team. Stay put."

He hung up and looked at the sisters. "I'm getting Luis protection. And the hunt is on for Duncan.

***

Pelin invited Luis to come back to visit. She wanted to keep in contact, hoping they could become friends. Luis promised her he would return. After what he had witnessed, Pelin felt he must need someone to talk to. "I think you coming back will help us both."

"His name is Luis, and he saw everything. He even showed me a video he recorded on his phone of the entire incident, including the man walking away after shooting Kemal."

Shireen and the mayor were in disbelief. "I remember that man was one of the first people we saw when we drove into town. And yes, he was wearing the green hat with an emblem of a yellow farm tractor on it," Pelin told the mayor and Shireen. "That was the same man I saw on Luis's phone."

Pelin felt as if the weight of the world was on her shoulders after hearing and seeing what happened to Kemal. She imagined Kemal standing there with his hand over his heart, knowing that was the moment he realized he was going to die. "With his hand over his heart, he was probably saying his last prayer to his God."

Shireen wrapped her arm around Pelin's shoulder, pulling her closer. She knew Pelin was in shock after hearing the details of Luis's story. Shireen was also struggling after hearing what Luis had told her sister.

Stewart leaned back on the sofa; his heavy thoughts harden. The pieces of the puzzle were falling into place.

Pelin walked over and looked down at the mayor, worry filling her eyes. "I just pray he'll be okay," she said to the mayor.

"This is only the beginning. I'm sure there's a lot more we'll hear and see. But for now, we need to get that video; it's solid evidence," the mayor said. "Luis…he's brave, but he sounded scared. And he has a right to be, after witnessing what he did." As he spoke, Stewart was already contemplating their next move.

The three of them paused when they heard voices outside the gate, leaving them to wonder if anyone was waiting for Luis when he stepped outside. When the mayor peeked out the window, no one was there.

But just as Luis rode away on his bike, someone else showed up and stood by the gate.

"That's him. That's the same man I saw looking with binoculars on the same evening that Kemal was killed!" Pelin shouted.

Two days after Luis visited Pelin at her home, Pelin put on her coat and got ready to walk out the door. "Where are you off to?" Shireen asked.

"I'm going to the diner to wait until Luis gets off work." Pelin remembered Luis telling her that he and Diego finished at six on weekdays. She wanted to meet him before he went home.

"Do you think I'm going to let you walk to the diner alone?" Shireen worried. "I don't believe things have cooled down in town."

She wasn't convinced that Duncan acted alone, so she wasn't going to let Pelin out of her sight until more details surfaced.

The two sisters walked down the street, attracting many looks. Two women smiled and waved from their window. Pelin and Shireen had no idea who they were but politely waved back.

When they arrived at the diner, Pelin convinced Shireen to go inside with her. She wanted to see Luis's face as reassurance that he was okay.

The diner wasn't as crowded as when they last visited with the mayor. Pelin grew a little nervous when she saw the man in the red cap inside.

Pelin immediately recognized the man in the red cap. He was the same man she saw with Mr. Duncan on the first day when she and Kemal arrived in Weavers Valley. He was sitting with a small group, including the police chief. They looked at her and Shireen and burst into laughter. She wanted to turn around and leave, but something told her to stay.

"Let's get out of here," Shireen whispered, her heart racing.

Pelin was already holding her sister's hand and gripped it tighter. "No, I'm not leaving," she said, searching for a table.

All eyes followed them, and the murmurs grew louder. "That table over there is vacant," Pelin told Shireen. They did not wait for the waitress, as the sign at the door suggested.

"Those two just walked over and sat at the table without waiting to be seated," said a man who was watching.

"That's the problem with immigrants. They can't read or something," the man in the red cap said loudly.

That was the last straw for Pelin. Without a second thought, she stood and looked directly at the man, addressing him and everyone else who was listening.

"Let me be clear!" said Pelin.

Everyone working in the kitchen came out to see what the commotion was about, including Diego, Luis's brother.

"I can read, and I can write. That's how I make my living," she told the man and the others. "I'm not an immigrant, and neither was my husband. We didn't come here by boat or by scaling a fence. We bought tickets and arrived on a plane. We wanted to escape the bigotry in our country, but I believe we made a mistake and arrived at its birthplace."

While Pelin spoke, Luis made a panicked dash out the back. He ran across the street to the mayor's office and pounded on the door.

When the mayor opened the door, he saw Luis standing there breathless. He knew something was wrong.

"You need to go over to the diner now. I think there's going to be trouble!"

There was no need for Luis to tell the mayor who he was talking about. From the urgent look in his eyes, the mayor could sense that Pelin and Shireen were at the center of what was about to happen.

"Mrs. Pelin, she's over there screaming at the chief."

Stewart closed the door and hurried behind Luis. When they arrived, Pelin had just taken her seat and was sliding her chair back into place. The chief of police sat with the man in the red cap and his group of followers.

Mayor Stewart walked straight over to the table where Pelin and Shireen sat. "Is everything okay?" He spoke loudly enough for the others to hear.

Before Pelin could answer, the chief said, "There's no problem with her. The young lady just needed to get a few things off her chest."

"Okay, if he says there's no problem, then there's no problem," Shireen told the mayor. "My sister basically told them to get off her back. That's a nice way of saying it." Shireen was proud of her sister for standing up to the bullies.

The mayor sat with the two sisters and listened to more of what they had to say about the treatment they had just received. He was relieved that there was no trouble. He looked around for Luis, who stood by the door leading to the kitchen with Diego. Then he glanced over at the rude men at the table and shook his head, but not in disbelief. But he was disappointed in his police chief.

When Pelin saw Luis out of the corner of her eye walking by the window, she stood and excused herself from the table. By the time she caught up with him, Shireen had joined her. "Luis, hello, it's me, Pelin." He turned and waved for her and her sister to follow him and Diego down the street toward the trail. Meeting on the trail was less visible to anyone back at the diner.

Feeling confident and safe, Pelin followed the boys onto the trail. However, it was Shireen who looked around after each step they took. She didn't want to go too far into the forest with the sun going down. Pelin reached for her sister's hand, knowing she hadn't been in a forest in years.

A lump formed in Pelin's throat as memories of Kemal flooded her mind. She couldn't help but imagine him standing there saying his last prayer at sunset. Pelin wondered what thoughts must have crossed his mind in his final moments. Her chest tightened, and she fought back the tears that threatened to spill from her eyes.

She started a conversation to take her mind off Kemal. "How are you two?" Pelin asked. "I understand that it probably wasn't a good idea to come to the diner, but I was worried about you Luis." She was concerned that anyone else might have seen him witness Kemal's murder. She had these thoughts because the town was so small that it would be hard for anyone not to notice what went on from day to day.

"It's no problem. Everyone here is nosey and always peeping out their windows, spying on others. Including my mother and sister," Luis said as he looked around to ensure that no one was watching.

Pelin opened her purse and took out the white envelope. She handed it to Luis while Diago looked on with a friendly smile. "This is for your troubles and the information you shared with me. Promise you won't open it until you get home. Open it with your mother. I'm sure it's something you all could use."

Luis and Diago promised not to open the envelope until they got home. Pelin and Shireen turned and began to make their way back to the street that led them home. Just as they exited the forest, the police chief eased alongside them and rolled down the window of his cruiser. Pelin looked over at him as he sat in his car and smiled. In return, the chief gave the two women a harsh look.

Shireen grew anxious, unsure why the chief drove up beside them. But Pelin refused to be intimidated by the chief's actions. She had gotten used to being followed and had had enough. Therefore, whatever the chief's reason for driving beside them, she was not afraid. It surprised Shireen when her sister stopped and put her hands on her hips. "May I help you?" Pelin asked. Shireen could not believe that her once quiet little sister had become so bold.

The police chief narrowed his eyes and stared back at Pelin, causing Shireen to shiver. "You ladies caused quite a stir back there," he told them. "I'd suggest you not poke around where you don't belong."

Pelin held her ground, her voice steady and unwavering. "The diner is open to the public, isn't it?"

The chief smiled with a sparkle in his eyes. "Just remember to mind your own business." With that, the chief sped off, his tires screeching against the pavement.

Shireen exhaled the breath she had been holding. "What was that all about?" she asked Pelin.

"We can't let him scare us. I have to stay here until Kemal's murderer is found guilty. If you don't feel safe, you can go back to New York."

"And leave you alone? Is that what you want?" Shireen asked Pelin.

"No, I'm just a little frustrated right now. And I miss Kemal."

Pelin didn't like the idea of the chief following her and saying, "Mind your own business."

"I'll show him about business," she told Shireen.

When Luis and Diego arrived home, Luis stopped before going inside and looked at the envelope in his hand. It felt bulky and weighty. "What do you think is in here?" he asked Diago, who shrugged but was just as curious. "I don't know, but we'll find out when we get inside." They looked around nervously, let their bikes fall to the ground, and ran up the stairs.

Inside, their mother was preparing dinner. She looked up as her sons walked through the door, noticing the envelope in Luis's hand. "What's that?" she asked, wiping her hands on a towel.

Luis handed her the envelope. "Pelin gave it to us. She said that we should open it together."

Their mother's face softened with concern. "Pelin...that lady has been through so much." She took the envelope and sat down at the kitchen table, her hands trembling slightly as she opened it.

Inside was a stack of cash and a note. The note read: "Thank you for your courage. Use this to help your family and stay safe. We'll get through this together." —Pelin

Luis and Diago's mother looked up, tears in her eyes. "This...this is too much. There's no way we can accept this amount of money from that poor lady who just lost her husband."

She had an arm around each of her sons. "This is $1,000.00; we have to give it back. This kind of money will attract attention. You know everyone in this town is watching their neighbor. What if someone saw her give it to you?" Their mother did not want to accept money from someone who just buried her husband.

Pelin and Shireen were back home. The encounter with the police chief was still fresh in their minds. Pelin sat down at the kitchen table, her thoughts racing. "We need to be smart about this. The chief is watching us, and we can't afford to make any mistakes."

Shireen nodded. "And we need to find out more about Duncan and why the chief is so interested in us. There's something bigger going on here," said Shireen.

—43—

The crisp morning air carried the scent of bacon and coffee from the diner across the street from the mayor's office. The *Maggie Valley Times* and a day-old copy of the *Wall Street Journal* had been delivered to the office doorstep. He stooped to pick up the two newspapers and tucked them under his arm without glancing at the headlines.

As he entered the diner, the bell above the door jingled, announcing his arrival. The mayor sensed something was different when he walked inside; more people had gathered there than usual. As he made his way to his reserved table, he could feel all eyes on him.

The waitress approached and poured him a warm cup of coffee. "Morning," she said, walking away without further conversation. She had always greeted the mayor with a smile and some small talk. Her abrupt "Good morning," the lack of the usual friendly chatter, heightened his sense that something wasn't right.

As he unfolded the *Times* and read the bold headline, "Weavers Valley Former Mayor Charged with Murder," his stomach turned. Although he already knew the facts, the harsh reality didn't sink in until he saw it in bold print. Mixed emotions flooded his mind as he read about the man he'd known all his life. Memories of looking up to Mr. Duncan as a teenager resurfaced.

"I cannot believe what I just read!" the mayor muttered under his breath, but it was right there in bold ink.

"God help us..." the mayor whispered, while looking at the headline and still in disbelief. He knew of the charges; he'd been briefed days earlier. But seeing it printed on the front page made it all too real.

Weavers Valley Former Mayor Charged with Murder. The words didn't just accuse a man; they tore at a legacy.

Duncan had been a mentor, a fixture, someone who once told him, *"Integrity isn't negotiable."* Now those words meant nothing.

He laid the paper on the table and leaned back in his chair. This wasn't a shock; it was something heavier. He was seeing the other side of a man he grew up respecting.

John Duncan had been a guiding light for Weavers Valley for twelve years. He was the kind of mayor people could talk to on the street. His words once carried a lot of weight. But in his last term, whispers had started to creep through town. Folks at the diner spoke in low voices about how he seemed slower, or even forgetful. Others said he'd lost the fire that had once made him fight for the town's future.

By the time election season rolled around, the gossip had increased. People were saying that maybe, just maybe, it was time for a change.

When the ballots were counted, the younger Johnny Stewart had won easily.

* * *

A vacant chair at the round table where a group of regulars sat served as a stark reminder of the void left by Duncan's absence.

Everyone in the diner looked at the mayor, waiting for him to comment on the article about Duncan. Luis and Diego stood near the kitchen door among them.

Tension filled the diner, with each table grappling with the news that one of their own, a pillar of the community, was being held for murder. One of the men from the round table stood up, pushed his chair back, and walked over to the mayor's table, his voice carrying through the diner.

"Those Muslim friends of yours came here and caused a lot of trouble. They have torn the fabric of our community apart," he told the mayor, and waited for a response. "Don't you think it's time we ask the two that are still here to leave town?"

"No!" the mayor said, dismissing the man's suggestion. After a moment's hesitation, he stood and declared, "I don't believe chasing anyone out of town is the right way to respond to this. Those two ladies here are not the ones charged with murder."

Gasps echoed throughout the diner. They could not believe the mayor was defending the Muslims against one of his own.

The man turned and walked back to his table. "For the life of me, I don't know what has gotten into you."

There was a long pause before anyone spoke again. Stewart then walked to the center of the diner. "I suppose you're waiting to hear more." Luis and Diego peeked out from the swinging kitchen doors, curious about what the mayor would say next.

From the look on his face, it was clear he was still disturbed by Duncan's arrest. He knew everyone wanted to hear his thoughts.

With his stomach churning, he began to speak. "I feel much the same as most of you. Shocked. I find myself at a loss for words," he said in a somber tone. He promised to investigate the matter and do what he could to seek Mr. Duncan's release from jail, and to ensure he received a fair trial.

The mayor felt driven to express his outrage at the unfair treatment Pelin and Shireen had received for a crime they did not commit. He wished to tell the patrons that everyone should have the right to travel and live wherever they wanted in this country, regardless of how they looked, dressed, or worshipped. He wanted to assert that everyone should also have the freedom to write a book without fear of persecution.

However, Mayor Stewart knew that the timing was not right for him to voice these opinions to an audience that had gathered seeking answers about Duncan's fate.

The man who wore a red MAGA hat, a longtime friend of Duncan, pointed a finger at the mayor. "How do you feel now about having those Muslims come here and wreak havoc on our lives? One of our own is behind bars because some foreign writer is running from the law. She's a coward who wrote lies about her government. Now she's without a country or a husband, and we will not allow her to live among us."

Once again, the mayor found himself in a precarious position. He knew it would be impossible for Pelin to understand his desire to seek the release of a man who had killed her husband. He realized that addressing this troubling situation would require a careful mix of understanding of everyone's feelings. That would take logical thinking, and a commitment to doing what was right in the eyes of the community. Would this allow him to do what was right in terms of the law?

The diner's atmosphere grew more oppressive by the minute. The tension was thick. Whispers turned to murmurs, and murmurs to debates that rose in volume as patrons grappled with the implications of John Duncan's arrest. Some expressed sympathy for the man they had known and respected for years, while others voiced their anger and resentment towards Pelin, blaming her for the town's troubles. A majority wanted Pelin gone and Mayor Stewart to resign.

Amid the chaos, thoughts whirled through Stewart's mind, spinning faster than he could grasp. He was searching for a way to bridge the gap between the townspeople's feelings and the law. The unquestionable fact was that a man they respected had murdered an innocent person. He knew that healing the community's wounds would not be a simple task, but it was one he was determined to undertake. With a heavy heart and a sense of purpose, he felt he had said enough.

As he walked to the door, all eyes followed him. The bell jingled, and Mayor Stewart took a deep breath before walking out. He had never experienced anything like this in Weavers Valley, either as a private citizen or as mayor, but he was ready to face it. He took one last look at the headline that had shaken Weavers Valley to its core and walked out, prepared to confront the darkness threatening to engulf his beloved town.

When he arrived at his office, he was surprised to see Pelin and Shireen waiting outside his door. They had received a text from Luis, saying there was a meeting about them in the diner.

"What was the meeting about down at the diner?" Shireen asked before he could take a seat.

He held up the newspaper for them to see. "They saw this in the papers this morning and wanted to know what was going on," he explained to the two sisters. "Everyone read the article, but they needed to know my take on it." The mayor wasn't being entirely truthful. He assured Pelin and Shireen that he would do what was right for the community. As a friend, he also promised to stay committed to seeking justice for Kemal.

"I understand that you have a job to do, and you need to be careful in how you go about it. But maybe you can find out more information by talking to some people around here. You might discover if they know anything about what is behind Kemal's murder. I am thinking it wasn't just Duncan," Shireen told the mayor.

"No! I shouldn't say a word to anyone here about this case. That might work in the movies or in big cities, but the people around here won't say anything that might incriminate one of their own, especially when an outsider is involved." Stewart didn't want to say it outright, but he did.

"The people around here never see others for who they are; they only see race, gender, or religion—insider or outsider. Remember how Kemal always reminded you about trust? Well, I'm reminding you to be mindful of the people around here."

Later in the day, the three of them sat preparing for the drive to Asheville, where they were to meet with the lawyers who volunteered to help her understanding her rights in America in the aftermath of Kemal's death, now that she was sole owner of the property. Her phone rang; it was Luis. "Mrs. Korkmaz, can you meet with us on the trail after work?" Luis and Diego's mom wanted the boys to return the cash. She felt they should not accept it.

"I'm going to Asheville for a meeting today. Is it okay if I contact you as soon as I get back?" Pelin asked.

"It's okay, I understand, and I will tell my mother."

As soon as they stepped into the real estate attorney's office, the receptionist greeted them with a warm smile, "I am glad they finally made an arrest."

Pelin froze, though she already knew. That was old news, but hearing it again was upsetting.

The attorney came out to meet them with a brisk handshake and a wry smile. leading them down the hallway. "I understand that the arrest of Mr. Duncan has been casting a shadow over the whole valley.

Pelin's heart skipped. She wasn't there to discuss the murder; she was there for advice on how to move forward now that she was the sole owner. Due to her long day, Pelin texted Luis, asking him to come to her home instead of meeting somewhere else. Luis arrived with an older woman, whom Luis introduced as their mother. "She wanted to come," he explained. Their mother didn't want them to accept money for simply doing the right thing. She had also wondered whether a witness accepting money was a bad idea: it would put his testimony under suspicion.

Pelin and Shireen wanted to convince Luis's mother that they should keep the money. "It is money that Kemal's family and I put together as a reward for anyone with information about his murder. Now it's yours. Without your son's bravery, we wouldn't know anything. It's not hurting us."

"I raised my boys to be kind and honest. They can help you without you having to pay them."

Pelin found comfort in Luis and Diego's mother's words. Shireen recognized her as the person she had seen in the window, the one who had waved and smiled when they walked by her home.

Luis, Diego, and their mother left with the envelope of cash, much to the sisters' relief. They knew that if anyone in Weavers Valley needed it, it was this family.

They were still concerned that the boys and their mother may have put themselves in danger by associating with Pelin. However, as more information surfaced about Kemal's murder, it was also a moment of glimmering hope. Pelin believed that, thanks to people like Luis, his brother, and their mother, the truth would eventually be uncovered. She hoped it would bring justice and peace to the small town of Weavers Valley.

— 44 —

When Pelin answered the phone, it was the DA on the other end. She pushed her coffee cup aside, bracing herself for what the attorney had to tell her. An early phone call usually meant important news.

"Just an update," the attorney said. "John Duncan was an easy hire as a hitman. His hatred for foreigners and Muslims made him the perfect choice. Two Turkish men paid him to kill you and Kemal. We all know who he got first."

Within a day, FBI and SBI agents tracked Duncan down. Sloppy work made him an obvious suspect, and Luis's video sealed his fate. Following the money trail, investigators confirmed he had stopped while driving to Knoxville for more ammunition and supplies.

After hours of interrogation, Duncan confessed. The Turkish men had driven from New York, paying him $50,000 upfront, with the rest promised in Knoxville. "They must have sensed something was off," the attorney continued. "They never showed up with the rest of the money."

Pelin let out a deep breath. "By now, Turkish government agents have likely helped them disappear. They were probably hiding in the embassy or on their way back to Turkey."

She appreciated the swift response from authorities but wished they had acted sooner. Too late for Kemal.

Pelin struggled to process what she was hearing. "Do they know who the Turkish men are?"

"No identities yet," the DA said. "But the CIA is close."

"The men rented a car with New York plates. When they arrived in Weavers Valley, Duncan confronted them, just like he did with you and Kemal, demanding to know why they were there."

Sensing his hostility, they played to it, offering him a large sum of cash. From there, it was easy. Duncan agreed to the job, and the three of them planned the attack.

Pelin's stomach twisted. She remembered the uneasy feeling she had had when she first saw the two men in the red and green caps.

"The FBI says Duncan's confession matches the video you saw," the attorney continued. "He spotted Kemal praying on a bench. 'An easy target,' Duncan called him."

Tears welled in Pelin's eyes.

"The plan was for him to lay low in a hotel until things cooled down," the attorney added. "But the others never showed with the rest of the money."

There was a pause.

"Pelin, are you there?"

"Yes." Her voice was barely above a whisper. She wiped her tears.

"I know this isn't what you wanted to hear first thing in the morning," the attorney said gently.

Pelin sat silently; she knew that the agents had been following her and Kemal for two years, but she never thought they would track them all the way to Weavers Valley.

"Shireen was surprised to learn that Turkish agents paid Duncan. She called last night asking if I had any updates. When I told her I did, she insisted I call you right away."

"I'm glad you did," Pelin murmured.

A buzz interrupted them. The attorney looked at her phone. "I just received a text from the state prosecutor. The two Turkish men were last seen boarding a flight to Istanbul. They boarded the plane with Turkish passports and government credentials."

Pelin had suspected as much. But her mind was elsewhere. "Will they ever have to answer for what they did?" she muttered. "It's international now."

"There's still a lot we don't know."

Pelin hesitated, then asked, "Do you realize this all started because of my book?"

The attorney sighed. "It's come up, but no one's focusing on it. Not yet."

"They should." Pelin's voice was firm. "That book is the key to everything. I must have exposed something they didn't want the world to know."

The attorney exhaled. "Duncan kept yelling at the FBI about your writing, saying you were spreading lies about your government and that he wouldn't let you do the same in America. The chief FBI agent working the case thought it was strange."

She didn't have more details; the prosecutor was withholding evidence, waiting for Turkish authorities to cooperate.

"One investigator told me those two men were just part of a larger operation," the attorney added. "At least two dozen agents were after you and Kemal."

Pelin ended the call, her mind reeling. She sat in silence, staring at her untouched breakfast. The eggs were cold, the bread hard. She pushed the plate away, pressed a hand to her stomach, and doubled over.

Shireen walked into the kitchen and froze in place. "Pelin?"

Pelin wiped her eyes. "It was the phone call." Her voice shook. "I can't believe they followed us here."

Shireen sat beside her. "I was afraid something like this would happen the moment I read your book."

"So, the FBI confirmed it was the government?"

"They said the Turkish government employed the men." Pelin's grip tightened on her coffee cup. "But I need to know who gave the order."

Shireen took her hand and held it tightly. "We'll find out."

Determined to uncover the truth, the sisters combed through every lead, pressing Luis and Diego for more details. They left messages at the attorney's office, demanding answers about the two Turkish men.

A sticky note from an FBI agent sat on Pelin's desk; a case number was scribbled on it. She considered calling him but remembered her attorney's warning: the FBI was keeping the investigation sealed to prevent leaks.

By evening, the sisters sat on the porch, watching the sun dip behind the hills of Weavers Valley. The fading light reminded Pelin of Kemal. "I miss him so much," she whispered. "He kept me steady, even when I didn't know I was shaking.

Shireen placed a comforting hand on her shoulder. "I know. He inspired so many."

"But not the people here," Pelin muttered.

The mayor had warned Shireen that some locals wanted Pelin gone.

"She has every right to be here," Shireen had told him. "Kemal's blood is in this soil. Neither of us will leave until justice is served."

Pelin woke before dawn; she couldn't stop thinking about how Kemal died. But this morning, something else stirred inside her—a determination. She walked into Kemal's study. His presence lingered in the neatly stacked books and the scattered notes on his desk. With teary eyes, she sat down and ran her fingers over his handwriting. These were his last words.

She began to write, and as the hours slipped away, she poured their shared experiences onto the pages. She documented their struggles as journalists and the dangers they faced in exposing the truth. She emphasized the numerous risks Kemal undertook, demonstrating his courage and determination. Pelin reminded herself of the enormous price he paid for doing what he thought was right.

At one point, she could almost feel him there, guiding her toward the finish line.

Finally, she emailed Kemal's former boss, explaining her intentions. The moment she hit send, relief washed over her.

This was what Kemal would have wanted. Pelin stood and picked up his framed photo from the bookshelf, pressing it to her chest. "I miss you," she whispered. "I won't stop until justice is served."

She found Shireen in her study, deep in thought. They had mapped out their next steps the night before, and now, they were ready. "We'll start with the rental car company," Shireen said. "See if they left any clues."

"I'll call a friend in Istanbul," Pelin added. "He can hire a private investigator to dig on the Turkish side."

For the first time in months, they felt something other than grief. They were on a mission to find answers. The wanted to ensure that the men whoever was responsible for ending Kemal's life would face justice. No matter how deep they had to dig, no matter the cost, Pelin swore she wouldn't rest until the truth was uncovered.

With a steady breath, she braced herself for the battles ahead.

It had taken a full year, but the truth finally came to light; it was proven that the Turkish government had orchestrated Kemal's murder. Despite political obstacles, a handful of dedicated officials in the U.S. Justice Department uncovered new evidence. There work led to the arrest of two Turkish men who conspired in the killing. The chief prosecutor now had proof that powerful institutions were working to silence democratic voices, but the full story could no longer remain buried.

After months of diplomatic negotiation, U.S. authorities reached an agreement with the Turkish government to extradite Adem Kaya and Hasan Demir. Both were accused of orchestrating the murder plot. The two men were transferred under federal custody and flown to North Carolina, where they would stand trial alongside Mr. Duncan. Prosecutors alleged that Kaya and Demir had financed the operation, paying Duncan to carry out the killing. The initial charge of solicitation to commit murder wasn't enough; the prosecutor was pushing for first-degree murder.

For Pelin, the past year had been the most exhausting of her life. Through it all, Shireen stood by her side, unwavering in her support.

"I couldn't have done this without you Shireen," Pelin said with her voice trembling with emotion. "Your strength has kept me going."

Shireen squeezed her hand. "You're stronger than you think. Kemal would be so proud of what you've accomplished."

Meanwhile, Pelin's latest novel, *Fragments of Freedom*, had skyrocketed in international sales. In its pages, she warned that the erosion of democracy in her homeland wasn't just a local crisis; it was a threat to the entire free world.

With her earnings, she reinvested in Weavers Valley, purchasing the town's beloved diner from Mr. Duncan's daughter, who needed the money to pay off debts and fund her father's defense. During the negotiations, there was no bitterness between them.

"I hope this helps," Pelin said softly, handing over the check. "Your father meant a lot to this town."

The daughter nodded, tears welling in her eyes. "Thank you, Pelin. This means more than you know."

Fulfilling a dream Kemal once had, Pelin expanded the diner, transforming part of it into the town's first bookstore. This addition created jobs and brought fresh energy to the community. Luis and Diego were promoted to manage the diner, while two recent UNC Asheville graduates were hired to oversee the bookstore.

Opening night coincided with the eve of John Duncan's trial. The trial had been moved from Weavers Valley to Asheville, due to its high profile . . . and the prosecutor's concerns about bias against Pelin, and Muslims in general.

The bookstore was crowded. Near the entrance, a prominent display featured banned books by LGBTQ and Black and Brown authors. A framed photograph of Kemal hung on the wall above, his dark eyes and warm smile watching over the room. Locals had shown up in force—some out of curiosity, others with quiet skepticism. The diner had been the heart of Weavers Valley for generations, and many worried about what Pelin's ownership would mean for it.

Mr. Thompson, a long-time regular, frowned as he surveyed the space. He finally approached Pelin, speaking loudly enough for others to hear. "What do you know about running a place like this?" His tone was threatening.

Pelin took a deep breath to center herself. The night was already nerve-wracking, but she met his gaze calmly. The room quieted as people leaned in to listen.

"I know how much this place means to you," she said. "Don't worry; there won't be many changes. The kitchen staff is staying, and the menu will remain the same."

The younger residents murmured their approval, and slowly, one by one, the older patrons began nodding. It was a start.

Pelin exhaled, feeling the tension ease. Maybe the town was ready to move forward. Pelin added an addition to what had once been a large back storeroom. It now held polished wooden shelves and a reading nook with two armchairs. A glass partition separated it from the main diner. But the new addition could not block the scent of home cook meals and the fresh smell of coffee. A hand-painted sign hung above the entrance to the new space that read, The *Reading Room*.

Two women near the banned book section caught her attention. "How much is this one?" one asked, holding up *Fragments of Freedom*.

Another woman leaned in, whispering, "Would you sign it for me?" She glanced over her shoulder, as if afraid of being seen.

Pelin smiled. "Of course."

The woman's eyes lit up. "I've never had anything signed before. And I've never met an author!" She held the book close, then discreetly tucked it into her purse.

"There's no charge," Pelin said. "It's a gift."

Another woman approached Shireen. "I wasn't sure about this at first," she admitted. "But seeing what you've done, I have to say it's remarkable. This town needed a fresh start after all the bad press and terrible events."

"Thank you," Shireen replied. "But this was all my sister's idea."

More women in the crowd softened, approaching Pelin with quiet condolences. For some, it was the first time speaking to her. It was difficult, especially after Kemal's murder. Their thick Southern drawl blurred words she didn't quite understand. But Pelin felt the warmth in their gestures.

As promised, there was not much of a change in the diner, except for new tables and chairs. The locals sat in their usual seats, and so did the mayor, alongside four of the town's regulars. One chair sat permanently empty.

"Kemal would have been proud, to see how you upgraded this place," Stewart told Pelin. His eyes flicked to the banned books section. "That's a brilliant idea. You're giving a voice to those who've been silenced."

"That's the goal," Pelin said. "Governments everywhere are trying to erase the history of marginalized people. If I can help push back against that, even in a small way, I will."

The women in the room far outnumbered the men. That alone told Pelin everything she needed to know. It was the women who were ready for change.

"Shireen, can you believe how many people showed up?" Pelin murmured.

"I knew they would," Shireen replied. "I just met two women who drove down from Maggie Valley. And a family from Black Mountain."

Before Pelin could respond, a tall woman in elegant attire approached.

"Mrs. Korkmuz?" she asked.

"It's Korkmaz," Pelin corrected.

"My apologies. I'm a journalist from *The New York Times*." She smiled warmly. "I flew down to cover your story."

Pelin shifted uneasily. "I don't think I'm worthy of that kind of attention."

"You are," the journalist insisted. "At the *Times*, we encourage artists whose work has been banned to share their stories."

Pelin forced a smile. "I appreciate the support."

She was about to excuse herself when she noticed a man near the entrance. Tall and lean, with red hair and a dull gray suit, his loosened tie gave him an air of casual authority. He had been watching the room with keen interest. Shireen, sensing something, motioned Pelin over.

"This is Mr. Langley," she whispered. "He's with the State Department."

Pelin's stomach tightened. She cleared her throat and offered a polite handshake.

"Congratulations on the bookstore," Langley said. "I flew down from Washington today."

His smile was easy, but something about him felt off.

"I'm not here on official business," he added quickly, noting her wariness. "I read your book. Had to come meet the author for myself."

Pelin exchanged a glance with Shireen. Neither of them relaxed.

"Was it really worth the trip?" Pelin asked, forcing lightness into her tone.

Langley's expression shifted. "Your book didn't just make waves; it rattled some very powerful people." His voice dropped slightly. "Powerful and dangerous, and I hope you're ready for what comes next."

Before she could respond, his phone buzzed. He checked it, straightened his tie, and nodded. "We'll talk soon." Then, just as swiftly as he arrived, he disappeared into the crowd.

Shireen's face had gone pale. "What was that about?" she whispered.

Pelin shook her head, wondering. "I don't know. But I don't like it."

Mayor Stewart had been watching from across the room. He rushed over. "Are you okay?"

Pelin hesitated. "A man from the State Department just introduced himself."

The mayor's expression darkened. "Why was he here?"

"He said he was impressed with my book." Pelin glanced at the clock. Less than an hour before closing. She forced a smile.

"If he was really a fan," she said with curiosity, "he would've asked for a signed copy."

She turned back toward the crowd. Right now, she had a store to run, but deep in her gut, she sensed something was off about Mr. Langley. The same instinct that had warned her the night Kemal died now was warning her to be mindful of Mr. Langley.

As she moved through the crowded room, smiling and chatting with customers, part of her stayed alert and watchful. The photograph of Kemal seemed to follow her with its stare, a bittersweet reminder of all she had lost, and everything she still needed to protect.

— 46 —

The moment Pelin stepped into the courtroom, she braced herself for the grueling testimony that would unfold. For two weeks, she had sat on the hard wooden bench with her eyes fixed on Duncan. Shackled at the defense table, he never once looked at her. His lawyers fought aggressively, trying to sow doubt, but no argument could erase the footage the jury had seen of Duncan pulling the trigger.

Tension hung thick in the air as both sides chipped away at their cases while witnesses took the stand. Some were tearful, others angry. Many in town still wished Pelin and Kemal had never come to Weavers Valley, convinced that if they hadn't, Duncan would still be a free man. But not everyone saw it that way. Across the aisle, some blamed Mayor Stewart instead, considering him responsible for welcoming the outsiders in the first place.

Pelin had heard the brutal details of Kemal's murder so many times that she feared they would haunt her forever. The only comfort was Shireen, who never left her side. Pelin's chest tightened at the sound of Kemal's name. Shireen handed her a tissue while her own eyes were filled with tears.

As promised, Tarek had flown in from London to be there. He had never set foot in an American courtroom before, and everything about it felt foreign yet painfully familiar. He had grown up hearing stories about the flaws of American justice, but today he hoped to witness something different. Still, his anger simmered beneath the surface. He caught himself looking at Duncan and clenching his fists. He could be heard muttering something under his breath, prompting an immediate reprimand from the judge. The jury filed back into the courtroom. They hadn't taken long, which said more than words could. No one looked at Pelin. Not yet. She sat still, with her hands clenched in her lap, trying to read their expressions. Then it was time for the verdict. The judge's gavel cracked against the wood, sending a jolt through the room. Shireen reached for Pelin's hand as the judge cleared his throat. Silence filled the room, the air heavy as everyone held their breath.

"Mr. Robert Duncan, for the crime of first-degree murder, this court finds you guilty." The judge continued, "And for their role in abetting this crime, this court also finds Adem Kaya and Hasan Demir guilty of first-degree murder." A collective exhale swept through the prosecution's side. Lawyers exchanged quiet nods, relieved that their months of work had not been in vain. Tears slipped down Pelin's face, and Shireen squeezed her hand. Across the room, Mayor Stewart shook his head, still in disbelief that Weavers Valley's former mayor had been found guilty of murder. He turned to the sisters and murmured, "It's over. Finally."

But before the judge could adjourn, Duncan suddenly lunged forward, forgetting his shackles. His voice exploded through the courtroom. "Those two men!" He pointed frantically at Adem and Hasan, who sat frozen in horror. "They didn't hire me! I've never seen them before! They don't even speak English!"

Gasps rippled through the crowd. The defense attorneys stiffened; their carefully built case had just shattered. Pelin took a deep breath. "What did he say?" she whispered. The mayor leaned in. "He's claiming the real masterminds aren't in this courtroom." A chill ran through Pelin. If Duncan was telling the truth, then the real killers were still out there.

The judge's face darkened, but his voice remained firm. "If the defense wishes to appeal based on this claim, they may do so. But for now, this court is adjourned." The gavel struck one final time.

Duncan slumped back in his chair, his face pale. He opened his mouth as if to say more, but the bailiffs seized him before he could.

Pelin's stomach churned. The victory she had just felt now seemed hollow. The murmurs in the courtroom turned into a buzz of confusion. Reporters scribbled furiously, townspeople whispered in hushed voices, and the defense attorneys exchanged tense glances.

Outside, the chaos continued. "I hope the defense has the sense to appeal," muttered Mr. Thompson, one of Duncan's supporters. "This whole thing's a hoax."

But for Pelin, it felt like a weight had finally been lifted and justice had been served. Tarek stood beside her on the courthouse steps; he let out a breath he hadn't realized he was holding. He had come prepared for the worst, fully expecting another case where a man walked free after killing someone who looked like Kemal. But for once, justice had won. He turned to Pelin, whose face was wet with tears. He pulled her closer and gave her a firm hug. "This is for everyone who couldn't be here," he whispered. For Kemal's mother, who had aged years in grief before his death. For Kemal's nieces and nephews, who still asked when Uncle Kemal was coming home.

Pelin's phone buzzed. She glanced at the screen; it was a thumbs-up emoji from Diego. She smiled through her tears. Without him and Luis, this verdict would have never been possible. The trial had drawn international attention, not just because of its location but also because of the Turkish government's suspected involvement. Reporters swarmed outside the courthouse, shouting questions, cameras flashing. Tarek stepped in front of Pelin and Shireen, shielding them. For that Pelin was grateful. She had no interest in talking to the press. Justice had been served in the courtroom, but no verdict would bring Kemal back.

In the days following the trial, Shireen prepared to return to New York. "You need to come with me," she pleaded. "You need a break from this place. The diner and bookstore will be fine without you for a while."

Pelin closed her eyes. The past two years had been a blur of grief, change, and reckoning.

"Thank you," she said softly. "But New York isn't where I need to be right now. I have work to do here. Before that phone call two years ago, I was writing for democracy. I need to get back to that."

Shireen's expression tightened. "You can't keep exposing the government's injustices. Look where it's gotten you." Her voice rose with frustration. "There's still an active warrant for your arrest in Turkey!"

Pelin met her sister's look, without hesitation. "Kemal gave his life supporting me in this fight. That alone is enough to keep me going." She exhaled. "If I keep pushing, something has to give—either me or the regime. And I have no intention of backing down."

Shireen searched her sister's face, hoping for a sign that she might change her mind. But she saw Pelin's resolve, looking stubborn as ever. After the past two years, she hoped Pelin would walk away from this battle, leave to find peace in New York, London, anywhere but Weavers Valley or Istanbul. But Shireen knew, deep down, that nothing would make Pelin abandon this fight.

Pelin wasn't entirely sure what her future held beyond writing and running the bookstore. But she remembered a conversation she once had with Kemal. "I'll go home when the time is right," she had told him. "Only you will know when you're ready," he had replied.

For now, the bookstore and diner would keep her occupied. And whatever she decided, she would do it for herself and for Kemal.

— **47** —

Six months had passed since Kemal's murder trial, and still, there was no word of an appeal. Pelin had spoken with her attorney multiple times, but every conversation ended the same way: the case was closed. The verdict had been rendered. The past could not be undone. Yet, to Pelin, nothing about this felt like closure.

Her time in Weavers Valley had changed her in ways she hadn't expected. She had arrived as a woman on the run, desperate to escape capture—or worse. Initially, she and Kemal had been outsiders, unwelcome in this quiet town. Their skin color and religious beliefs set them apart, making them the subject of whispers in the streets and doors shutting in their faces. They had endured it all, right up until the night Kemal was stolen from her forever.

Now, standing on her porch, she traced the railing with her fingers, her eyes were locked on the winding trail across the road. It was the same path she and Kemal had walked when they first arrived, and the same one where he'd lost his life.

This town was supposed to be nothing more than a hiding place, a temporary refuge from the threats that had forced her out of Turkey. But somewhere along the way, it had become something more.

Among the towering pines and early morning fog, she had slowly begun piecing her life back together. The grief never fully left her. Some days, she felt as if Kemal was there, walking beside her. Other days, her ache was so painful that she could barely breathe.

She had learned to survive in this place that still held his blood in its soil. There were days when she was welcomed with open arms; other days, she was met with suspicious glances and hushed whispers.

"That foreign woman, the troublemaker." Some would say nasty things about her. But she had made up her mind: she would prove them wrong. That determination nearly faded when she stepped into the diner one morning.

Luis spotted her immediately and waved her toward the kitchen. He looked around, ensuring no one was watching. The typical relaxed expression on his face was gone, replaced by something that sent a chill through her. When she arrived, he leaned in close. "Mrs. Korkmaz, this is getting serious. You can't stay here."

Pelin's eyes widened. "Say something, Luis. Tell me what's going on." He lowered his voice to a near whisper. "Immigration officers were here earlier. A half-dozen, maybe more. Sitting right out there, drinking coffee and asking questions." He paused and looked around. "They're not just looking anymore; they're hunting for you."

Pelin's stomach tightened. She knew what it meant to be hunted. She had spent years running from government forces that saw her as a threat. But why were U.S. immigration officers looking for her? All her documents were in order. She was here legally. Unless… something had changed. Maybe it was the trial. Perhaps she had unknowingly violated something while seeking justice for Kemal. Or maybe it was due to the new administration's changes in immigration policy.

She had no idea why U.S. immigration agents would be looking for her. A familiar dread slid down her spine, cold and relentless. For a moment or two after the trial, she had allowed herself to believe things were getting better. She had bought the diner and built a life. But now, it was happening all over again. Her heart started beating faster. "Did they say if they were coming back?" Luis shook his head. "They didn't have to. You know how this works. Stay in one place too long, and they will find you."

Pelin swallowed hard. She had no plan. Nowhere to go. Fear was starting to take over, but she forced herself to stay calm. Luis must have seen the panic in her eyes; he placed a reassuring hand on her shoulder. "You're not alone, Mrs. Korkmaz. My family is here for you." She gave him a grateful smile. "Luis."

He cut her off with a shake of his head. "Listen, Diego called my mom. She's already on alert. She wants to help." Pelin hesitated. "Luis, your mother is kind, but won't that put her in danger?"

"She's been through this before. Even after she got her green card, they continued to harass her. But now? She's one of the best housekeepers in town. People respect her." He hesitated before adding, "You, on the other hand… people want you gone. If they find you, they'll take you, and we're not letting that happen." Pelin opened her mouth to protest, but Luis held up a hand. "You have no choice," he said firmly. "I know you've spent your life fighting to stand on your own. But this? This is too big. You can't fight it alone."

She exhaled slowly. "Are you sure? I don't want to put your family at risk." Luis nodded. "We have space. You'll be safe."

"Thank you, Luis. Truly." She reached into her purse to call Mayor Stewart, but Luis quickly stopped her. "No. Don't." She froze. "Why?"

"The mayor has a lot on his plate. He's fighting to keep his job and uphold the law. I don't know what he can do. He's probably already been contacted by immigration."

Pelin hesitated. She wanted to believe Johnny Stewart would help her; he had before. But Luis was right. This time, the mayor's hands were tied. Luis didn't wait for her to decide. "Come on, we need to move. Diego's waiting out back."

They slipped out through the kitchen door and into the alley, where Diego stood scanning the street. When he saw them, he waved. "We have to be careful," he murmured. "They might still be watching."

Pelin barely breathed as they made their way toward her house. Every passing car and every set of footsteps sent her nerves on edge.

When they arrived, Luis and Diego entered first, checking each room before waving her inside. Pelin moved quickly, stuffing a bag with clothes, her notebook, and the worn photo of Kemal she kept by her bedside. Before leaving, she took one last look around. This place had never truly felt like home, but it had been hers. Luis touched her arm gently. "We should go." She nodded. "I'm ready." Together, they disappeared into the night, making their way toward the Navarro home, where Luis's mother waited to shelter her.

Pelin knew it would only be temporary. Once she was settled, she pulled out her phone and called Shireen. "They came looking for me," Pelin told her.

Shireen exhaled. "They came for me too and ransacked my place. I didn't tell them anything, and eventually, they left."

Pelin sniffled and couldn't say anything.

"First your sister," an officer had told Shireen, "Then we'll be back for you."

"How long will you stay with the Navarro's?" Shireen asked.

"They said I can stay as long as I need. But who knows how long that will be?"

"I'm calling Johnny."

"No. Don't," Pelin said firmly. "It's not legal for him to get involved. His job is to enforce the law, not break it.

—48—

One week after hiding in the Navarro family home, Pelin stepped out to go to the diner. The street was nearly empty, as if everyone knew something was about to go terribly wrong. A gust of wind sent a shiver through her body as she walked toward the diner. This would be her first visit there since staying with the Novarros.

She never saw it coming. A dark van screeched to a halt in the middle of the street. Before she could react, the doors flew open, and three uniformed immigration officers launched themselves at her. They yanked her arms roughly, forcing her to the ground.

Pelin hit the pavement with a force that knocked the air from her lungs. Her cheek scraped against the asphalt as a knee dug into her back. A voice that she recognized barked orders. All she could do was focus on the pain in her wrists as someone fastened cold handcuffs around them.

She had no idea what was happening. Once she could breathe normally again, she screamed at the top of her lungs. Everyone who heard her stopped in their tracks, and those inside the diner rushed toward the commotion outside, including Luis and Diego, with looks of horror on their faces.

"Stop! Don't hurt her!" Luis shouted at the officers. He took a step forward but froze as three more officers jumped out of the van with their guns drawn.

The crowd grew as word spread that Pelin was being arrested by ICE.

"Leave her alone!" A woman's voice could be heard shouting.

From his office window, Mayor Stewart saw the commotion and felt his stomach drop. He jumped from his desk and ran down the steps two at a time. By the time he reached the street, it was too late.

Mrs. Navarro stood frozen beside her sons, tears streaming down her cheeks. "I am so sorry," the mayor murmured as he placed a comforting arm around her shoulder. He wanted to say more and do something, anything. But the words wouldn't come, and there was nothing he could do.

On the ground, Pelin stopped resisting. There was no use; she was outnumbered. She lifted her head, and that's when she saw him. Mr. Langley.

The man from the bookstore opening. The one who introduced himself as a representative of the U.S. State Department. He stood at a distance, his mouth moving as he barked orders to the officers. Pelin wasn't surprised; she had sensed something was off about him the moment he spoke that night.

When the officers lifted Pelin from the ground, some in the crowd held their breath. Pelin turned toward the Novarros, her face was streaked with dirt, but her voice was steady. "It's time," she said, as if accepting what had happened.

She was ready to go back to Istanbul, and if this was the way she had to go, then she was prepared.

Luis clenched his fists. "No," he whispered, pain tearing through him.

"Call Shireen; we planned for this day," Pelin told Luis. He swallowed hard, understanding what she meant. The power of attorney. The instructions, the bookstore, and the future she had prepared for, knowing this day would come. "I will," he choked out, wishing there were more he could do to help, but there was nothing.

The police chief stepped forward, his voice flat, showing no sympathy. "Everyone, return to your business." But how could they? How could they pretend nothing had happened?

Mayor Stewart turned away, already tapping the buttons on his phone. His voice was heavy but controlled; beneath it, anger simmered. "Shireen," he said. "It's happening. I'm sorry. We did everything we could."

Pelin was already being led away. But she didn't struggle. And she did not cry.

"She had become part of the community, and I always thought that she would be safe here. And now, she's gone," said the mayor.

—49—

Pelin returned to her homeland feeling like a stranger, and the absence of Kemal made her return even more difficult. In the hands of the agents, she was uncertain of what lay ahead. The guards remained stone-faced and silent, offering no hints about her destination; they were simply following orders to transfer her to a women's prison outside the city. Suddenly, she was plunged into darkness, but she was determined not to let the guards see her fear. She had never faced such a terrifying situation before. All she could do was cling to her prayers and hope this nightmare would end.

Once outside the terminal, the agents forced her head down and shoved her into the backseat of the minibus. A female agent placed a blindfold over her eyes, cutting her off from the world and leaving her feeling isolated and helpless.

Amid it all, she recalled her mother's calming voice, which brought her a moment of peace. However, the realization that she might never see her again deepened her worries. She knew she had to be strong—for herself and for Kemal.

Back in the airport terminal, Shireen's desperation grew as she sought information about Pelin's arrest and destination. Approaching airport security, she was visibly shaken.

"Excuse me, can someone please tell me where my sister has been taken?" she pleaded.

The officers barely glanced at her, dismissing her pleas. "Ma'am, please step away from the desk," one of them said.

Frustration boiled inside Shireen. She raised her voice. "This is ridiculous! I demand answers! Why won't anyone tell me what's going on?" The officer repeated, "Ma'am, step away from the desk." Shireen turned around, her eyes fiery red. "Fine! If you're not going to help me, I'll hire an attorney and get to the bottom of this!" she screamed, her voice echoing throughout the terminal as she walked away.

* * *

"Turn left here," the male agent instructed the driver. Pelin heard a ship's horn blowing and inhaled the salty sea air. "Cross this bridge, turn right at the light, and drive straight for forty-five kilometers," he continued giving directions.

With the smell of the sea, Pelin realized they were near the Bosporus, where Kemal's ashes had been scattered. Silently, she whispered his name, wanting his ashes to know she had returned.

The minibus finally drove through the prison yard gates. Once inside, the gates clanged shut behind them. The agents removed Pelin's blindfold. The sudden glare of sunlight blinded her momentarily, and she couldn't shield her eyes because her hands were still cuffed.

"Step out," the agent commanded. Pelin stumbled out, feeling weak and nauseated. She looked around and saw women in tan jumpsuits, all staring back at her, recognizing her as a new intake. "Follow me," the female guard instructed her. The guard grabbed her arm and lead her through two eight-foot-tall steel double doors opened by a guard monitoring a camera.

"Once you are processed and changed out of your street clothes, you will be assigned a cell," the stocky male agent said. He and his female companion signed paperwork and handed Pelin over to the federal prison guards. "Soon you will come face to face with the man who ordered your arrest," the female agent told Pelin before turning and walking away.

The officers at the booking desk informed Pelin that she had been brought to Kandra Women's Prison, where she would remain in federal custody while awaiting a court date.

Pelin knew a bit about the prison from her work with women who had served time there for various reasons. She recalled a case years earlier, where a woman had been tortured and sexually abused in Kandra. The prisoner had been found dead in her cell, allegedly by suicide, at the age of 28.

Despite the urgent request, investigators were told that no investigation was ever conducted. The only information they received was that the young woman was quietly whisked away, her existence nearly erased. She had been placed in solitary confinement until the chilling day her lifeless body was found. The mystery surrounding her death deepened, leaving behind an unsettling silence and many unanswered questions.

Thinking about this case heightened Pelin's anxiety. At night, she was tormented by nightmares, haunted by the thought that she might never see the outside world again.

"They're going to kill me if I have to stay here—just like they did to the young woman and to my father," Pelin muttered to herself. She lay awake for hours contemplating her future. The oppressive atmosphere of the prison was overwhelming, filled with the sounds of women screaming, fights, and cell doors slamming throughout the night.

* * *

Six months passed, and Pelin was jolted awake from a deep sleep—not by an alarm clock, but by the voices of women in neighboring cells. She had almost forgotten where she was until she heard the guards shouting for everyone to get up and get dressed for breakfast.

"Ms. Korkmaz, eat your breakfast and gather your belongings. You are being released today by orders of the Minister of the

Interior." Tears streamed down her face. The women she had spent the last six months with all clapped their hands and wished her well.

She took one deliberate bite of stale bread and one sip of bitter black coffee. Wasting no time, she stuffed her possessions into a large clear trash bag. The last item she packed was her precious manuscript, the one she had started on the plane six months ago and finished within the cold walls of her cell during her detention.

The impatient guard yelled through her cell window, "Hurry, or you'll have to spend another night."

As she was escorted from her cell, tears of joy streamed down her cheeks. She was told her backpack and other items would be mailed to her within days of her release.

"There will be no court date," the officer said. Pelin hoped this wasn't a dream from which she might awaken at any moment.

The booking officer thrust a final document onto the table and asked Pelin to sign it. Her hand trembled as she scrawled her name in ink, smudging it slightly. She followed the officer through the double doors and down the long walkway, out through the prison courtyard.

The sunlight was blinding as she stepped outside, the blue sky a stark contrast to the gray walls she was leaving behind. Pelin blinked, tears welling in her eyes. She took a few tentative steps outside the gates, feeling her freedom was almost too good to be true.

"Pelin!... Pelin!" When she turned, her heart sank. She saw Shireen standing across the street in tears, waving a white scarf. Shireen was with Aylin, and to Pelin's surprise, Emir, the owner of the Turkish coffee shop she and Kemal had frequented in London, stood with them. He had flown in to secure her release.

Pelin took a deep breath and walked toward them. She was free—truly free. After embracing Shireen and Aylin, she turned and looked at Emir. She saw the happiness in his eyes.

"You came," Pelin said.

"I have been with you since day one," he replied, his voice catching slightly. He stepped closer, close enough that she could see the spots of amber in his dark eyes. "I was the anonymous caller."

The revelation washed over her like a wave. The anonymous tip that led her and Kemal into exile. The mysterious Turkish businessman.

"Why?" she asked, though somehow, she already knew the answer.

"Because truth deserves protection," he said simply. "Because what happened to Kemal should never happen to anyone ever again." He hesitated, then added softly, "And because history should not be erased, and books should not be banned."

Acknowledgments

This first acknowledgment reaches all the way back to my earliest days at **Brown Summit High School**—a small, segregated school tucked into the heart of North Carolina. Though modest in size, it was vast in knowledge and rich in care. I was fortunate to be nurtured by teachers and staff who felt more like family than faculty. They planted the first perennial seeds of learning in my mind—seeds that continue to blossom, year after year. Their dedication to seeing students like me succeed left an imprint I carry with me to this day.

I am deeply grateful to **Thekla**, whose unwavering support helped bring this book to life. Without her belief in me—especially during the times when others thought I would never finish anything—I might not have found the strength to see this project through. She stood by me, reminded me of my worth, and never let me forget that the dream was possible.

To Scuppernong Books, my **local Indy bookstore**, thank you for providing a space where I could share not just this story, but many others over the years. Those open mic nights were more than events—they were lifelines, moments of community and connection that kept me grounded and inspired.

Also, to the many **writing workshops and critique groups** I've had the privilege to be part of—your guidance, honesty, and encouragement helped me stay the course. There were countless moments when I doubted myself, when I questioned whether I was "good enough" to publish anything at all. But you reminded me that every writer has a voice worth hearing—and that persistence is part of the art.

At last, one of the important people behind the scenes, my editor Ann Klefstad.

This book stands as a testament to all of you. Thank you, from the depths of my heart.

J. R. Slade

9 798218 683290